# MUSIC YOU WILL NEVER HEAR
## REVISION

# OTHER BOOKS BY THE AUTHOR

*Music You Will Never Hear*
A Modern Greek Tragedy
iUniverse.Inc
2005

*Too Good Cooking*
Morris Press Cookbooks
2008

*Of Bears, Mice, and Nails*
*Outhouse Chronicles*
iUniverse.com
2010

*Life In A Troubled Land*
*Mirupafshim (Good-bye)*
iUniverse.com
2012

*The Boy That Was Shanghaied*
True Stories
iUniverse.com
2014

# MUSIC YOU WILL NEVER HEAR
### REVISION

## — A Modern Greek Tragedy —

ANGELO J. KALTSOS

*Angelo J. Kaltsos*

iUniverse

# MUSIC YOU WILL NEVER HEAR
## A MODERN GREEK TRAGEDY

iUniverse books may be ordered through booksellers or by contacting:

iUniverse
1663 Liberty Drive
Bloomington, IN 47403
www.iuniverse.com
1-800-Authors (1-800-288-4677)

Cover photo: William Goudas on steps of Fort on Fort Hill, 1943-44, Roxbury, Massachusetts. Photographer Ziko Agnagnos.

ISBN: 978-1-4917-9421-0 (sc)
ISBN: 978-1-4917-9599-6 (hc)
ISBN: 978-1-4917-9422-7 (e)

Library of Congress Control Number: 2016908156

Print information available on the last page.

iUniverse rev. date: 6/10/2016

# DEDICATION

I dedicate this book to my immediate and extended family, and especially to my uncle Christie who passed away in February 2004.

# CONTENTS

# ACKNOWLEDGEMENTS

I would like to thank all of the following individuals that encouraged me to go forward with the original version of this story and helped me put my thoughts together: William Acheff, Susan Anderson, Carol Melzar, Cheryl and Alan Rice, Tina and Skip Warren, and lastly, Cindy Simmons, who originally said I should write this story. To the individuals that I was able to locate and interview, my deepest gratitude goes to each and every one of you.

A notable thanks goes to Rebecca Orr for her generous gift of a laptop in the winter of 2004. This allowed me to utilize a word processor instead of my pencil and typewriter, and to make duplicate copies of my work more affordable.

My deepest gratitude goes to my editor Sarah Perry for her journalistic suggestions and editing this revision, while in the process of writing her own manuscript.

To my uncle, who has passed away, I want to give my thanks for the encouragement and interviews that allowed me to write this sensitive family story. Last but not least I want to thank the one character in this story named "Stew." This enjoyable and informative individual passed away in September 2004.

I also want to thank Brian McGrory, editor of the Boston Globe, for giving me permission to include images of headlines and pictures printed during the period of the crime you are about to read.

# PROLOGUE

The inspiration for writing the first version of this story occurred many years ago, during the latter part of August, 1997, when nights become cool and days are still warm in the mountainous region of northern New England where I now live. It is the time of year when the attacking insects disappear, and a time when the fall harvest from vegetable gardens yield an abundance of food.

I like the prospects of gardening and weeding, and bug control is a part of my second nature, but seeing that I don't use chemical controls, it becomes a daily chore. Either on your knees or bending over, it is a time when one's personal thoughts become internal without any outside interference. The act of meditation comes into play. Gardening delivered the proper temperament I needed to prepare myself for writing this story.

My prize garden reward comes from a patch of sweet corn that usually produces twenty-seven to thirty-six dozen ears of delectable sweet corn. I suppose the reader wonders what a patch of corn has to do with this story you are about to read. Well, one of my personal rewards is to share this corn with friends and neighbors.

On one of those sharing days, I set up a long table and folding chairs aside my cabin, surrounded by the forest and a fire in my fire pit, which has a metal grate situated atop the red-hot wooden coals. Sitting on the grate were ears of corn still wrapped in their natural sheets of husks, thus securing the internal water and sweet juices of the yellow and white kernels; they were picked as the hot coals were developing. There is something to say about the soil that produces such a sweet tasting corn.

There was a basket of corn sitting next to the fire-pit for replacements, and on the table there was butter, salt, beer, wine, soda, and napkins in a heap. I invited a group of friends to dive into the feast and feed their hunger from the sweetness of corn. They also came to enjoy the company. It is always a good time for laughs, stories, and local news. After bellies were full and most of the company had departed, a group of four were left sitting around the fire relaxing as the approaching darkness descended upon us.

Having attended to the comfort of my guests and also having devoured at least half a dozen ears of corn, I thought that I would entertain my guests with a story. Why I thought of this one particular story that came to me out of the dark, no pun intended, is hard to explain to you; never mind me.

Many years have gone by since that night with my friends, and the idea of relating this one particular story still eludes me. This story is one that I had never divulged to anyone in decades, even to my closest friends. Of course, my wife and elder family members were privy to those events, and the younger generation were told many years later as they matured, and even then not in complete details. Relating all the particulars now will reveal it in depth, and it will also reopen the time and events to those of the family still alive who witnessed it all, which includes my sister and me.

The guests who were sitting around the fire had been intimate friends for a couple of decades. As I was writing this, it drew me back to that one day, and I questioned why I divulged this secret, this family secret. The only answer I have is that I trusted their friendship and that the story I was about to share didn't connect me directly to the tragic incident, but it did connect me because of my relationship with the individual directly involved, and of course, to all the members of that immediate family.

As I recall that August night in 1997, I remember sitting by the fire relaxing, and saying, "Would you like to hear a true story?" The response was positive, so I went into a twenty to thirty minute monologue relating the most important parts of the story, watching their keen interest and quiet listening as they swallowed my words.

After finishing of what I felt was enough of the story, so that they had a good interpretation and would be aware of a past incident that took place in my youthful years, I sat back and waited for any kind of responses that they might throw back at me.

Cindy Simmons, one of my lady friends asked me, almost to the point of finishing, "Is that a true story?" I had assumed someone would ask, or say, "Yeah right," or "you're full of it," or whatever.

I replied, "Yes."

She then said, "Well, I think you should write a book about it."

I thought then and there that maybe it would make a good book. After my friends retired to their homes, and I secured the fire and condiments, I went inside. The thought of a book filled my brain, and returned to me again and again. I vacillated between not writing about it and writing about it. After all, the story had been a family secret for fifty years.

Three years later, when I decided that no immediate harm or personal damage would be done to my family, the thought of that book reentered my mind, and I said to myself, "I'm going to try and write that book." I also believed that the younger generation, sometime in their life, would like to know the facts of one of their past relatives, and what affect it had on the immediate family and the extended families during that period and the following years.

To my relatives, I hope you find this story interesting and not offensive. To those that think I should have kept this incident a secret, I apologize. I'm sorry if you feel that I made an ill judgment. I do know that the past is the past and one cannot deny that event even though it was an evil act, but if it helps the general populace to understand the effects of such a hideous crime, then so be it.

I rewrote this non-fiction story to give a true account of the place in which this crime occurred. It also allowed me to include more anecdotal stories. The original novel was published in 2005.

It was difficult to write this story about a close relative that killed an individual while committing a crime and as it happened that individual killed was the second police sergeant in the history of the Boston Police Department at that time period to be killed by gunfire, October 1946. The results of this crime is that it became a disgrace for the family of the killer and a family secret for over fifty years, but a thought to ponder. If you research through your own genealogy for a generation or maybe many generations you probably have someone either infamous or maybe famous in your own past. But with this thought, it didn't take writing this story less difficult.

To the family who suffered such a great loss, our family is deeply sorry.

# CHAPTER I
## Funeral

Two thousand people attended service at Saint Theresa's Church, West Roxbury, Massachusetts, to pay their final respects for a slain officer shot on Wednesday, October 2, 1946, at 9: 30 p.m. He was one of the few officers killed in the line of duty in Boston (the second police sergeant, the seventh officer since 1926, and the eighteenth since 1912) by gunfire.

Rolling through the streets of West Roxbury was a long line of family and friends following the black Cadillac hearse and flower cars, and behind them were Boston police motor vehicles. Entering the smooth gravel road of Saint Joseph's cemetery, they were met by the din of motors filling the air and a bugle sounding notes of despair. Led by the Boston police commissioner and the superintendent, one hundred police officers, Boston deputy superintendents and captains, color bearers and guards, a firing squad, and nineteen officers in VFW uniforms attended this funeral on October 4, 1946.

A fellow officer, killed while on duty, was a passenger in the hearse and this officer was on his last ride on this earth. Only a few days earlier, he was sitting with his wife and two young daughters having dinner. Sergeant William F. Healey of 28 Albright Street, West Roxbury, went to work thinking it was just another day like most days. He did not go home for dinner ever again.

Sergeant Healey, a member of the Boston police department since 1928, had been awarded the highest distinguishing Medal of Honor for duty during the 1938 hurricane that struck New England without pre-cautionary warnings. Sergeant Healey on September, 21, 1938 saved the life of six police officers marooned on a police boat. He was able to maneuver the boat to safety. The bullets that struck Sergeant Healey on October 2, 1946 were not received as precautionary warnings; they led to his demise.

To be struck down by a panicked individual and to have no warning to protect oneself was one of the dangers of his profession. Sergeant William F. Healey was buried on this day.

# CHAPTER II
## The Family

World wheat crops were the largest since 1940. The Second World War had ended, most soldiers had returned, and some were still returning from overseas destinations. The country was turning to a post-war economy and the populace was enjoying the peace. I was in my junior year at Boston English High School; one of Boston's all-boy prestigious schools. I had just spent the summer in Saco, Maine, a rural farming community in the southern part of the state. I had a job working on a dairy farm, with twenty-eight milking cows milked by hand, two medium-sized chicken houses full of chickens to be fed, about one hundred very hungry turkeys, and a few pigs eating all the scraps for fattening up their hams, for feasting during the winter months. The farm also raised crops to feed the livestock and a family of four: the mother and her three children, two girls and a boy. The boy and I did all the farming chores and sold sweet corn in South Portland to Ma and Pa grocery stores, and also house to house. After we finished selling the corn, we would go to Old Orchard Beach and ride the roller coaster over and over. We were both sixteen years old. The year was 1946.

I returned to the city of my birth and to my grandmother's home, which was located in the Roxbury section of Boston, Massachusetts, at the end of summer, to return to school.

My grandmother lived on the second floor of a three-story gray wooden clapboard building located at 118 Cedar Street, Roxbury. It housed six families, three on one side and three on the other side. It is an empty lot today.

The three flats on our side of the building were occupied by two Irish families, one below Ma, and one above her, and on the other side of the building were two Polish families, one on the first floor and the other on the third. In between the two Polish families was an English family. My grandparents are Hellenesmos, otherwise known as Greeks. Three of the six families were fairly recent immigrants from the early 1900s. Ma arrived in 1920. I called my grandmother, Ma.

Each apartment had six rooms, and my grandmother's flat, as we called it in those days, was on the corner of a small side street (Cedar Park) that was situated on the bottom of Fort Hill. It was an old Victorian building that had at one time natural gas gaslights. The old pipes and outlets could still be used in most rooms. I know, because I had lit them when no one was at home, although they no longer had glass globes.

It was a friendly community, as all the adjoining neighbors got along. They would join together for tea and coffee, gossip and conversation, and the children played together. The surrounding neighborhood was of similar make-up, and I supposed it would have been classified as blue collar. Everyone knew everyone, and every mother was yours, if you know what I mean. It was a safe area; we didn't lock our doors except at night. Robberies were unheard of.

The front of the first floor of this building was very high above the street below. From the street you had to climb two long flights of stairs to reach the first floor. The rear of the building rested on a very steep bank. The walk up the hill to reach the rear entrance was much easier than climbing the many stairs to reach the first floor, never mind the second or third. Everyone used the rear entrance, except salesmen or strangers. Our flat's front door was always locked because of its nonuse.

School was in session for about a month, and everything had been going great for me. I liked my subjects and my teachers, so far so good. I even had a job after school on Fridays and Saturdays. I worked with a young local war veteran selling ice and oil. My job was to deliver block ice for iceboxes, and kerosene for heating and cooking. Hardly anyone in the neighborhood had electric refrigerators, and few had central heating or could afford the coke or coal.

It was not unusual to take one hundred pounds of ice on your back, using metal tongs, up three flights of stairs, then to return with five or ten gallons of kerosene, and repeat this all day. Most customers averaged thirty to fifty pound pieces. The one hundred pound pieces sold for one dollar and the kerosene at about nine cents a gallon. I made my money on tips; my pay was $2.50 a day. I was not paid by the hour, and I liked my boss very much.

The neighborhood was mostly three deckers, as they call them in this part of the country. Streetlights were the old gas lanterns made of iron poles that were painted jet black, and they had a large circular glass globe that was twice as high as it was round. This globe circumvented the flame.

Occasionally, the neighborhood boys, including myself, would shimmy up the pole and lower the flame being naughty. Once in a while the flame would go out and the city workers would have to relight the flame, and of course make the flame higher when needed. They used small ladders. The pole stood about ten feet tall. It was crowned with an elaborate spike, and at the base of the globe there was an iron handle bar. Main cross streets in the area had electrified lights; one 750 watt incandescent clear glass bulb under a metal shield hanging from a wooden pole.

It was a predominately white neighborhood, although some black families lived in brick row buildings, diagonally across the street from the local corner store that every neighborhood had. Their front doors had brass plates for numbering, and they were highly polished. The families living there kept mostly to themselves. There never were any problems, and at times the older black boys would play softball with my age group, and also the older crowd. The rest of the area had numerous ethnic populations, mostly from Europe.

The local corner store was owned and operated by an Armenian family. They had a wooden enclosed telephone booth inside where many neighbors made their telephone calls, including my grandmother's family. A telephone call cost five cents.

The streets were fairly clean, as tenants picked up trash, and they even swept the sidewalks, unlike today in large urban areas. Soldiers, sailors, and marines had returned from the war, and everyone was quite proud of their sons and daughters that had served in the armed forces. Everyone worked for the war effort and for victory and peace. It was time now to forget the past and go forward. Although lost ones would never be forgotten, and heartaches would linger for a long time, people were looking toward the future. Some veterans returned to their old jobs, and some were using the G.I. Bill for educational funding that was offered to all veterans by our government. The economy was fairly strong as manufacturing goods changed from military to consumer. The war recovery was in full swing.

I had been living with my grandmother off and on for two years. My grandfather had died four years earlier; 1942. Also living in the house was my aunt Madeline, two uncles: Gregory and William (Bill), and my older sister Dorothea (Dolly). As I had not lived with my mother since I was about eighteen months old, my grandmother was my only female link to a mother. Her name was Penelope.

My grandmother and grandfather came from Sofratica, a northern Greek mountain village. It wasn't a very large village, but it was considered a central location that had an ancient connection with the past. They both came from prominent families. The two families were educated, and had family members, past and present, that were doctors, judges, merchants, and landholders, as well as a priest, my great grandfather. All the marriages were arranged, and one marriage partner, my mother's father's mother, came from a local family of questionable background. They were noted for being thieves and undesirables. The only reason for this strange arranged marriage was that she was very pretty, and not of the same character as her family. At least, that is what my grandmother told me.

Ma arrived in this country as a young woman of twenty-five with a ten-year-old daughter from Northern Epirus, now a part of Albania since 1912. Her husband left for America soon after their daughter was born to start a new life in the Promised Land. It was over nine years before he could send for his wife and child. That child was my mother Rita. They settled in the Roxbury section of Boston where other villagers from their home had settled. Three of Ma's brothers had arrived earlier, so even though her new life was somewhat difficult, she at least had family here.

On arriving in America in 1920, my grandmother spoke no English, and her first effort to learn was difficult. As time went on she became more fluent, but with an accent. My mother, who was ten when she arrived in America, attended school and learned quickly. She never had an accent. After Ma had been here for ten years, she went to night school to learn to read and write, and to get her citizenship. She had gone to school in her village and finished the eighth grade, a situation not common at that time, especially in that part of the world. I don't know where my grandfather learned English, but he was very proficient in reading and writing. He was educated and had finished high school in the same village as Ma.

Grandfather was a barber, and owned a barbershop in downtown Boston on Kneeland Street. He had two other barbers working for him. His name was Thomas. He was always dressed in a suit and tie. Grandfather wore a felt hat during the winter and a yellow straw hat in the summertime, which was fashionable at that time. People used to say that he resembled Harry S. Truman. Grandfather died at the age of 52 from a heart attack.

After arriving in America, Ma had her second child in 1922, a daughter named Madeline. Then came four boys: Gregory in 1923, Christie in 1924, William in 1926, and Nicholas in 1927; my sister was born a year later. William was born with a heart condition. Of course, at that time knowledge and medicine for such problems was limited. The only treatment was rest and no physical activities. He was told from the onset to never run, play ball, or do any heavy lifting.

Until he was six or eight years old he remained in institutions. The family had to take public transportation to see him, and it was an all-day event.

Christie remembered visiting him, but when Bill was a baby Christie was only two years older. Christie couldn't understand why he was home and he had to go there to visit his brother, so Christie thought he was really sick. Christie told me that he thought Bill had a leaking valve. That was the terminology that they used, heart trouble and leaking valve, which also my grandfather had. The family didn't have an automobile, so they didn't visit as much as they wanted to. Having a leaking valve there was no reason why he couldn't have been home theoretically, but that's what the doctors thought in those days.

When Bill finally came home he went to public schools. Being sedentary, he was always somewhat overweight. He grew to be 5'10", with straight black hair, dark brown eyes, a round face, and a beautiful smile that showed perfectly straight white teeth. The ladies thought he was handsome. He had a gentle personality, and disliked violence. I don't think he was ever in a scuffle with other boys. Of course, he had two older brothers to protect him, and his sister Madeline.

Bill didn't finish high school, and when he was eighteen he moved to Brooklyn, New York. He never had a job until he moved to Brooklyn, where he found work as a doorman in an upscale apartment on the upper West Side of Manhattan. Bill lived a few blocks from my mother and her husband Dominic in the Bay Ridge area of Brooklyn. He rented a room in a private home on 83rd Street. Bill would walk to 4th Avenue and 86th Street to take the BMT 4th Avenue train to Manhattan to go to work. The cost was ten cents.

Bill returned to his mother's home about one year later, settled in, and never looked for work. During the war years, he obtained a guitar and started to learn on his own. He studied classical music and later on he learned to play some jazz. By 1946 he had advanced quite a lot. He wanted to attend The New England Conservatory of Music, but neither Bill nor the family had the finances for him to attend.

I played the violin, and I was trained to play classical music, so we used to play together sometimes. I would play from my sheet music and he would play from his. It was great fun. I had been playing for six years, and was playing in my high school orchestra. I thought we sounded pretty good. I don't know what the neighbors thought. They never said anything or complained.

# CHAPTER III
## The Errand

It was a Thursday when I returned from school and went into the kitchen to get a cold drink of water from the icebox. Ma was in the kitchen sitting at the table. Dolly was at work and Madeline was in her bedroom.

I asked Ma, "Is Bill home?"

"Yes, he's in the front."

Carrying my glass of water, I headed down the hallway. Bill was sitting on the couch with his left foot on a hammock. It was wrapped in cloth.

I asked, "Hey man, what happened to you?"

"Oh, I just hurt my ankle. Would you get me a glass of water?"

"Sure."

I did an about face and headed down the hallway again. I returned with his water in my hand, and I passed him the glass.

He asked me. "Would you do me a favor?"

He seemed anxious and I replied, "What is it? I plan to see my buddy."

He continued in almost a whisper, "Would you go over to Vine Street, and go to Jocko's (George E. Larson) house?"

Vine Street was two miles away: I could walk or take a trolley, two in fact, because one trolley only went to a terminal where I'd have to make a transfer and then take the one heading toward Vine Street. Then I'd have to make the return trip. That would be a total of ten cents, five each way. My pockets held some small change, but I didn't want to use it in this way.

I pondered for a moment, but Bill interrupted my thoughts and said whispering, "I really need you to do this for me, I can't go myself," looking down at his injured foot. "I'll give you two bits."

A quarter would pay for the trolleys, and I'd have fifteen cents left over to buy candy, ice cream, or a ride to school; any one of them for a nickel. Not bad, besides, I would be going to my old neighborhood. Maybe I'd see an old schoolmate from my junior high days. I hadn't been there in two and a half years. Bill knew I knew the area very well.

I asked, "When do you want me to go?"

Without hesitation he said, "Now!"

I was a little surprised, but he seemed urgent, and I wanted to help him. He was my favorite uncle, but he felt like an older brother.

He continued, "When you get to Vine Street look around for the cops, especially in unmarked cars. Jocko might be in trouble, so if you see anything suspicious just keep on walking and come straight home. Don't run!"

Hey man, this is getting intriguing, but for a city kid not too surprising. As a sixteen-year-old I knew my way around. Not that I'd been in any trouble, but that was a city kid's way of life. My blood was flowing with excitement. It was like being in a flick with James Cagney or Humphrey Bogart.

I replied, "Yeah, no problem."

He went on to say, "Go to 120 Vine Street, second floor, and ask to see Jocko. When you see him, ask him to come over as soon as possible."

That was the end of the conversation; he didn't say another word. Bill hobbled into his bedroom, and then he stood at the bedroom doorway, hand held out. I took the two bits and left. I was on a serious mission. I had no idea what or why he wanted to see this guy, but I only knew it required my immediate attention.

Everyone in the house had met this guy, Jocko, and he was well liked. He was two to three years older than Bill, taller and thinner. He had sandy colored hair, hazel eyes, and was kind of frail looking. I don't know how strong he was, but I used to wonder, at times, if I could take him, you know, in a scrap. That's the mind-set of a sixteen-year-old city kid. Life was tough sometimes on the streets. I was thin and not too tall, but carrying ice and oil had built up my body. I guess I thought I was tough, oh well.

I said goodbye to Ma and left quickly. She never asked where I was going. I always went where I pleased, and came home when I wanted. I was on my own in that sense.

I had to walk to Elliot Square, grab a trolley to the Dudley Street station, and get a paper transfer when I got on. I loved those old trolleys, with a metal pin on the floor for clanking the bell for "Get out of my way." And the hand controls for speed and stopping. The left hand had a control with a big round wooden knob that went in a half circle, mounted on a flat metal piece, from left to right for speed. The right hand control piece was for stopping. It also was mounted on a flat metal piece with a shorter handle, and a shorter movement, with no knob on the end. The conductor used this with quick movements from left to right. You could hear air hissing from the brake control arm; I always wanted to drive a trolley.

I arrived at the Dudley Street station and waited for the Uphams Corner trolley. There were always lots of trolleys during the daytime, so I didn't wait long. I went up the two wooden steps that unfolded, and then stepped up to the trolley floor. I handed the conductor my transfer and sat close to the front door on a wooden bench. It was another ten minutes to my stop. He made every stop to pick up and discharge passengers. I looked at the young ladies riding the trolley, but did not make any eye contact. I got off at my stop, stepping on the wooden steps again. It was at the end of Vine Street. I had taken this ride many times before moving to Ma's home. My old school was only a few blocks away as this area was my old hangout.

At my stop, there was the Vine Street library on one corner and homes on the other corner on Dudley Street. Vine Street went up a hill (Mount Pleasant) as soon as you got off. It was lined with mostly red brick row houses on both sides. I looked at the library where I'd gone many times and headed up Vine on the right-hand side. It was a gradual climb, and Jocko's building was almost to the top, on the opposite side of the street.

I walked, scanning the street and the buildings. There were a few vehicles parked sparingly on the street. In those days most people didn't have autos. The street was void of any people, and I saw no signs of the police. Before Jocko's building there was a cross street. I approached it with trepidation. It would be a good spot for the police to sit, as they could see Jocko's place from there. I looked both ways, checking for anything suspicious. I was on the right-hand side of the street, because it would have been easier to keep on walking to the top of the hill then take a right onto

Mount Pleasant Street. This street circled around to the right and then went back down the hill to Dudley Street, where I could get the trolley back to the house, as quick as possible, not missing a beat, but that would be unnecessary--the area was clean.

I crossed the street and went into the 120 Vine Street building, up one flight of stairs, two at a time, and knocked on the door that was on the right, at the head of the stairs. It was a wooden door with a large pane of glass covered with a white cotton curtain that you couldn't see through. No one answered, so I knocked again, louder this time. Someone inside answered, "Who's there?" It was a woman's voice.

I asked, "Is Jocko home?"

"No!"

I waited and thought that someone would open the door, but maybe they were waiting for the police to arrive. They didn't ask if I was the police or who I was.

I said loudly, "I have to talk to Jocko; I have a message from William Goudas. He wants to see Jocko as soon as possible."

The same person replied, "Okay, we'll tell him when he gets home." I didn't know if that was his sister or his mother, but I felt that I had met my obligation.

I said, "Thanks," and turned around.

They didn't respond, so I went down the stairs, through the front hall door, stopped and looked around. The coast was clear and nothing had changed. I felt secure and headed down the street toward the same trolley stop, but I would go across Dudley Street and head the other way. I don't know if he was home or if they looked out the window, but I never turned around to show my face. I'm sure they knew I was young, and if Jocko was home maybe he knew who I was. The entire round trip took about an hour or so.

I said hello to Ma, who was still in the kitchen where I had left her, but was now standing over the old black iron cook stove that was converted from coal to kerosene with a wooden spoon in her hand and stirring something in a pot. Then I went down the hallway to see Bill.

He was sitting on the couch reading a newspaper. I don't know where he got the paper, but I didn't ask. I said, "Hi."

He didn't return my salutation. He only said, "Did you see him?"

"No."

I then proceeded to tell him everything that happened, repeating their conversation and mine. After all, it was brief and there wasn't much to tell. I also told him that I saw no police, marked or unmarked. I could see a look of disappointment and concern on his face. Jocko had a telephone, but we didn't. The nearest public phone was at the corner store. With his injured foot, he was in no condition to walk there. The store was owned and operated by a family named Guzellian, and they also lived above the store. The parents had two boys: one was about my age, and the other was a few years older. They also had a daughter who was even older. They all took turns working in the store. They had a great selection of penny candy.

I wondered what Bill wanted me to do now. He only said, "Thanks," got up and went into his room. I turned and left. It was now my time to go out and play before dinner and homework. It would be getting dark soon.

The evening would be one filled with normal activities. The family members coming home from work, would eat, and then go out, Gregory that is. Dolly and Madeline usually didn't go out during the weekdays. Usually, we would listen to a couple of radio programs and then go to bed.

When I returned in an hour or so, Gregory and Christie were there, as was my sister. Ma had taken some food to Bill's room. The other family members would divide eating between the kitchen and the dining room. There was no set routine of who ate where. My two uncles and I ate at the large round oak table in the dining room, and Dolly, Madeline, and Ma ate in the kitchen. The dining room table was made of thick oak that had four large carved lion's claw feet resting on the floor. The top could be lengthened with a piece of matched wood that fit in-between when you pulled the two separate top pieces apart.

We sat around the table, talked about our day, and about the police sergeant who was the second police sergeant in the history of the Boston Police Department killed downtown by gunfire the night before. It made big headlines in all the papers. The city hadn't lost too many police in the line of duty up to this time. It was major news, and there was a big manhunt for the killer or killers.

After supper, Gregory went out, probably on a date. Christie hung around for a while and talked to Madeline and Ma. Before Christie went out, he walked to the parlor and saw Bill sitting on the sofa with his bandaged foot resting on a hammock, playing his guitar. Few words were said, and Christie returned to the kitchen in a few minutes.

Dolly was in her bedroom, after doing the dishes, fixing herself up. We all know how young ladies are. Ma sat at the kitchen table, and Bill stayed in his room. I sat at the dining room table and did my homework. When I finished, I put on the radio that was in the dining room. Christie had already gone out by then. Madeline and Dolly came in to listen to one of our favorite programs.

After one of the programs ended, I went into the kitchen, and just about then Bill came limping into the kitchen, sat down at the table and told Ma that he wanted some more soup and a cup of coffee. It was getting late and bedtime was approaching. Of course, Ma catered to him as she always had since he came home from those institutions. Sitting down, he didn't say anything; he was just being quiet. Ma started to prepare his food.

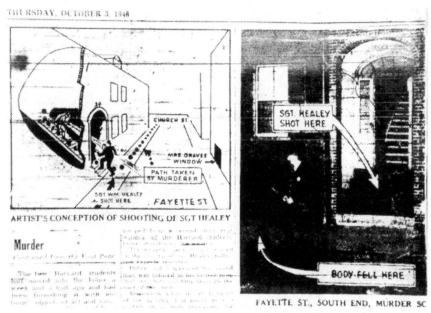

*Boston Globe Oct-4-1946*

# CHAPTER IV
## Knock on the Door

Ma, Bill, and I were in the kitchen, and Madeline and Dolly were in the back bedroom, the last room in the rear. Bill was sitting at the kitchen table in his pajamas. He had stayed in the house all day. He said he had twisted his left ankle and had trouble walking, and he had it wrapped in a cloth bandage. No one suspected anything, even though it was all right the night before. I guess we all assumed that he injured it getting out of bed. It was about 8:00 p.m.

The kitchen was an inner room to the rear of the flat. My grandmother was making coffee and warming up the soup we all had for supper for Bill. I was standing next to the black cook stove watching Ma. We heard this loud banging on the door in the front of the apartment. Ma looked at me with a surprised look, as I did with her. Bill showed no response, as his eyes were looking down at the table. Again, there it was again, a knock, a loud knock on the front hallway door. Actually, there were many loud repetitive knocks in rapid succession on the door. Really? Seeing as it was dark out, who would be knocking on the front door at this time of night?

I said, "I'll get it."

I walked down the long, narrow hallway. It was dark and twenty feet long, and the front door was on the left on the interior side of the building almost at the far end of the hallway. It was a double wooden solid door, and I don't remember both doors ever being open. A low watt bulb encased in an opaque scalloped glass globe hung down from the middle of the ceiling in front of the two doors. It had a cotton pull cord that had a small round clear glass ball on the end. I pulled the cord and then unlocked the door and opened it. No one had a key to this door except Ma.

As I opened the door wondering, I faced a man about my height, 5'7" and wearing a felt hat, which was common in those days. The light entering the stairway hallway was dim, but I could see that he was dressed in a dark suit and tie. In that quick instant I couldn't see anyone else.

By the time I noticed others wearing dark clothes, this man asked, in a tone not friendly, but also not discourteous, "Is William Goudas home?"

By the time I could respond, "Yes," he was stepping forward with a pistol in his hand, aimed at me.

"He's there in the kitchen," I said, pointing left down the hallway.

I noticed Bill looking down the hallway while still sitting at the table. Then everything happened very quickly. This man in civilian clothes came through the door, pushed me against the wall, turned to his right with the pointed gun still in his hand, and said sternly and loudly, "Don't move or I'll shoot."

He went darting toward the kitchen. My uncle rose slowly and sat down before he could stand erect. At the same time, another suited man rushed in and then uniformed police by the numbers. The police immediately scattered all over the flat, pouring into all the rooms as fast as they could. Some of them had guns in their hands. It was very frightening, to say the least.

I could hear Madeline and Dolly let out screams of terror. Ma never uttered out a cry. She was usually internal with her thoughts. If she did utter a moan I never heard her. Someone yelled, "What's going on?" It was probably my aunt Madeline.

Bill was immediately handcuffed with no Miranda rights invoked. That was before the court's decision on Miranda. I was removed from the hallway to the parlor, all the way to the front corner of the house. My sister came running down the hallway crying. She was wearing a bra and full slip, also a skirt, but no blouse. She was eighteen years old, with long brown wavy hair, large brown eyes, a round beautiful face, and a great figure. She stood at 5 feet 1 inch.

Between tears she said to me, "Go get Gregory and Christie."

At my sister's request I replied, "Okay. I'll go to the corner."

One of the officers nearby gruffly replied, "You're not going anywhere!"

I got the message and didn't move a muscle. With the police everywhere in the apartment it was a ubiquitous situation and I was too afraid to resist. I swallowed hard and slouched against the wall.

Gregory was probably at a girl's home in another neighborhood. He never stayed home.

Christie was not living at his mother's, but he visited a lot after work. He was at the local corner where the young men from the war would gather under the electric streetlight to play cards, or go to a local bar called Napoli that sold pizzas and Italian food. A large cheese and pepperoni pizza sold for fifty cents.

Christie was a good son. He had always worked to help with the family's expenses before entering the Marines. He stood at 6', the tallest one in the family. He was of modest build, with a narrower face, lighter brown eyes, and light brown straight hair. Of all the boys, he was the most stable, caused no problems within the family, and he had an even temperament.

As far as I knew, especially in this country, no one in the family had ever gotten into any serious trouble. One wonders, does it run in our blood? Are we cursed for something that happened a long time ago? Maybe it was payback time. Our passions run deep. Curses are part of our heritage, but I do know we are hardworking, honest, not troublemakers, and getting more educated. The family had to overcome the language barrier, the results of being poor in this country, surviving the depression, and World War II.

# CHAPTER V
## The Arrests

I asked the policeman standing next to me, "What are you doing here, what the heck is going on?" His response was a blank stare, like "shut up, kid." When I opened the door I wasn't shown a search warrant. Maybe Ma was shown one, and I'm sure Madeline would have asked for a search warrant.

Madeline was a strong-minded woman, and during the war she worked at the Hingham shipyard. The shipyard transported the ladies to their workplace after most of them traveled on public transportation to arrive to a specific bus stop. She did what was considered, at that time, man's work, putting hot rivets into metal plates on the sides of ships. Madeline was considered tall for girls at that time. She was slender in stature, with dark blondish wavy hair and brown eyes, and she was strikingly attractive. And those legs, all the men checked out her Betty Grable legs. She was very outspoken, but not rude, and she had a good head on her shoulders. She was twenty-five.

The police search was in full swing. You could hear bureau drawers being opened, closet doors being opened. Seat cushions in the parlor were upturned and hands shoved deep into the couch and chairs. There were three pantries off the kitchen. One housed the icebox and shelves for canned goods, condiments, etc. Another contained dishes, pots and pans. The third held the sink and drain board for washing dishes, and was also used for food preparation. The flat had numerous nooks and crannies, and closets in every room. There was a small bedroom off the parlor in the front of the flat that looked down to the street far below. This was Bill's room. The police literally tore this room apart leaving nothing unturned or unopened. The whole house was completely ransacked.

They removed all the 78 rpm records from the windup gramophone that sat atop the floor model Zenith radio that had AM and short wave. It housed a twelve inch speaker that could boom, and when Ma wasn't home, it boomed either jazz, big band, or classical.

With all the commotion inside the apartment, I didn't realize they were also searching the cellar below us. The cellar was cluttered with litter belonging to the tenants on that side of the building. There were three furnaces, coal fired, but the coal bins were cluttered, as they hadn't held coal in years. I can't imagine rummaging through that dirty, dusty mess.

All the building's tenants, when they either heard the ruckus or the word passed around quickly, came out to see what was going on. That would account for about twenty individuals, if everybody was home. I can imagine their conversations were inquisitive and stupefying, and the police in sheer numbers would have been startling to anyone.

It probably was only ten minutes after I let the police through the door when Christie returned to the house. He was at the neighborhood corner meeting with his pals. They were trying to organize a neighborhood (Highland and Cedar Street) group and call themselves the Highlanders; our age group was called the Red Skins.

One of the men in the group who lived on Highland Street near Fort Hill Avenue was studying to be a lawyer. They were using him for legal counseling. This man later in life became a mayor of Boston. His name was John Collins.

Christie's meeting ended quickly, as someone noticed the police in front of the building. The distance from the corner to the house was approximately 550 feet, and one of the street's gaslights was positioned right in front of our building, so the commotion could be seen. He rushed home with some of his buddies following, running up the side hill, skipping up the back stairs and walking into the kitchen. If he had to identify himself before entering the first floor entrance, it didn't seem to hold him back.

It was about then that the police allowed me to leave the parlor with little concern for my movement. Where could I go anyhow with the police surrounding the premises?

Bill was still in the kitchen, but he was standing at the entrance to the long hallway, surrounded by uniformed policemen and Lt. James U. Crowley, who was holding Bill by the arm very securely; Bill was handcuffed. He was the first officer I had let through the front door along with Joseph B. Dawson. Both of them were members of the Bureau of Criminal Investigation.

As soon as Bill saw his brother, he spoke quickly in his mother's tongue. Before the police interrupted the conversation, a message was given. The police then handcuffed Christie and arrested him also.

Madeline stepped into the kitchen when she heard Christie, but by then they took the two brothers out the front door and into the paddy wagon. She stood there sobbing and yelling, "Where are you taking them?" It was about 8:30 p.m.

During this whole ordeal, which was like a horror flick, no one in the family knew why the police were there, except Bill. When we asked, they just ignored us as if we weren't even there. The air of frustration was getting intense. Madeline was very outspoken, but they ignored her outcries and removed her from the room.

I was taken away by the police also, but my stay at the local precinct was brief, but I was not handcuffed. Somehow they quickly realized that I was too young and I didn't fit their MO. They were looking for older men. Although I was sixteen I looked much younger; in fact I've never looked my age. I didn't go where they took Christie or Bill. They were taken to Station 4 (Berkeley Street) downtown. I was taken to the local precinct at Roxbury Crossing (Station 10). After some questions about my age, where I went to school, etc., they said I could go home. I said it was late and it was a long walk. The detectives brought me up to the front desk and the sergeant in charge told two policemen to take me home in a squad car. I felt relieved and was glad to be going home, but when I returned, the police were still in the house. They finally left, leaving the house in a mess and us too. All this commotion took about three hours, but it felt like twenty. It was now 11 p.m.

When it got to be about midnight, we were all exhausted and tired of talking and crying, so we decided to go to bed. I had to go to school, and my sister had to go to her job at the bank. We figured that we would find out what was going on in the morning. We had no phone, so what else could we do at that point?

I had just fallen asleep when there was a knock on the back door. This door was always locked when we all went to bed or when the lights went out. Everyone had a key to this door. My aunt Madeline got up, slipped over to the door and asked, "Who is it?"

"Police, open up, open up!"

The police invasion started all over again. Dozens of police surrounded the building, and of course, they entered the flat. Not even an hour had passed since they had left. What did they want now? Of course, the neighbors probably had gone to bed like us, but with all the commotion, who could sleep? The police were on an important mission, and they obviously didn't care who they disturbed, so the neighbors were up again, only this time they were in their nightclothes and slippers and looking very disturbed. I was very sleepy and was still lying down when one of the officers came over to my bed, but a detective told him, "He's too young; the men we're looking for are older."

Just about then, Gregory returned home, walked into the kitchen and was immediately handcuffed. Of course, he knew nothing of the previous events. Maybe somebody yelled something when he appeared in the area. Before anyone could get a word in, he was gone, zipped away. If they gave him a reason, I didn't hear it.

Outside, they had set up portable floodlights. They had gone into a small shed that housed the tenant's trash barrels in the rear of the building. Trash and garbage were strewn everywhere. The cops were searching an empty house lot behind the shed that used to have a house, a ghost house. That's what the local kids called it. It was torn down about the time the Second World War broke out.

After an hour and a half of searching, the police packed up their gear and left as quickly as they'd arrived. In the meantime, they had talked to Ma and my aunt in another part of the house away from my sister and me. They told her everything, and they answered her inquiry, as much as they could or would. She was told why they were there twice, and the reason they arrested Bill and her brothers.

Madeline was sobbing and had great difficulty trying to explain the situation to my sister and me, and telling us what the charges were, especially against Bill. We listened intensely, gasping as the words flowed from her lips, interrupted by sobs. N-o-o-o, her explanation was unbelievable. Not my uncle Bill!

Bill and I were playing music together for a couple of months, but it ended quickly, very quickly. He was sitting in jail and I was devastated, the family was devastated, and the crime he was alleged to have committed was terrible.

Now we had to deal with this relative in jail. Oh man-oh man, what were we to do? I had no idea where to start, but I knew someone in the family, someone, somewhere, would know what to do. I didn't think it would be my grandmother, nor my sister or me, maybe my uncles or my aunt or one of our relatives. Someone called my mother Rita, who was living in Brooklyn, the next day. I was told that my mother and her husband Dominic were coming to Roxbury. They were going to drive their four-door 1939 Pontiac, black with bullet headlights; as we said in those days, it was a big bomb. They would be here in a day or two. What a relief. "Dominic will know what to do," Madeline told me, when I returned from school the day after they arrested Bill. Help was on the way as I went out to see my buddy. I had to talk to someone my age.

# "A Gun Went Off in My Hand"

# ADMITS HE SHOT OFFICER, SAY POLICE

**Abp. Cushing Flatly Condemns Slav "Trial" of Abp. Stepinac**

A Roxbury youth has confessed he murdered Police Sgt. William F. Manley during a Fayette-st. burglary last Wednesday night, police declared today.

Boston Globe murder scene 10-3-1946

**X FREE**

# Point Blank Shots Fell Father of 2 In Fayette Street

Sgt. William F. Healey, 49, holder of the police department's medal of honor for heroism, was shot and killed last night by a burglar who was surprised while ransacking a house at 24 Fayette street, in the nightclub and theater district.

The police sergeant, running to the house in response to a call for help, was shot at point blank range as the burglar emerged with a suitcase filled with loot. A bullet penetrated the policeman's heart and he was dead on arrival at City Hospital.

Within minutes after the shooting at 9:36 P. M., nearly 20 police cars converged on the area. The killer was seen fleeing along Fayette street, and later was nearly captured by a police cruiser squad near Berkeley street. Although nearly a dozen suspects answering the slayer's description were rounded up late last night and early today, the murderer was believed still at large.

### Holder of Department Hero Medal

Sgt. Healey, who leaves a wife and two daughters, was awarded the department's honor medal for his rescue of the crew of a gasoline boat during the

**$50,000 FUR**

*Boston Globe 10-3-1946*

ROBERT KANE, 17, who witnes
fatal shooting.

*Boston Globe 10-3-1946 Robert Kane-witness*

*Boston Globe 10-4-1946*

# CHAPTER VI
## The Crime

G regory and Christie were released early the next morning. They were not implicated in Bill's troubles, which the police found out during the night's investigation. They were only implicated at first because they were adults and Bill's brothers. Ma and Madeline were told more of the details of the crime by the police at headquarters.

The major news story that had been in all the local newspapers and on the local radio stations the day that Bill said he had hurt his foot, was on Thursday. The killing had taken place around 9:30 p.m. on Wednesday night not far from where the Coconut Grove fire had killed 492 people in twelve minutes on November 28, 1942.

Madeline had a date at Coconut Grove that night with a Boston College football player, if Boston College's football team had won their game with Holy Cross. Boston College was rated number one in the country, but they lost 55 to 12. Boston College cancelled their celebration. Madeline stayed home. This area is now called the Bay Area, near the central section of the city.

Two of the three major Boston newspapers: the Boston Globe, the Boston Herald, had the following headlines:

"POINT BLANK SHOTS FELL FATHER OF 2 ON FAYETTE STREET" *Boston Globe*

"THIEF KILLS POLICE SERGEANT" *Boston Globe*

"FLEEING THIEF KILLS POLICEMAN" This headline was reported in the *Boston Herald* late city edition on Thursday, October 3, 1946, which sold for three cents.

As reported in one of the papers: "A city police officer, William F.

Healy, 49, was killed by a thief exiting a doorway of a three-story brick building, after looting a college student's home. The thief was trying to make his dramatic escape when he encountered the officer. The officer was killed instantly when one of two bullets fired by the thief entered his heart. The other shot hit him in the side of his body. The officer had his revolver in his hand, but was unable to use it in his defense. The thief dressed in a brown overcoat, black pants, and a dark felt brimmed hat with the brim pulled down over his brow was witnessed by two neighbors who had heard shots and screams before the officer was killed. The neighbors lived across the street."

The following information is my interpretations mixed with true facts that describe the events leading up to the crime and about the events of the crime. I have written what I think what internal or external thoughts or conversations that might have taken place among the individuals involved in this story.

One of the witnesses was a young man of seventeen, who lived in the basement apartment. The other witness was a middle-aged woman who lived on the second floor of the same building. They both witnessed the thief carrying a fairly large suitcase in his hand running down the street toward Church Street, where the nearest trolley that could take him toward home was nearby. The officer was lying on the red brick sidewalk, slain.

By the time the police responded, and the area was thoroughly searched, the unknown assailants involved in the robbery had made their getaway. The caper hadn't gone off as the thieves expected; now they were on the run for their lives.

There were four individuals involved in the actual crime scene on that fatal night, the driver of the getaway car and three other persons. One of which was Bill.

Bill had met this man called Fritz O. Swenson Jr. (Jake) at a nightclub in the city. They befriended each other and started to see each other frequently for about two or three months before the big robbery. Jake used to come to the house to see Bill. We, in the family, didn't know much about him, but no one liked Jake from the get-go. He had this sly manner about him, and tried to act slick. He talked out of the side of his mouth like he just stepped out of a gangster movie. A real bad character! Jake was 5' 8", medium build, straight dirty blonde hair, acne-scarred face, beady eyes, and a harelip. He was two years older than Bill.

He would attempt to be friendly and say hello, but you got the feeling that he didn't mean it. No one in the family had much to do with him, only saying a passing hello. My sister said she was afraid of him. Bill just passed it off and defended his friend's demeanor. When Jake came to visit, we would all leave him with Bill, and he would take him down the long hallway to his room. Jake never made long visits. Maybe they were making plans to meet each other somewhere else so they could talk in depth, away from the family.

Soon after he was paroled, Jake was working doing a roofing job on Fayette Street which was next door to the place of the robbery. A new tenant was moving in, and Jake observed large quantities of silverware and antiques being moved into the apartment; "A good haul." This looked like a good caper for the boys, he thought. Right up their alley. He put the idea into his memory bank for a future heist.

We had never met the other men involved in the robbery; thank heavens for that. One crook was enough. Jake's scoping gave him enough information for the gang to make the necessary plans and establish the time and date for the robbery. We did learn that he wasn't the ringleader, but just another crook, with a lot of experience under his belt.

Their plan was to go there and use one person disguised as a Western Union messenger and gain entrance by false pretenses. They set the date for a Wednesday evening about 9 p.m. By the time the robbery took place, Jake had already finished the day job on the roof for the company he worked for a few weeks earlier, and he was now working somewhere else, far from that scene.

On that ill-fated night, Bill had gone to bed fairly early. Ma had also gone to bed at the same time. She fell asleep quickly, and when Ma slept she had a very loud snore that would wake up the dead. We used to laugh about it. She slept in a bedroom to the right of that long hallway bordering the parlor. My sister and aunt, plus me, slept at the other end of the house next to the kitchen; it had the black iron wood-stove that now burned kerosene. With it lit, it spread some heat into our rooms. Madeline and

Dolly slept in the back bedroom, and I slept in the dining room. We all went to bed about a half-hour after Ma and Bill. It was about 8:30 p.m., which was our usual bedtime during the weekdays.

Bill, realizing that we were all probably asleep, or knowing we were too far away to be able to hear him, tiptoed out the front door and made his way down the long flight of stairs to a waiting car on the street far below. He left the flat's front door unlocked (because he didn't have a key) to get back in knowing no one would ever check, as there would be no reason to.

I'm sure he wore no shoes as he slipped quietly down to the building's front door, because he wouldn't want the first floor neighbors to hear him. He got into the waiting car with three other men, and they drove away unheard by anyone, at least not by any of us.

The 1941 black Plymouth sedan which Jake Swenson rented for $35.00, motored through the low-lit city streets meeting a few other autos and passing the slow-moving yellow electric trolleys going in different directions. A driver would sometimes straddle the iron trolley tracks for a smooth ride as the auto swerved slightly trying to stay on. It always felt good, especially after jostling over the gray granite cobblestone surfaces.

On the way to the caper, the man driving the car gave Bill a 32 caliber automatic foreign revolver. This man was Big Joe (Joseph E. MacEachern, 38). Big Joe was older than Bill and had large shoulders. Big Joe was wearing a naval peacoat and black wool knit hat. He only said hello. Jake did all the talking. Jake then told Bill that his seat companion was Joseph. Joseph F. Moore was older and looked larger than Bill, but not as big as Big Joe. He appeared to be Big Joe's age, but a few years younger. Joseph only nodded as their eyes met in the dim light. Everyone was wearing dark clothes and hats of one kind or another.

No one shook hands. Joseph sat behind Big Joe. Driving to their destination, Jake went over the details: where they were heading, what they were going to steal (it being a home burglary), how they were going to gain entry, which person was going where in the building once they entered, and the details on exiting the building. Big Joe was to wait in the car out front for their getaway. The ones going inside had guns, flashlights, and gloves. This wasn't their first caper, but maybe it was the first time all together.

They arrived at their destination, easing down the narrow one-way street, looking to see if anyone was about and if there were any lights on in the house at 24 Fayette Street. The street was clear of pedestrians, and there were only a couple of cars parked on the opposite side of the street. Slowly and quietly Big Joe stopped the car and Jake got out, gently shutting the car's right-side door.

The robbers planned on gaining entrance to the premises using a fake Western Union telegram and to then holdup the residents. Jake had chosen himself to present the fake Western Union telegram to the occupants of the house.

The residence was one of those red brick homes, three floors with five steps under an arched closed opening leading to the front door. To the right of the door, there was a round polished brass doorbell with a button in the center. The door had narrow panes of glass covered with a lacy, yet opaque, white cotton linen.

Jake rang the bell a few times. No one answered; the place was empty as far as he knew. He then skipped down the stairs, turned to his left and ran down the street, passing two doorways, then went around to the back of the buildings and down the alley to gain entry at the rear. He hopped over an unpainted wooden picket fence, kicked in the first floor rear door, and then ran through the apartment, opening the front door. Joseph and Bill were already waiting in the front stoop huddled against the front door, knowing that Jake was going to let them in. Big Bob relaxed as he witnessed his cohorts enter the apartment. He knew Jake knew his stuff. He had a lot of confidence in this small time petty thief. He knew Joseph was okay, but this was Bill's second job with him, and he didn't know how capable he was. The last job went somewhat okay, but he knew the kid needed more experience. He knew Bill would get that experience, being along with Joseph and Jake, two experienced men.

Bill stayed on the first floor while Jake went up to work the attic and Joseph was to work the second floor. It was a three-story single family home with the third floor being an attic that had half the floor space of the rooms below. The attic was set back behind the front of the building, so no one could see it from the street below, unless you were across the street looking up, and then you could barely see the top half of the attic.

The three men were in the process of gathering jewelry, money, antique silver pieces, watches, and other expensive items from tables and shelves. They had collected and filled six of the owner's suitcases that they found in the house. The operation went very smoothly and quickly. It was almost time to leave and then get into the car waiting out front to make their getaway. Ten to fifteen minutes was what they allocated to gather the loot; anything beyond that was risky.

The neighborhood was an upscale area with narrow streets and little traffic. Maybe one car went by in all the time they were inside. Fayette Street was a narrow one-way street, with parking on one side, red brick buildings, red brick sidewalks and black-poled gas lights that lit the area, so it was not well-lit; an advantage for robbers.

Bill was in the parlor making a last look-see. The parlor was in the front of the building. At the same time, two males and a lady friend were walking down the sidewalk returning from a late dinner engagement, and were about to enter this same building unaware of the robbers inside their apartment stealing their valuables. The younger of the two men, Gene Metz, 24, a former school teacher, came from a wealthy respectable Florida family and was attending Harvard University. His roommate, Joseph W. Fulton, 25, was also going to the same school. He was from Colorado; they were graduate students.

Their lady companion, Theresa Zezzos, 23, was attending Radcliffe Graduate School (now part of Harvard University), a women's college in Cambridge; she lived in Hough's Neck, Quincy, a southern suburb close to the city. The dinner had been joyous; little did they know what was in store for them inside the well-decorated, furnished three-story apartment.

Big Joe was calmly sitting across the street out front and saw the approaching trio. He slouched down in the car so he would go unnoticed. They didn't look towards Big Joe, as they were busy talking. When they got in front of the home, they turned and slowly went up the steps to enter number 24 Fayette Street where Big Joe's cohorts were performing their act of criminality. After the three entered the building, Big Joe started the car and left his buddies to fend for themselves. It was *amscray*, as we used to say for wanting to leave a scene, rather than say, let's go. When Big Joe saw a policeman on the corner, he proceeded with caution. The officer gazed at him as he turned the corner, but suspected no foul play. Big Joe's timing was perfect. In a few moments, all hell would break loose, but he was well on his way out of there. He would go home and wait and wonder.

Gene Metz climbed the five steps leading to the front door. He inserted the brass key into the lock, opened the heavy wooden door, and entered the dark vestibule with his two companions following directly behind. Gene then turned to his right, reached around the opening of the parlor door, and threw the light switch for the crystal chandelier hanging from the plaster ceiling. Gene and the others were met by Bill carrying a full grey suitcase in his left hand. He reached into his pocket in the flash of an eye and pulled out his automatic weapon. It was retrieved just as the light went on.

Gene told the police, "I put the key in the door and walked into the vestibule; the front door closed automatically. I reached for the light in the living room and as I did I heard a voice say, "This is it, don't move or I'll shoot you!"

Joseph Fulton grabbed Theresa Zezzos and shoved her against the far wall of the vestibule, out of the gunman's line of sight. He then very quickly darted out the door. On seeing this, Bill fired a round at him, but missed him completely. Fulton went yelling down the street toward the officer, who had been standing at the opposite corner of the street. Fulton assumed the policeman would still be in the vicinity and would react hearing him yelling, "Help, help, police. There's a burglar in the house."

The officer, somewhat confused in his first reaction, stopped a motorist who was heading in the same direction as Fulton. Realizing quickly that this was not the burglar, he waived the motorist on and started down the street toward the burglarized home while Fulton yelled, "He's got a gun, he's got a gun." The auto was the second car that had driven down the same street, the two seemingly close to one another.

As Fulton was going down the front steps, Bill hurried toward the parlor door, the suitcase in one black gloved hand and a gun in the other gloved hand. He went to pass by Gene Metz when Gene, very daringly and bravely, closed the parlor door on Bill's right arm, the one with the gun. Bill pulled with his gun arm and freed himself instantly, pointed the gun at Gene and fired, but missed. Gene lunged at Bill and they went down rolling on the floor. Bill had let go of the suitcase, but not the gun. Somehow, the gun went off again, striking Bill in his left foot. This had no effect on his demeanor. Managing to point his gun at his opponent at close range, Bill angrily said, "I'll shoot you if you don't let me out of here." Right about then Bill, with a lot of force, struck Gene on the left side of his head with the gun, striking him in the eye. Gene had no choice but to let Bill go. Bill rose quickly when he felt the release of Gene's hold on him. As all this was going on, Miss Zezzos stayed in the vestibule, too afraid to do anything but scream.

Joseph Moore, hearing all the commotion downstairs, quickly broke a lock on a small pantry window and squeezed through. Proceeding onto a small and narrow ledge, he leaped diagonally across the yard onto a shed roof. On landing, his leg crashed through the roof, but he pulled himself up, leaped over a picket fence and sped through the alleyway. When he crashed through the roof, he dropped his gun, which was fully loaded with eight bullets. When the police located the gun, there were no fingerprints on the gun or on the window.

In the meantime, Jake, alerted by the fracas coming from the front of the house, managed to go out the rear door, unnoticed by anyone, the same way he entered. He went scurrying over the same wooden picket fence that Joseph had gone over, or was about to go over. Whether they went over at the same time is not important, but I assume that they were on each other's heels. Bill was on his own; it was every man for himself.

Officer Healey finally reached 24 Fayette Street with his pistol in his right hand. As he arrived at the front of the building, he was about to place his right foot on the bottom step when he met Bill coming through the doorway reaching the top step. These five steps were the only objects separating life and death. They were facing each other at a very close range, their minds going in different directions. One saying to stop and the other saying go. The two of them had similar motives, stop or I'll shoot, one for the law, one not for the law.

The light from the vestibule was on and it outlined the burglar exiting. As the sergeant was about to cock his service revolver, Bill saw the right hand of the officer with a gun, and he quickly fired off a round from his foreign automatic striking the officer in the aorta, which fed life blood into his heart. As Sergeant Healey was falling backwards, Bill shot again at the falling policeman, and hit him again, but on one side of his body. This was not the fatal shot. The first one did all the damage necessary to end the poor man's life.

Bill ran as fast as he could past the officer and past two neighbors from across the street, who had both heard the screams and shots. Louisa Graves, landlady of 29 Fayette Street, witnessed Bill lugging what looked like one hundred pounds of loot. The woman was looking out a second floor window. A young renter of seventeen, Robert King, who came up out of his basement apartment, witnessed Bill running and lugging a grey suitcase. Bill ran as fast as he could, never looking back.

Joseph Fulton was still at the corner where he alerted the officer, and he witnessed the officer going down after a shot was fired. There wasn't anything he could do except to go back and see what to do next. He also wanted to see if his friends were okay. Of course, he saw Bill running with the suitcase in hand going in the opposite direction. He still had the memory of just being shot at, and after seeing the officer go down, he had no intention of running after Bill. No way! By the time Fulton returned, the seventeen-year-old boy was at the officer's side to see if he could assist him in any way, but Fulton's instinct told him it was useless.

Bill made his way toward the nearest trolley line, dumping his loot in an alleyway, hoping to return and retrieve it later; how naïve. Bill ran up Fayette Street and crossed Church Street until he reached Arlington Street, then he headed up Cortes Street reaching Berkeley Street (a police cruiser was nearby, but suspected nothing), and then onto Columbus Avenue, where he boarded a trolley car heading towards Egleston Square. He got off at the Cedar Street stop and went up the steep hill which leveled off when he crossed Centre Street, and then from there he walked to his home, which was nearby.

Of course, the police found the stash and returned it to the occupants who were robbed. The police also found five spent shells, but only four bullets were accounted for, two in the slain officer, one in the vestibule wall, and the fourth lodged in the front room door frame. Where was the fifth? The tenants were unaware that the fifth was imbedded in Bill's foot, and the police could only speculate. Bill knew where it went.

By the time the police were notified of the crime and had come in force to cover the area, Bill was well on his way, stepping onto a trolley heading home. He finally arrived home after a five-minute walk from the trolley. He then went up the long front flights of stairs and into the flat unnoticed and unheard. This would have taken at least forty-five minutes to an hour from the time he ran from the crime scene. Of course, everyone was fast asleep. Now he was in real deep trouble, not only for shooting a policeman, but also because he had shot himself in the left foot while fighting off the tenant. A double whammy!

When Bill finally returned home, he went directly into the bathroom. I'm sure he thought, "Oh boy, everybody is asleep, and I'm in deep trouble. If those guys got away, and I can get this foot fixed, no one will know I went out, I'll be okay. I better look at this foot."

Bill pulled the bathroom cord and turned on the overhead light, a bare 100-watt bulb, enough to light the small bathroom, which contained a sink, a commode with a water closet (used for flushing) above, and a tub. A shower would have been a luxury. Also jammed in there was Ma's washing machine, with a ringer attached. Bill removed his bloody shoe and sock. Bill's foot was covered with blood, and when he washed it off, he could see the bullet lodged between his last two toes. Bill hadn't realized that the bullet was still in his foot. He assumed it had passed through the shoe. He took a double edge razor blade and tried to extract the bullet.

When he couldn't accomplish this, he put on the bloody sock and his shoe with a hole in it, where the bullet had penetrated, or he went shoeless again down the front steps. Bill changed clothes and immediately left the house quickly, using the front door. Bill went over to his friend's house. This friend was not part of their gang. His name was George E. Larson (Jocko). Bill traveled the same way I had gone the very next day. He got Jocko out of bed, as late as it was, and told him his secret. A secret is no longer a secret once you tell even one soul. He told one soul, Jocko.

It was reported that Bill told Jocko, "I just shot a policeman. There's a bullet in my left foot, can you help me take it out?"

The reason he asked Jocko was that Jocko had attended college and studied premed, but left school for reasons I don't know. Jocko was working at Boston City Hospital as a medical assistant, and he had access to medical equipment. Bill thought that Jocko would know what to do-- he could probably remove the bullet and dress the wound, plus he was one of his best friends.

When Jocko heard Bill's tale and his condition, he wanted nothing to do with the situation and totally refused, in no uncertain terms, to treat him on the spot, but conceded he would help when he got the necessary medical items from the hospital. I'm sure Bill was desperate, and Jocko was desperate to get him out of his house as soon as possible.

It was quoted in the local newspapers after Bill's capture that Jocko told him to stay home, and he would come over and give him medical aide.

Jocko knew he had no intention of following up on his promise, especially when he found out the next day that the officer had been slain. Jocko would have then become an accessory to the crime; a felony.

Bill left completely disillusioned, and probably hid his anger at Jocko's refusal to treat him immediately, but he didn't want to alienate Jocko. He needed his help, knowing he couldn't go to any hospital or doctor. The hospital or the doctor was obligated by law to report any gunshot wounds. He returned home, having to leave the bullet in his foot, hoping that Jocko would come over tomorrow. The best he could do for the time being was to bandage his foot and go to his room. Returning home again, no one in the house heard a thing.

Did Bill go to sleep, did he cry, did he stay up all night, or most of the night? I'm sure he was a nervous wreck. He had just shot a cop. He had no idea how serious the wound was, but I'm sure he didn't think that he had killed him. There were three witnesses at the scene and two more that he was unaware of, and he had no idea what happened to his other partners in the building, or the getaway car and the driver. Maybe they were captured and were now talking. What a dilemma! I can't imagine being in this position. Can you?

All the newspapers in the city came out the next morning with the story, plus it was on all the local radio stations. I'm sure Jocko was paying attention to see if what Bill had told him the night before was true. As reported, a policeman, not only a policeman, but a police sergeant was shot and killed by a thief. Jocko soon realized that Bill was the culprit. I don't know what time of day Jocko found out, but when he did, he called the police department after confiding with his mother and sister about Bill's visit and what Bill had told him.

Jocko called the police and told them that he had information that might be useful in solving the shooting of a policeman. He was told to remain home and they would send homicide detectives over right away. He finally got to talk to Captain William Bell of the Bureau of Criminal Investigation. He talked about Bill's visit to his home, and said Bill admitted that he had just shot a policeman. The police, obviously, took this information, but did not act on it immediately. They had to investigate into it further to make sure it had merit, as it could be from a crazy person.

It must have been somewhat of a difficult decision for Jocko to make, but any upstanding citizen would probably make the same decision with reservations. After all, Bill was his friend, and now his life might be in danger, for Bill was not the same person he thought he was. His friend is now a killer, a police killer.

After the police had interrogated Jocko at length, they had gathered enough substantial information to form a force and go to the address given by the informant and arrest the culprit for the murder of one of their officers in the line of duty. The case wasn't solved, but they had a very good lead, from a seemingly reliable person. One day later, and almost to the hour of their comrade's death, they headed to our house to arrest the man alleged to be the killer.

The next day after the arrest of William Goudas, newspaper headlines read:

"CITY YOUTHS HELD IN SERGEANT'S KILLING" *Boston Globe*
"One Wounded Toe Firing At Healey, Police Say"

"COP KILLING SUSPECTS HELD" *Boston Globe*
"Two Men Questioned in Healey Death"

# Police Spur Hunt for Moore, Third Man in Healey Murder

Police last night intensified their efforts to find Joseph F. Moore, 32, of Dorchester, missing third man wanted in connection with the murder Wednesday night of police Sgt. William F. Healey.

Teletype messages were sent out with descriptions of Moore supplied by the two men already under arrest for the Fayette street house shooting, William Goudas, 20, of Cedar street, Roxbury, and Fritz O. Swenson, 23, also of Roxbury, and every clue, no matter how flimsy it appeared on the surface, was being studied.

A tip earlier in the day sent a squad of detectives led by Lt. James V. Crowley to an apartment on Highland street, Roxbury, but the mission produced nothing. Information that a man named Moore was living in the apartment proved to be correct, but it was not the man wanted by police.

## FOOT GANGRENOUS

Meanwhile, Goudas, who police say has confessed to the fatal shooting, remained at City Hospital with a gangrenous infection from a bullet wound that resulted when the youth shot his own left foot Wednesday night. Police quoted Goudas as saying he had shot himself while wrestling with Eugene Mets, owner of the apartment house where Sgt. Healey was killed.

So serious had the infection become by last night that Dr. Henry Nigro, executive night surgeon, declared it was doubtful that Goudas could be arraigned for murder in court tomorrow as scheduled. One postponement already had been made, Both Goudas and Swenson, who has admitted complicity in the burglary that preceded the killing, originally were to be booked yesterday.

Swenson will be charged with murder despite Goudas' admission that he fired the fatal shots, as will Moore, on the ground that Swenson and Moore were committing a felony at the time of Sgt. Healey's death. A fourth man, who drove what was intended to be the getaway car, however, will not be implicated in the murder charge, but merely for being an accessory, according to Lt. Crowley. Like Moore, the fourth man is still at large.

## BULLETS IDENTICAL

Ballistics experts yesterday said that the slug removed from Goudas' foot and the bullet that killed Sgt. Healey both came from the same gun, a .22 caliber barrel with four lands, four grooves and a right twist.

Despite the fact that Goudas directed police to a Roxbury field where he said he had buried the automatic following the shooting, the gun was still missing last night.

Goudas told police he had removed two remaining bullets from the automatic, then had buried it in soft earth in a vacant lot at the rear of his home.

This explanation led police to believe that, since the field where the gun was supposed to have been buried, was used by children at play, the weapon may have been uncovered and carried away.

Detectives agreed that Goudas probably had been telling the truth about where he had disposed of the automatic since one of the two bullets the youth said he had removed from the gun and thrown aside was found in the field.

announced that he had informed Prime Minister Attlee of it in advance. But when the British Foreign Office confirmed today that Attlee had sent a reply to President Truman and hinted that the communication was a strong one, the White House declined to reveal its contents or even comment directly on it.

In line with the White House attitude, the State Department made no comment on the situation today.

## 2000 Attend Rites, For Sgt. Healey, Slain Policeman

Close to 2000 persons yesterday crowded into St. Theresa's Church, West Roxbury, to pay final respects to Sgt. William F. Healey, policeman who was slain Wednesday night by a fleeing burglar at a Fayette street house.

Scores of police, in and out of uniform, and hundreds of neighbors. Heading the official police delegation were Commissioner Thomas F. Sullivan, Supt. Edward W. Fallon, three deputy superintendents and all 22 captains of the department.

Burial was in St. Joseph's cemetery, West Roxbury.

## Contributions Total $1115 to Police Fund

Police Com. Thomas F. Sullivan announced last night that police and private organizations had to date contributed $115 to a fund for the benefit of the family of Sgt. William F. Healey, slain Wednesday by a burglar.

He added that other citizens wishing to contribute to the fund could send checks to him.

Contributions received last night: R. H. White Company, $100, Charles Raymond, president of R. H. White Company, $50; Lt. George P. Sullivan, $10; Joseph O. Lawrence, $50; William Q. and John A. Pearson, $5.

*Boston Globe 10-4-1946 Search for associates*

# Goudas, Pal Face Murder Charge Today

## Confession Said to Involve Four in Crime

Police sought two more desperate fugitives in Greater Boston last night, while a bullet that may prove his death warrant was extracted at City Hospital from the foot of William Goudas, one of two Roxbury youths under arrest and who allegedly have confessed to the murder of Police Sgt William F Healey Wednesday.

The bullet was lodged in the left foot of Goudas, 20, of 118 Cedar st., Roxbury. Police said Goudas admitted having accidentally shot himself ~~only seconds before the murder~~, during a ~~wild fight with~~ Harvard ~~student who had~~ surprised him robbing the student's apartment at 24 Fayette st., South End, Wednesday night.

See SLAYING    Page 2

*Boston Globe 10-5-1946*

SLAIN POLICEMAN AND TWO WHO SURPRISED BURGLAR ASSAILANT—Sgt. William F. Healey (right) was shot in Fayette street while rushing to the aid of Eugene Metz (center), Harvard student whose room was burglarized. Miss Theresa Zezzos (left) was with Metz and another friend, Walter J. Pelton, when they surprised burglar.

*Boston Globe 10-6-1946*

# Sgt Healey Fund Reaches $23,573

### Police Association Gives Check for $500

The Boston Police Relief Association, with a check for $500, led yesterday's list of contributors to the Sgt William F. Healey Fund, which reached a total of $23,573.10 last night, Commissioner Thomas F. Sullivan announced.

*Boston Globe 10-16-1946 Fund*

PRINCIPALS IN SOUTH END SHOOTING—Left to right, Theresa Zezzos, Harvard post-graduate student present at the shooting; Sgt William F. Healey of the Warren-av. station, the victim, and Gene Metz, 24 Fayette st., who escaped assailant's bullets fired in his apartment. Note bruises on Metz' face.

*Boston Globe Thursday 10-3-1946*

# CHAPTER VII
## Interrogation

The following information is what I presume what took place in the integration room and what was told to me by Bill. Bill was not forthright with information about his arrest or the crime until many years after his parole, and of that it wasn't much. I can only write what I remember of what he told me.

On the night of the arrest, Bill was taken into a room and seated at an empty table. The two detectives who arrested him were also in the room. One sat down facing him, the other one stood close by his side. It was time to grill him to see if they had the right man. Of course, the bandaged foot was a good place to start. They had already been told that he had shot himself and the bandaged foot looked promising.

He was told to remove his shoe and the bandage. When they inspected the shoe closely, they could see what looked like a bullet hole.

"Okay, now remove the bandage," one of them told him.

He removed the bandage and exposed the bloody wound. Well, it wasn't a sprained ankle. So far so good! Jocko's information was holding up. They asked him how he got the injury. He refused to say anything. Then the questions came rapidly, but he refused to cooperate. He denied the accusations and the inquiries, which made the detectives extremely angry; after all, one of their best had been shot dead. They were getting nowhere. They wanted a confession, and they wanted it now. Investigating officers Lieutenant Francis G. Wilson and Police Sergeant Charles Hewitt grilled Bill for a full confession.

Whatever method they used, and however long it took, they finally got Bill to confess. Of course, the bullets from the body of the officer and

Bill's foot would be checked for a ballistic match, to see if they were fired from the same revolver. This would be more than circumstantial evidence for the trial against Bill.

He told them how they robbed the home, that he shot the sergeant and himself, how that came about, and the names and addresses of his accomplices. When they asked him where he had hidden the gun, he gave them a cockamamie story. Whatever it was, it wasn't the truth, but it got them off his back.

There had been rumors in those days that the police used physical force to obtain confessions. Whether this was true I really can't say--it's only what I had heard. What really transpired in that closed room away from public scrutiny one can only guess. I can only tell you what my uncle told me when I asked him what happened when he was arrested.

Bill told me that he was interrogated fiercely and they used physical force. I remember asking, "Well, how did they do that?"

He told me, "They beat me repeatedly with a rubber hose." Now that's a strong accusation to make, but I have no way of knowing the truth, nor do I not want to believe what he told me. I do remember seeing such activities in the movies, but those were movies.

When I consider whether Bill was deserving of the beating, my thoughts waver. He murdered a policeman, he was caught in the act of armed robbery, and he terrorized the inhabitants of the building with a pistol. The basic fact is that he took the role of an evil man. Would he have confessed without force? Who knows? The reality of the situation demanded the truth, and that's what they received. And I'm satisfied with that.

With names and addresses, the police went out into the city to arrest the gang. Jake was arrested at his home at 12:30 a.m. as he was returning home from his girlfriend's house. The other two men were on the lamb, so an all-points bulletin was put into effect for their arrest.

Thinking that the gun was still located in the house, or in the surrounding area, the police sent another force of officers back to search and try to recover the murder weapon. That's why they returned to our home around midnight.

After Bill's confession, they had all they needed for the time being. It was time now to attend to his wound. When they had examined his left bloody foot they could see the bullet lodged in between the toes. For the first time, the Boston police department used a fluoroscope to record the bullet found in Bill's left foot. The bullet would be removed and compared to the bullet from Sergeant William F. Healey's body.

Bill was escorted under heavy guard to Boston City Hospital's emergency room. The doctor removed the bullet lodged between his toes, in his left foot, and handed it to the detective standing in the room. Gangrene had already developed in the wound. The detective carefully put the bullet in a small paper bag that was labeled for identification. The nurse in attendance bandaged the foot after applying iodine. Bill was not hospitalized, but was taken back to headquarters and put into a cell for the night. The nurse had given him a pair of crutches to enable him to walk around. Very little conversation went on between the doctor and Bill. The doctor performed the surgery and left with only a nod to Bill after he was through.

The investigating officers retired for the night, but they still needed to find the gun. It was the one vital piece of evidence to wrap up their case. They would continue the investigation in the morning after they had a night's sleep and a cup of coffee before returning to work.

Bill got up the next morning and had breakfast, then two officers escorted him back to the same room with the bare table; the same arresting detectives then confronted him. Bill knew what they wanted. He knew that they wouldn't find the pistol. They were looking in all the wrong places. Bill thought to himself, as he stared at them with tired eyes, "Should I tell them what I did with it? I've already confessed to everything and I've squealed on my buddies. I can make it easier for myself if I tell them the truth this morning. What should I do?" Complicated thoughts raced through his mind. "Maybe I can stall them with another phony story." He had stuck to his original story far too long, and he could witness the frustration in the two men. They were getting nowhere, and he knew that this was only going to get worse.

The morning inquiry had started at 10 a.m. and now it was noon, and the detectives decided to take a break and begin again after lunch. Maybe they would initiate a different strategy when they returned. They definitely were not going to give up. Bill was escorted to his cell, walking with his crutches. They fed him a bologna sandwich with a glass of milk for lunch.

The clock on the wall in the room with the bare table read 1 p.m. The two detectives returned to resume the questioning. About an hour went by; they finally got Bill to tell them where he threw the gun on his return trip home after the incident at Fayette Street. They believed this new story. He convinced them that he was now telling the truth. They rounded up a force of police and headed to the area where he said he threw the gun.

It was on a Friday, two days after the crime, and I was on my way home after spending one of my strangest days in school. Boston English was abuzz about the murdered cop. I told no one of my troubles at home. Seeing that my last name was different from Bill's, no one put two and two together. None of my neighborhood friends went to the same school, so my classmates never associated me with the captured killer. I was thankful for that. I didn't want to be bombarded by questions, stupid or otherwise. Of course, none of my teachers knew where I lived except my homeroom teacher, Mr. Simmons. He never said anything, probably to protect me from my classmates. I applauded him for his thoughtfulness and his consideration.

I got off the trolley at Columbus Avenue, at the far end of Cedar Street, returning from school. As I was nearing home, one of the local boys my age came running towards me and said, breathing hard, "They got your uncle in the alley."

"What alley?"

"The one behind Doctor Brown's place."

"Really?"

"Yeah, they got him sitting with crutches, and there are police everywhere," he said, as I went running with my school bag bouncing off my back.

This alleyway was called Linwood Alley, but "the alley" for short. It was located diagonally across the street from our apartment building. It was a large area where every kid played cops and robbers, cowboys and Indians, aggies, tag, and hide and seek.

The alley was a lengthy block long, and was situated behind row houses on three different streets. It was rectangular in shape. There were no buildings in the alley, only the rears of the red and yellow brick apartments. Doctor Brown's large Greek Ionic columned ten-room house sat at the far end with its back facing the alley. The home was painted pure white, quite a contrast to the brick buildings nearby. Doctor Brown's house was older than the surrounding homes.

I reached the alley panting. There was a large crowd mulling around the alley entrance, which was large enough to drive a truck through. The police were trying to keep the people from entering into the open area. I recognized familiar faces as I pushed my way through. I could hear someone say, "Hey, they got Bill in there."

I was surprised, as was everyone else in this mingling crowd. When I was finally cleared of the crowd, I could see twenty or so uniformed police swarming over the area, heads down, intently looking for something. I overheard someone say they were looking for a gun, Bill's gun. Bill had finally relinquished the whereabouts of the murder weapon. He told the detectives that he threw the gun in the alley as he passed through on his way home.

I walked briskly toward my uncle when a uniformed officer said loudly, "Hey, where do you think you are going? You can't go over there."

I told the cop, "I'm his nephew and we live together across the street. I just want to say hello!"

This officer wasn't searching, but just standing there obviously doing guard duty, or on crowd control. He looked me over and said, "Follow me, but don't get too close. Don't touch him!"

Bill was sitting on a chair with his foot resting on a wooden crate that had probably been found in the alley. He had a set of crutches in one hand. When he spotted me he managed to squeak off a smile, trying not to look scared, but you could see the fright in his eyes. I said, "Hi, how are you?"

"Okay."

"How's your foot?"

"Okay, they removed a bullet."

I briefly talked about how Ma was doing and about the family. It wasn't an easy conversation. In the meantime, one of our friends went to our apartment and told Madeline that Bill and the police were over in the alley. She hurried over, and after she got through the crowd, she became hysterical when she spotted her brother.

She started yelling at the police, "He's innocent, he's innocent let him go."

Madeline was getting too rowdy; two cops approached her to remove her with force, if necessary. It was evident that she was not going to cooperate.

Luckily, Christie also came through the crowd, and when he witnessed Madeline, he went over to her and wrapped his arms around her. He said something in her ear and whisked her away. That didn't stop her from yelling, "He's innocent, let him go." She was also crying uncontrollably.

I didn't know what to do, and Bill just sat there. He had no control of the situation. The police continued with the search. They never found the weapon, so a judgment call was made to stop the search. They had spent well over an hour looking. I assume that they figured someone probably found the weapon and was not about to give it up for whatever reason. The alley was heavily used, and if he threw it on Wednesday night, some forty hours ago, anything could have happened to it. They did go through the crowd and ask if anyone had seen the gun or had found it, and if so, asked them to please return it to the police. No one came forward.

One encouraging fact was that two unspent 32 caliber bullets were found next to the heavily trafficked wide gravel path. This was very promising. These would be evaluated to see if they matched the bullets that they had from the crime scene. They would now have to wait to see if the pistol would be brought to headquarters. What else could they do?

They told Bill that they were through searching and they were leaving. One of the officers removed the crate, and as Bill was rising, we both said good-bye. We had no idea when we would see each other again. A few tears flowed from my eyes. I loved this man very much.

Bill was told to go toward Doctor Brown's house. There were only a few people standing at that end of the alley. Bill looked at me, surrounded by police, and found his way to the opposite alley entrance. Bill never turned around for another look. He was taken back to his lonely cell. His confined life's ordeal had just begun.

# Bullet Wound in Foot Betrays Suspect

ROXBURY YOUTHS HELD IN SLAYING—Fritz Olaf Swenson, 23 (left), and William Goudas, 20 (right), with Police Sgt Charles Hewitt (center) after six-hour grilling at Station 4, climaxed by alleged confession of Goudas. Inset (lower left) shows bullet hole (arrow) in shoes worn by Goudas.

*Boston Globe 10-4-1946 Criminals sitting and shoe with bullet*

# Bullet in Youth's Foot Like One in Slaying

A bullet removed from the left foot of William Goudas, 20-year-old alleged slayer of Boston Police Sgt William F. Healey, was declared today to have been fired from the same foreign-made revolver with which the officer was slain.

Ballistics expert Edward Culpin reported to Commissioner Thomas F. Sullivan that the bullet extracted yesterday at the Boston City Hospital was found to have "four lands, four grooves and a right twist."

This indicated that it was fired from a foreign-made weapon. The bullet which found Sgt Healey's heart and killed him almost instantly bore the same markings. According to Culpin, the bullet taken from Goudas' foot by Dr. William F. Hickey was "in very good condition."

## Schacht and Fritzsche Freed by Americans

NUERNBERG, Oct. 5 (UP)—United States military government ended an 11-hour argument German police today by releasing Hjalmar Schacht and Hans Fritzsche from American house arrest, promising them protection from arrest by German authorities.

Franz von Papen, the third man leader acquitted by the international tribunal Tuesday, remained in the Nuernberg prison awaiting formal reply to his request to enter the British zone.

Nazis

(Continued on Page 3)

*Boston Globe 10-5-1946 Bullet in foot*

**FATAL BULLET COMPARED TO OTHERS**—At right is the .32 calibre bullet removed from the body of the slain Sgt William F. Healey. In center is the one extracted from the left foot of William Goudas, confessed slayer of the policeman, and at left is an unfired shell of same type found near Goudas' Roxbury home, 118 Cedar st.

*Boston Globe 10-6-1946 Bullet*

# CHAPTER VIII
## Hiring a Lawyer

Seeing Bill in the alley the day before was not easy for the family or for me. There wasn't much we could do except wait for my mother and Dominic. We tried our best to do what was usually routine on the weekends. I went to work delivering ice and oil. My boss said he was sorry for the family trouble. The other kid that worked with us didn't say anything. I guess he really didn't know what to say. Ma and Madeline went food shopping, taking the trolley. My sister stayed home as she was too upset to go out. Gregory did what he always did. He went out. He never stayed around too much anyway. Christie came later in the day to check on Ma and Madeline.

Dominic and Rita arrived mid-afternoon on Sunday in their Pontiac. We were all home except Gregory. Christie arrived at noon. Ma had cooked lamb and roasted potatoes and carrots, and we also had salad and bread. This is a typical Sunday Greek dinner.

Of course, there was feta and olives plus yoghurt (always made by Ma). It's spelled yogurt today, commercially.

We were happy to see them coming through the back door. Dominic was dressed in his usual pinstriped sharkskin wool suit. His skin color was olive and his hair was black, the same color as the suit. He stood at 5' 6", of medium build, but strong in stature. Dominic's eyes were dark brown, and when he looked at you, they penetrated right through you. His shoes were so highly polished they would reflect the sun, and the same thing with his hair. It was slicked back with hair grease, which was the style at that time. Dominic also brandished a thin lined mustache. He represented the typical Hollywood tough guy in his early forties. If he didn't like someone he would call them, "that dirty degenerate rat bastard."

My mother, who was adorned in a stylish dress and a small hat perched on her head, came dragging in with a worried look. She looked like she had cried all the way. It was good to see them, but they didn't come for a friendly visit. After the "Hellos," Ma asked if they were hungry––there were plenty of leftovers. My mother said, "Yes." We all sat around in the dining room while they ate and small-talked about their road trip.

Rita had been living in Brooklyn for a dozen years and in Manhattan before that. I didn't get to see her until I was six or seven after she left our family when I was a baby still nursing. I knew very little about her, so it was still a novelty to see her. I just sat there and studied her. I hadn't seen or talked to her for fourteen months. Even so, we still didn't exchange many words.

She was small in stature being only 5' tall, with the family's round dark brown eyes, a round face, pretty facial features, and olive smooth skin. Her hair was curly like mine. She was thirty-six years old. I did discover that she had a strong personality and a temper. She worked as a stitcher in the sweatshops of Manhattan factories. She was an excellent cook in the Greek and Italian styles, combining her heritage and my father's, and Dominic's in her cooking.

After they finished eating and Ma was making demitasse for Dominic, I decided to go out and leave the older folks alone. I knew they had a lot to talk about, and it would be easier if I just left. Besides, what input could I have? I would find out later what happened. I said my good-byes and went across the street to see my closest friend, the only person that I could confide in.

The family decided to let Dominic see his friend's connections (Mafia) in Boston. They would know of a good criminal defense lawyer. They also discussed the lack of money. Even if we all pitched in everything we had, it wouldn't put a dent in the money needed for Bill's legal defense. Dominic said he would help to retain a lawyer, but more money was needed. A good lawyer was very expensive, there'd be no pro bono. Dominic told them that he could stay for a while, but someone had to raise money. Christie promised he would try to come up with something. Dominic said they were going to stay with his cousin, who lived a mile or so away, and make connections over there as they had a phone. They might also know of a good lawyer. If not, Dominic knew who to call for advice in another part of town.

I knew that Dominic was of questionable character. He worked as a union boss on the Brooklyn waterfront. It was a carpenter's union, and it was these union bosses that oversaw who worked for the day. They also handled the union dues.

Dominic told the family he would come back on Monday or Tuesday with a lawyer's name. Christie and Dominic could then go and meet with this lawyer. He asked Christie if he could get off of work. Christie said that would not be a problem. Rita and Dominic left the house when the sun started to set. Ma didn't say much. I guess she figured all was lost anyhow for her son. What could be done now? She pondered. He wasn't coming home again.

Dominic called Christie Tuesday night. Christie was living downtown in a rooming house at 675 Boylston Street in Copley Square. At that time, it was the only residential house in Copley Square. He had a bedroom and the use of a kitchen. To reduce his rent he removed the trash and did some minor maintenance.

Dominic talked to a lawyer and arranged for a meeting on Wednesday. Dominic arranged to meet at Christie' place and then proceed to the law office, which was seven blocks away. Christie looked forward to this meeting, but was apprehensive because of the lack of funds. He had a job, but it didn't pay all that much. At twenty-two years old he was still trying to figure what to do with his life. The war and his injury had taken a toll on him. Christie informed me as to what happened at the lawyer's office.

Wednesday arrived and Dominic and Christie went to meet with the lawyer. Christie was nervous, but Dominic was cool as a cucumber. He strutted into the lawyer's office as if it were his. Christie trod behind, troubled. After the usual introductions, and the shaking of hands, the lawyer told them to be seated. He was already informed about the case.

The main two reasons for this meeting were to see if he would take on the case and how much he would charge. The latter reason was of most importance; there were other lawyers.

This lawyer's name was Juddins (no one remembered his first name). He was a lawyer for mobsters, but this would be his first cop killer trial.

It wouldn't be cheap! Juddins immediately said, "I have to have money up front before I even talk to you."

Dominic asked, "How much?"

"Four thousand dollars."

"Dominic responded, "Four gees?"

Juddins answered with a pronounced nod.

Dominic got out of his chair, reached into his pocket and pulled out a wad of money. It looked as if it would choke a horse. He peeled off the four gees, handed it to Juddins who sat down and never blinked an eye.

With the money in his hand Juddins counted it and said, "Okay, I'll take the case. I'll get in touch with you in a few days; in the meantime, I'll go and see the client." That was it, end of conversation: zip! He was hired. A mob mouthpiece!

While they were meeting with the lawyer, I decided to see if I could see Bill. I had never gone to see anyone in jail before. I purchased a nickel bar of candy, which would cost about one dollar today. It was either an O'Henry or a Hershey bar. The police station, which was also police headquarters, was about six blocks from Boston English High School, so I could walk there after school, and then I would take a different trolley car to get back home.

I climbed up the few granite steps leading into the solid stone station house. I was nervous and wondered if they would treat me funny because I wanted to see a killer. Stepping through the double green thick wooden doors, I passed a few cops mingling around the entrance. A long paneled desk was on my right, somewhat raised. I stopped and faced the cops sitting there; one of them was a sergeant. Our eyes met as he looked down at me.

He said, "Hey kid, what do you want?"

"I want to see my uncle."

"Who's your uncle?"

"William Goudas, we live together. I just got out of school and I thought I'd come here to see him."

"William Goudas?"

"Yeah, I want to see him, and I want to give him a bar of candy that I bought."

The sergeant probably thought I was crazy, daring, or just plain foolish.

He looked me over, saw my cloth school bag with the school's large light blue letter (E) over dark blue, and inquired, "Do you go to that school?"

"Yes, I just walked from there."

I guess seeing the school's insignia gave me some credibility for he said, "Well this is a little unusual, let me see the bar."

I took the cloth bag off my shoulder, reached in and retrieved the candy bar, and holding it up in the air. I said, "Here."

"Hand it up here."

I stepped forward and gave it to him. He turned it over as he felt the sides, squeezing it somewhat. Deciding that it was what it was, he handed it back to me and said, "Okay, you can see him this one time briefly, but don't come back."

I answered, "Thanks," as I stuck the candy in my shirt pocket.

He called to an officer who was sitting close by the desk, "Take this kid to see Goudas and let him give him the bar of candy."

We went through locked doors heading towards the rear of the building, passing officers guarding steel barred doors, and into the cell area that housed Bill. There was another officer there who led us to Bill's cell. Bill was lying down with his eyes closed.

When I saw him, I said loudly, "Hey Bill, hi."

He looked up and had this surprised look on his face, and then he smiled. I'm sure he couldn't figure why I was there or how I even got in.

He said, "Hi, Angelo."

I reached into my pocket, pulled out the candy bar, and was about to pass it to him when the officer that led us to Bill's cell said gruffly, "Hey, give me that."

The officer who walked in with me told the other cop, "Sarge said it was okay."

"Yeah, well, I want to see it anyhow, give me that!"

I handed him the candy bar and he did exactly what the sergeant had done, and then he handed it back and said, "Okay."

He turned around and left as I passed the candy bar through the metal bars, and Bill took it with a wide grin on his face.

As the cop was leaving he said, "Don't take too long."

The cop that brought me in to see Bill stayed by my side. I asked Bill how he was doing, how his foot was, and how the food was.

He replied, "Okay," to all the questions. I didn't know what else to say. It was an awkward situation, and Bill didn't seem to be in a talking mood. Then the cop said, "Let's go."

We said our good-byes, and I turned around and left. I can't say I felt good seeing him in jail, but he deserved being there. I didn't see him again for two years.

# STRIKE CLOSES FISH STO
# AS MEAT HITS NEW LO

## POLICE HUNT SECOND PAIR
## IN SERGT. HEALEY SLAYING

| Goudas, Pal Face Murder Charge Today | Truman-Attlee Row Flares Over Palestine | | Singer Says She'll Wed Joe DiMaggio |
|---|---|---|---|

*Boston Globe 10-5-1946 Indictment*

63

# CHAPTER IX
## Informant Attacks

The following articles appeared in the city's leading newspapers the day after the murder of Sergeant William F. Healey:

"Officers Warned To Be Extra Careful"

"Ironically the officers starting their tour of duty at 5:45 o'clock last night were admonished by the lieutenant in a roll call at the Berkley Station to be extra careful of suspicious persons because of the large number of crimes in the city recently, Sergeant Healey was one of the listeners and four hours later he was a victim of a murderer's bullet."

"At the time of Sergeant Healey's murder, his wife was attending a bridal shower for the daughter of another police officer. An officer interrupted the proceedings to announce that her husband had been injured and was in the hospital, and a patrol car was waiting to take her to her husband. When she arrived at the hospital, he had already passed away. Her two daughters, 12 and 14 years respectively, were taken to their grandparent's home directly from the bridal shower." *Boston* Globe

Sergeant William F. Healey, 49, was a veteran of World War I. He had been awarded the police department's Medal of Honor for rescuing lives in the 1938 hurricane. He was well-liked and respected by his fellow officers. A fund was established in his name to assist his family with their loss. He was given a hero's tribute and honored by a large outpouring of police from throughout the area, and by many friends and family at his funeral. The fund closed at $37,818 on October 24$^{th}$: a lot of money in those days. This would help the newly widowed mother of two financially, but not emotionally. Only time would heal the hurt.

Jocko, the man who assisted in the capture of the killer, was offered police protection after being assaulted and hospitalized. They said they would put him under police protection until Joseph F. Moore, Joseph MacEachern and Russell Swenson (Jake Swenson's brother) were captured. Unfortunately the protection offered Jocko did not help him the same night they arrested Goudas and Swenson.

Jocko was accosted by two assailants while returning home from finishing his tour of duty at the city hospital. It was 1 a.m. when these culprits jumped out of a black automobile and poured gasoline onto his left arm and then ignited it. With his arm on fire, one of them yelled, "Maybe that will teach you to keep quiet."

As quickly as they attacked, they jumped back into the still running auto and drove away screeching their tires, leaving with no lights on. Jocko managed to remove his jacket before any serious damage was done to his arm, but he did receive burns and had to be hospitalized overnight.

Three days later Jocko was accosted again. This attack took place a few blocks from his home, again at 1 a.m. while walking home from the hospital. Whether they were the same individuals is unknown, but they smashed a bottle over his head yelling, "Forget all you know about Swenson." They were driving the same black sedan. They also tried to run him down as he was crossing the street before jumping out to assault him.

I'm not totally knowledgeable about how Jake or his friends found out about Jocko, especially at the time of the first attack, but when they arrested Jake, I'm sure the word went out to his friends.

The assault on Jocko happened right after Jake's arrest at 12:30 a.m., a half-hour after his capture. One fact to consider is that Jake (102 Winthrop Street), and Jocko (20 Vine Street), lived three streets away from each other. How ironic! Whether they actually knew each other before this crime is not known, but it could be possible, although I can't imagine them hanging out together. Jocko and Jake came from two different sides of the street.

Based on the fact that they might have met through Bill, one must consider the following implications. Bill, after he shot the policeman, went over to Jocko's home to ask for treatment for the wounded foot. Bill could have gone over to Jake's house also and told him, or to whomever, what happened at 24 Fayette Street, and that he had stopped by Jocko's to receive treatment. Or, he could have telephoned Jake or Big Joe and given them the same information. Somehow, Jake or his cohorts became aware that Jocko knew of the slain policeman, and after the arrest of Jake, his buddies either knew or assumed that Jocko squealed to the police. Somehow, they also knew he worked at Boston City Hospital and would be getting home around 1 a.m. The only person that I'm aware of who knew all about Jocko was Bill. How Jake or the others found out is anyone's guess, but the above facts seem to warrant that Bill had to have informed his partners.

The attack on Jocko the same night of Bill and Jake's arrest gave Jake's friends the impetus to try and scare the stool pigeon into cowering. I do know, and can say explicitly that no one, and I repeat, no one from our family had anything to do with any attacks on Jocko.

The police decided that after the first attack on Jocko they better do something to protect him before they lose a star witness. He was put under protective custody until the two remaining members of the gang were apprehended. This brave citizen only did what his conscience dictated. It was obvious that outside forces were trying to intimidate him and to stop him from testifying. Maybe Jocko rejected the offer for protection the first time, but he probably accepted the help after the second incident. I know I would!

Our family never saw or heard from Jocko again, except for during the trial, and on two other somewhat awkward occasions. Christie was there when Jocko was put on the stand to relay his story. Christie also saw him again many months after the trial. Christie was approaching a bus stop at Roxbury Crossing just as the bus had pulled into the stop area. Standing in line to get on the bus was Jocko. He was the third person in the line; it was one of the few streets in that area that used buses instead of streetcars (trolleys). When Jocko saw Christie approaching, he took off at a rapid pace. He looked over his shoulder at Christie when he was about forty feet away, and then again, as he was quickly stepping away. Christie had no intentions of following him.

I did see Jocko once at the Warren Theater on Warren Street near Grove Hall in Roxbury, sitting with a young lady a few months after Bill's arrest. We made eye contact when I passed him on my way down the aisle to a seat up front with my young female friend. We both had surprised looks on our faces. When I was seated with my date, I turned around to look at him again. He and his date had disappeared. Their seats were empty.

A couple of months after the trial, I read in the daily paper that Jocko was attacked again. This time he was knifed and hospitalized, but was not in serious condition. The unknown assailant was not apprehended, as he fled on foot, unobserved. Three attacks and no persons were ever taken into custody. That was the last time that we ever heard anything about Jocko.

The police were now looking for three men, including Joseph F. Moore, 32, of Moreland Street, Roxbury, the other person involved with the robbery, and Joseph E. MacEachern, 38, of Millmont Street, Dorchester, and the driver of the getaway car and the actual ring leader of the gang. The third person was Jake's brother, Russell Swenson, 26. He was the hired chauffeur, at one time, of Gene Metz, the man that was robbed at Fayette Street, but before Metz moved to that address; an ironic detail of this story.

A few weeks prior to Healey's death, a robbery was committed in Dorchester, a southern suburb of Boston. At this caper, two foreign automatic pistols were stolen with some other goods. When the two men exited the rear of Fayette Street to get away, one of them dropped one of those stolen guns. The gun was discovered in the shed behind the building. The detectives were able to identify it as one of the two automatic revolvers stolen. Fritz and Bill were identified as implicated in that robbery in Dorchester. The prosecutor did not pursue that criminal act. It was murder one now.

It was revealed to the public that Fritz "Jake" Swenson was a recently paroled felon from Concord Reformatory, a state correction facility. It was also revealed that he had a rap sheet a mile long, and that he had also been detained in a juvenile detention center. His life of crime had started at a very young age.

On October 7, William Goudas and Fritz O. Swenson were arraigned at municipal court on murder charges, cases continued for a hearing on October 15, by Judge Joseph T. Zottoli. Joseph E. MacEachern (Big Joe) and Russell Swenson (Fritz O. Swenson's brother, 29) were indicted as accessories after the fact. Joseph F. Moore would be indicted after his capture.

On the day of their indictments, four officers were to leave for San Pedro, California, to return two of the three men on the lam. The lead officer was Lt. James U. Crowley, the same detective that arrested Bill. Two of the men to be returned were Russell Swenson and Joseph E. MacEachern. Joseph F. Moore was still on the loose and the police had no leads concerning his whereabouts.

Russell Swenson and Joseph E MacEachern left the city quickly, within an hour of Jake's arrest. They drove south in Joseph's car all night. Once beyond New York City, I'm sure they felt secure from being stopped by a roadblock. They finally landed in Miami, Florida, where Joseph sold his car, and the pair then flew to Los Angeles.

An informant called headquarters and told them that Joseph might have gone to Miami, and the informant also gave them a Miami address. The police then called Miami officials. The Miami police department, in their investigation, learned of a forwarding address that MacEachern had left in Miami, for mail to be delivered to a San Pedro, California home. All this information was forwarded back to headquarters in Boston. The detectives then called the San Pedro police and the two men were captured and held for extradition back East. Now there was one to go, Mr. Moore.

Joseph E. MacEachern might have been the ringleader, but to me he wasn't as bright as he thought he was. Can you imagine leaving a forwarding address even though it was in California? If you're on the lam then you break all ties with everyone you know. What do you care for mail, you are not going to pay any bills. Does that mean that someone back home was going to send him his mail? Don't you think the police would be looking for any lead to your whereabouts? Talk about a dumb crook.

ston
ton-
ing
read
ers,
the
con-
eeks
poly
any
cih-
ions,
npel
st in
at-
tion
ers.

Ph
nion
y to
un-
in a
'day

# Police to Fetch
# Boston Pair Held
# at San Pedro

## Court Continues Cases
## of Two Held Here in
## Sgt Healey Slaying

Awaiting the arrival of four Boston police officers, officials of San Pedro, Calif, last night held two Roxbury men in connection with the Oct 7 slaying of Police Sgt William F. Healey during the burglary of an apartment on Fayette st., Boston.

Lt James V. Crowley, Detective Thomas J. Conaty, both of the Headquarters Bureau of Criminal Investigation; Sgt Charles W. Hewett

*Boston Globe 10-7-1946*

# Man Who Tipped Police on Healey Slayer Slugged

Smashing a bottle over his head with the warning "Forget all you know about Swenson," two unidentified men shortly after 1 this morning assaulted George Larson, of 30 Vine st, Roxbury, who tipped off police last Friday to the alleged murderer of Police Sgt William F. Healey. The attack was at Albany st, near Dudley st.

Larson, medical assistant at Boston City Hospital, was on his way home from duty this morning when the pair drove up in a big, black sedan as he was walking along Albany st. He told police that they almost ran him down as he crossed the street, and when they missed, left the car and threatened him.

"One of the pair hit me over the head with a bottle and said: 'Forget all you know about Swenson,'" Larson told police.

Police learned that this was the second time that an attempt has been made to cow Larson since the night of the fatal shooting of Sgt Healey. Last Friday, while walking home from the hospital, he told police this morning, two men assaulted him, poured gasoline on his left arm, and ignited it.

See MURDER Page 13

# Sinatra, Wife Separate; No Divorce Planned

*Boston Globe 10-16-1946*

71

# CHAPTER X
## Where's the Gun?

Now that the police had four of the suspects in custody, what they needed to tighten the case was the pistol that killed their brother officer. Three separate searches had come up empty. A week had passed since the arrest of Goudas and Swenson when the department received a letter from a neighbor, possibly across the street from our home. The letter revealed that Christie had retrieved the gun from the Linden Street alley and thrown it in a pond. The police had to act on this tip.

The police arrested Christie again a few days later. He had been out with his cousin Jay and a few pals having some drinks. They used to go where Jay lived; there were beer joints there that they used to go to. Christie had my mother's Pontiac; he had it for quite a while. He learned to drive in it. In fact, he drove without a license. The reason I'm mentioning the automobile was the A-frame on the car, a bolt had worn, and once in a while the A-frame would drop and the front would drop down a little bit, and you had to jack it up, then knock the bolt a little bit to the side, and push the bolt back in. The bolt had worn a larger hole, and if you get it just right you could tap it back in and it would hold for a while. Christie returning from the beer joint had to fix it again.

Christie pushed the car off the road to fix it, by knocking that bolt back in, and then tighten the bolt. So naturally he got grease on his hands, and he had nice clothes on. He went home and parked the car in front of his building. Because somebody had written a letter to the police that Christie knew where the gun was, the police went to his home.

I remembered that building because I joined the Army when I lived there briefly with Christie. He didn't remember that. I asked Christie what happened and he related the following story to me.

Christie walked to the building's front door, and all of a sudden somebody pointed a gun right at him. There were two men there. They didn't have suits on. One had an Army type of shirt. He needed a shave and he had a soft felt hat on. Christie thought he looked like a bum, like a real bum.

He was a bit older than Christie, and he stuck a gun in his face. So, the first thing Christie said was, 'You caught me at a bad time.'

The gun was a 38 revolver. He could see the bullets in the revolver. So he put his hands up. He said to himself, I'm being robbed. He told them, 'Boy, you caught me at a bad night. I spent most of my money. I only got a dollar; you know you're welcome to the buck.' They then said they were police, they had gone there looking for him and the gun.

The other officer wasn't in uniform or he wasn't in casual clothing. Christie called it bum clothes. Christie used to get dressed up every day. So for him, if they weren't dressed up, they were in bum clothes. When he wore dungarees, because he was poor, he hated to be seen in them. He only wore them because he had to.

They brought him to the front room on the first floor and asked him a lot of questions. Of course, the other people of the house knew about it, because they had previously gone up to his room, and ransacked it.

Of course, they didn't find what they wanted. They were asking him about the gun. 'Where were you?' they said, 'Your hands are dirty? Where did you go, Willitt Pond?' He replied, 'What do you know about Willitt Pond?'

He used to go swimming there, it was the local's swimming hole. The cops knew about it for the person who had written the letter must have mentioned Willitt Pond. He had once taken a lady there parking. She lived across the street from his mother's house. So they cuffed him and brought him in.

They didn't show him a search warrant. Of course, they already had searched his room before he got home.

They saw his dirty hands and they saw a spot of dirt on his shirt, and of course, he was dressed up. They asked, 'Where were you digging?'

They were thinking he had dug someplace, and he hid the gun, that's why his hands were dirty. He told them 'That's grease on my hands.' he told them about his car breaking down, and why his hands were dirty. So, they took the car in and took it apart, just in case it was hidden in the car. They didn't find anything. They then put the car together. They did whatever they wanted then. Evidently they realized of course, he had told the truth about why he got dirty, because they could see the problem with the frame. They had him in a cell and they kept walking over to him, and asking him. 'Where did you hide it?' They put him in a cell and left him alone for the night.

The next morning the same two officers returned. 'We got a letter, we know you did it' 'Christie asked them what letter are you talking about? I don't believe you got a letter, a letter from whom? You couldn't have got a letter from anybody.' So they showed him a letter. He tried to see the name, but they hid it from him. Christie never saw the name, but he thought he knew who it was. He was sure it was that girl who lived across the street that he had gone out with, because it wasn't far from where Bill said he threw the gun.

Christie told them, 'Well if you got this letter, somebody tells you what they think, and they certainly can't tell you what they know. I had nothing to do with it, and that's it!' With that they walked away. They returned again and asked, 'Did you throw it in Willitt Pond?' It seems they either interrogated people from the area, or the girl across the street that mentioned the pond. She had never been to the pond before he took her. Anyway, after all that, they left. Then he heard someone call his name. It was Gregory. Gregory said, 'Is that you, Christie?' Evidently he must have heard his voice.

Gregory was in another cell, but it wasn't next to his. Christie hollered out, 'You've been here all the time?' Gregory said, 'Yeah.' They talked for a few minutes, and Christie told him they were looking for the gun. Christie said, 'I guess anybody in the family might have it or whatever. I know I had nothing to do with it.' They were talking out loud.

They were talking in English because if they talked in Greek they would think they were trying to hide something. Usually when you do talk in Greek in front of people that don't know the language, it's saying you don't want them to know what you're saying. You have something to hide. So, that was it, they let them go.

The reason Gregory was there was the same reason Christie was. They were not formally arrested or booked. They arrested them because they thought with interrogation they would get one, or both of them to confess to knowing where the gun was. The police wanted the gun to finish up the crime investigation. The police also thought they either had it or disposed it, or they were hiding it, whatever the case may be. Well, they let them go, and they never arrested them again. In fact, they never bothered them again! Christie told me emphatically that he had nothing to do with the gun.

I had been talking to Christie about this subject, "Do you remember Buddy Mone, the kid I used to hang around with? He used to live across the street, on the hill out back."

"Yes."

"Well, when we went out to play or go somewhere right after Bill was arrested, for about a week some cops in an unmarked car used to follow us. Of course, we were on foot so we played games with them. We'd act as if we didn't see them, then we'd run down one of the alleys or into Farmer Brown's field. We would laugh to ourselves. Hey, we were just kids. It was fun, but a little bit scary. We knew what they wanted."

# CHAPTER XI
## Paying for the Defense

The problem now was how the family was going to pay for Bill's legal defense. Dominic put up the money to retain the lawyer, but that was only a temporary solution. He wanted the family to repay him as much money as possible. Dominic said that we should try to raise the money. No one in the immediate family had that kind of money or the resources to obtain it. Even if we all gave everything we had, it wouldn't put a dent in the money needed.

Family relatives, for the most part, wanted nothing to do with assisting us. Of course, they had sympathy for Ma and her children, but they wanted nothing to do with Bill's defense. He had shamed their family's name and reputation. His crime was disgraceful to the entire Goudas family, and to all the close relatives. Looking back into their history, they came from a respectable background, except for one of my great grandmothers, as I have previously written.

The idea that came forth was to hire a dance band, rent a hall, and hold a fundraising dance. Christie volunteered to take on most of the responsibilities. Gregory said he would sell tickets, but nothing else. People enjoyed dancing, and it would be a good way to raise money. During those postwar years, going to the movies and to clubs and listening and dancing to live music were the few sources of entertainment. There even were weekly dances held in our neighborhood for teenagers at a building similar to a boys-girls club. They used to play 78 rpm records.

Christie decided to use a name that would represent a social club. He came up with the name, the "Buccaneers." The idea would be that the Buccaneers wanted to raise money for their club. Of course, the money collected beyond the cost for running the dance would be used towards Bill's defense. Christie would go to businesses and ask for money for advertisements for a booklet that was to be handed out to the attendees as a dance program. Tickets were printed and sold prior to the dance for entrance at a cost of one dollar each. They were to be sold at the door also. Extra donations were accepted during ticket sales. Tickets were sold well in advance, so the advanced money could be used for the cost of printing the dance program, and to pay the cost of the band.

The band would play jitterbug music and the usual slow dances like the foxtrot. We liked to hold onto our partners more in those days, and these dances allowed us to do just that.

Christie went to a group of businesses to sell ads. Of course, he had never done this before, so he was somewhat nervous. Besides, what approach was he going to use to sound legitimate? As Christie started to sell ads he got more confident, especially after his first encounter.

Christie went to all kind of places to get ads. He remembered walking into Shaughnessy's Springs on River Street. He remembered having to go visit them before. It was a broken spring on Rita's Pontiac. They used to break more often than they do nowadays, and, he remembered walking in there and telling the front girl there, if he could speak to somebody here, we're running a dance for a really good cause. So she called over to this fellow, and he came over, and Christie said, 'We're running a dance for our group called the Buccaneers, and running this dance for a good cause. We're wondering if you'll take an ad.' The man reached in his pocket, he took out ten dollars, which you know is worth more than ten dollars now. He said, 'Here.' Christie told him 'I'll send you a program.' He replied, 'Yeah, I'd like to have one.'

Just like that, he gave Christie the money and didn't think much about it. Christie was glad that the man was so good about it. Christie had been doing business there, and he was telling everybody about this place and the man. I think it was the first place he tried, because he didn't know where to go or what to do, and he was surprised how easy it was to get people to throw in an ad when you tell them it is for a good cause. We did hold the dance, and we did make plenty of money. Of course, all the money went to Dominic. Dominic kept the bankroll in his pocket, because he was the one paying the lawyer.

Christie got mad at Dominic a couple of times. Dominic drank a lot and he was spending a lot of the money, money that Christie was making. What could Christie do? After all Dominic got the lawyer. Christie didn't have any experience like he would have had later on, because of his military service, and adjusting to civilian life. Christie would rather have had somebody else handle it.

Everybody in the house sold tickets except Ma. Even friends helped. Anyhow, some money was paid to Dominic from the ticket sales and also money from extra donations. A lot of the neighborhood crowd gave extra money. Bill was well-liked, and most of all, I guess, they felt sorry for his family.

Dominic never did ask the family to repay the whole amount. My mother, I'm sure, had a strong influence on that matter. Dominic and Rita returned home before the dance took place. She of course, had to go back to work at the textile factory. Whether Dominic was obligated like a regular worker to return to work, I don't know, but I doubt it.

I went to the dance, which of course was a huge success. Most of the people there were adults, but I had sold some tickets to some of my friends, so they all came. I do remember having a good time, and I danced with a couple of older ladies, not too old, maybe twenty or so, and of course, with any girls my age.

The dance band played great jitterbug music. Everyone was dressed to kill, and the ladies wore those silk stockings that had a seam running up the back of their legs. The more they danced the more crooked the seam would become. Then the ladies would go to the ladies room and straighten them out. During the war, women painted their legs with a color to imitate the silk, and they would paint a seam up the back of their legs. Silk was unobtainable during the war, because the silk was used for parachutes. I always thought that silk stockings were great until they became crooked. Most of the girls my age wore bobby socks.

At the time of the dance, we had all resumed our usual routine way of life. The dance did take up some of our time, but Christie took on most of the responsibilities. There wasn't much else we could do but wait for the trial.

All the crime subjects had been indicted except Joseph F. Moore. Christie and the lawyer were in contact with Bill. Dorothea didn't go during the trial or to see Bill because she didn't want to see him locked up, and of course, I couldn't see him. I was underage. Ma just stayed home and lived her life as usual. I guess she just gave up.

Gregory didn't want anything to do with Bill. He did sell some dance tickets, but that was all. Well, for whatever reason, you could say it was justifiable. Gregory never had anything to do with Bill again. No one said anything to him about it either. I guess we all understood and just kept it to ourselves.

Nicholas, the youngest brother, was away serving in the Merchant Marines during those troubled times. When Nicholas did come home to stay, Bill had already been tried and sentenced. Nicholas, like his brother Gregory, wanted nothing to do with Bill either. Maybe the two of them confided about the situation when they finally got together and gave each other their reasons for their avoidance. The family had to accept their privacy and their decision on this matter.

Nicholas was a big sturdy strong man. When he was fourteen years old he was the biggest kid on the block. He stood at 5'10", but as the years went by he never grew another inch, he just bulked up. The other kids caught up to him or just got taller. Nicholas had light blue eyes, dark brown curly hair, and the round family face. After he returned home from the Merchant Marines he got a job unloading sides of beef. Nicholas would pick up one side of beef and carry it on his back from the truck into the cooler. He did this until the truck was unloaded, and that took all night. And I thought a hundred pounds of ice was heavy.

# CHAPTER XII
## The Trial

The weeks since Bill's arrest had taken a heavy toll on the family. After he rehabilitated from his injury, he was brought to the grand jury and indicted for the murder of Sergeant William F. Healey, and for the home invasion and robbery of 24 Fayette Street. Standing beside him was his accomplice, Fritz O. Swenson. Ma accepted Bill's fate and didn't discuss the matter with anyone except Christie. She knew Christie would do whatever was necessary, and he had already showed his deep concern by working so hard on the successful fundraising.

Madeline was melancholic and she would have frequent periods of crying, and if my sister was home, the two of them would join each other in this saddened predicament. Gregory, as I had mentioned earlier, went on with his usual state of affairs. Of course, he never joined in with his sister in those melancholy situations, but neither did he rebuke the affection that she displayed for Bill. After all, this was her brother, even though Gregory was disappointed and thoroughly disgusted with Bill's crime and the effect it had on the family's integrity. Robbery he could accept internally, but using deadly force, such as Bill displayed, was against his moral principles. And that was that!

With the capture of Joseph E. MacEachern and Russell Swenson in California, and their ultimate return to face trial for their implication and association with Jake and Bill, they were indicted by the grand jury. Joseph F. Moore was still on the lam somewhere, someplace; an all-points bulletin was still in effect.

As the trial convened, I was completing my junior year of high school. To tell you the truth, I had little interest in going, but I obviously wanted to know what was going on. There was little coverage of the trial in the newspapers that I can remember, because daily events locally and internationally took up all the front-page sections. The murder was old news as far as editors were concerned. Other murders or the Palestinian turmoil took precedence in the news, even way back then. I did have moments of desire to attend the trial, but, as previously mentioned, I wanted to go to school.

I missed my uncle tremendously. He was, at the time of the crime, the closest male family member I had. He was more like a brother than an uncle. Four years difference in age, how could he be an uncle? Uncles are old like fathers, especially during one's teenage years. When I would return home from school, we would discuss my classes and my day. He always showed interest in my studies and in me. My father never showed this interest in the fourteen years that I lived with him. You can understand why I became so attached. I missed those discussions, those meetings, that human connection, that father-brother association we had established, even though he was now a criminal, an undesirable by community standards and even by some members of our family.

As I mentioned before, we would accompany one another playing music, either classical or even popular music from the thirties and forties from sheet music. There would be many sessions when we would discuss Greek and Roman mythology, World War II, Napoleon, Alexander the Great, The Pharaohs, and religion, especially our religion, Greek Orthodox. Although I didn't discuss my goal in life with my family or friends, deep down inside I wanted to be a priest, like my great grandfather. It was a secret, and I told no secrets.

The trial took place a few months into the following year, 1947. Attending, sitting, and listening were left up to Christie and Madeline, Christie mostly. Both Goudas and Swenson used the same lawyer simultaneously. No one remembered his first name, so I will refer to him here as Lawyer Juddins.

I don't know what Fritz paid Lawyer Juddins, but I assume he paid the same stipend, four gees, which made a total of eight thousand dollars. One would expect a lot of defense for that kind of money. For eight thousand dollars you could buy four or five single-family homes in a respectable neighborhood.

It seems that it didn't turn out that way at all. The mouthpiece (Sharton) that turned out to be most effective, for all defendants, was the lawyer that Joseph E. MacEachern hired for his own defense. When the trial convened, all three defendants, William Goudas, Fritz O. Swenson, and Joseph E. MacEachern, were tried at the same time, in the same courtroom before the same judge.

Goudas and Swenson were standing trial for second degree murder. The reason being, that the murder of Sergeant William F. Healey was not a premeditated act by any of the defendants, even Goudas. First degree carried the death sentence. Second degree meant life in prison with a chance for parole for good behavior. MacEachern was indicted by the grand jury as an accessory to the crime and the ringleader. No witness could place him at the crime scene.

Fritz Swenson's brother Russell was to have a separate trial for being an accomplice after the fact. Fritz Swenson's penalty did not carry a life sentence, although I do not know what he received, and in reality it doesn't matter. He was convicted.

Sharton, now this was a great lawyer. As with Lawyer Juddins, neither Christie nor anyone else could remember Sharton's first name, so I will refer to him as Lawyer Sharton. Christie said he was sharp as a tack. He was the whole defense, for Goudas and for Swenson, plus the man that hired him, MacEachern. He commanded the defense's two tables. Goudas, Swenson, and Lawyer Juddins sat at one table and Lawyer Sharton and MacEachern sat at the other table, but it was Lawyer Sharton that did most of the talking.

Let's briefly recapitulate the crime. Joseph F. Moore, William Goudas, and Fritz O. Swenson went into 24 Fayette Street. Goudas got into a scuffle with one of the tenants, a man. During the struggle Goudas was shot in his left foot, which required medical attention. Goudas went to one of his friends that had medical knowledge, and worked at the city's hospital. Goudas asked for assistance, but his friend refused. Goudas told him that he'd shot a policeman. The next day all the news sources in the city reported that a police sergeant had been killed. This friend of Goudas notified the police. It didn't take a rocket scientist to put two and two together. After the arrest of Goudas, he confessed, implicating the men inside and the man outside at the scene of the crime. When Swenson was arrested, he too implicated the same individuals.

Now it was their confessions against MacEachern's denial of any wrongdoing. MacEachern, after his arrest and return from California, never said or confessed that he was implicated with those other individuals in the robbery or the killing of Sergeant William F. Healey. He claimed he only knew them briefly. Goudas and Swenson both knew that MacEachern was the ringleader, and that he drove the black 1941 Plymouth sedan rented by Swenson for $35.00 as a getaway car.

Lawyer Juddins was kind of old compared to the other lawyer. Lawyer Sharton was much younger. As I have written it turned out that Lawyer Sharton was the best lawyer. In fact, MacEachern never stayed in jail after he was returned from California. Bill and Fritz were never released. They were refused bail.

They (the police) knew MacEachern was the ring master. He was the one that really ran it. He's the one who had those guys do the robbery, but he didn't subject himself to do the actual stealing or entering the home. He planned it, he ran it. Give those guys what they needed, and survey the property, whatever. Send in those guys to do the dirty work, but he ended up in court, and had the best lawyer. Of course, Dominic didn't know at the time when he hired Bill's lawyer, and Christie didn't know either, but they found out. Christie sat through most of the trial.

Christie told me that the inside of the court room looked like what you'd see in the movies. It had the jury off to the right-hand side, lawyer and prosecutor tables in front of the judge, and of course, all the defendants sitting beside the lawyers. There was a little, old, Italian guy, in the end, who was crying when the verdict was in, because he was sorry, because he didn't really want to be in the jury, but he was and when they announced guilty, the poor guy was screaming. A little, old, Italian man.

To Christie it seemed like it was high-profile, yet he couldn't recall reading what the papers wrote. It was so long ago, it seems that some things he wanted to forget.

It's hard for me to really tell you everything, because for some reason or another those days don't stick in my mind. Besides, I was only sixteen years old. Of course, I didn't go to the trial; I only got what was told to me. I don't know if it's because you try to push it out of your mind or you don't want to remember it, so you don't retain it, but it was dramatic.

As previously written, they were all tried at the same time. They didn't

MUSIC YOU WILL NEVER HEAR

do it like they do today, but Lawyer Sharton did almost all of it. Christie remembered one thing, when the defense was on, it was him. So he was the lead mouthpiece.

Those that went to the trial told the family that during the trial Bill was handcuffed, but he didn't look scared, but he was mostly expressionless, he was very expressionless. There were no outbursts by any of the defendants and Christie or Madeline had no problem getting inside to the trial. Madeline went fewer times, but there were a lot of people there. The trial went on for several weeks. Swenson was not given the same sentence; it was a little less than Bill's, but a long sentence, because he was there, and he confessed to it.

MacEachern got off because they couldn't connect him. They couldn't connect him physically. The only thing they could have done was to get the words of the two who insisted during the trial that he wasn't there.

Christie asked Bill afterwards, 'How come you two are taking the rap and he's going to get off?' Bill replied, as a matter of fact, 'We're still going to take the rap and what difference is it going to make if we say he wasn't there, what difference is it going to make?'

Were we surprised at the verdict? No. When he was indicted and going to trial, we did expect a worse verdict. In those days the state still used the electric chair. That's what we were worried about, but once they were trying for second degree, we didn't expect anything worse, simply because they weren't trying for first. The fact that it wasn't premeditated, they knew it wasn't premeditated, so they didn't try to make it premeditated, so they went for second degree. That's why he got life. The lawyer was trying to get it down to third degree, to get a lighter sentence, because it was unintentional, but it wasn't an accident. If he had shot at one person and hit another person they might have turned it into a third degree case, but not in this case.

Gregory wasn't interested in any of that, and Nicholas wasn't around at that time, but he would have wanted to stay away from it too. The verdict is that Bill commits a serious crime, kills a policeman, and is given a life sentence.

The family wondered what Ma's reaction to all of this would be. I never asked her, but Christie told me, "Ma wasn't a talkative person. She didn't say a great deal on this. I remember one time; she sort of said in a statement and sort of a question, like, 'Well he's no good then.' According to her mind thinking one way and putting it into English, sometimes didn't match what she was exactly thinking. I think she was probably more or less saying anybody who would murder somebody else has to be a bad person, has to be bad."

What was her reaction to the penalty when he was convicted? She never really showed. She never showed emotions a great deal. I think because where she came from, and her background. In her country bad things happened, and it was part of her life. Good things happen and it is nice, but tragedy happens, because they did come from tragic backgrounds, the wars (World War I and the Balkan War of 1912), the Turks, and they accepted it, that's what happens.

Christie was there when he was found guilty. It went exactly as he expected. He knew he wasn't going to get off.

So, how did Christie feel inside? Because of his age, he couldn't feel the same as an older person. When you're younger you're much more careless, and the fact that he had gone through a war and people were dying, and at that age it just didn't affect him as much, as much as it would have, if he was older. Naturally he was disturbed by it.

What did he feel like when he found out what he did? Wow, my brother is wanted for murder! Christie was terribly disappointed that he would even go do robbery basically. It didn't surprise him somewhat that he robbed, because they didn't have a great deal, and he wanted to go to the New England Conservatory. But if Gregory robbed, it wouldn't have surprised him at all.

And what did Christie feel about Nicholas if he did it, especially where Nicholas used to be a real teaser. He used to be a terrible aggravator, but he always worked and always had money, so he would have been shocked if Nicholas did such a thing.

Nicholas was aggravating all the time and Bill used to step in and stop him. Christie used to just look at him, as he was trying to antagonize him. One time Christie was laying down, Nicholas went over to him and put his hand over him, but he didn't touch him. He knew better than to touch him, but he figured he'd get as close as he could. Finally Bill couldn't stand it anymore, and they started fighting. They were fighting instead of Christie. I guess Bill couldn't stand it. So, with that kind of attitude,

Christie thought Bill shot first because with that sort of instinctive attitude, somebody points a gun at you and you have a gun, even though you're doing something wrong to begin with, you still protect yourself. It's natural. Bill didn't have much patience, and with no job training, robbing would be an easier way to have money. What a philosophy. He had everybody fooled.

After the trial Christie went home and had to tell Ma of the verdict. It was in the afternoon. She was in the kitchen cooking or she was in the kitchen doing something, and he told her. Her attitude was along the lines, he got what she expected, something along that line.

Gregory never did say anything about the crime to anyone like, what a jerk! He just did it with actions, not with words.

Nicholas was the same, but Madeline never felt that way about her brother. She was very hurt by the whole thing. We knew how sensitive she was. She would visit him whenever she could. She never gave up on him, and of course Rita, my mother, lived in New York, so she never came up much anyhow. I do remember her visiting though.

The family's reactions were split on the incarceration of Bill, and of course his violent crime. Not that anyone accepted it, but we had to move on in our lives. We were all still very young, so to speak, and we had to look to the future. Our matured lives had just begun; we were getting better jobs, more money, and new places to live. Marriage and children were not too far in the future. Ma and the family were starting to separate and move on. Ma found a smaller place to live at the Cathedral Projects, off of Washington Street near Holy Cross Cathedral, which would help to alleviate the sorrows from having lived in the place where they were founded. She still had all her children alive. After the turmoil of war, one son had lost his freedom, even though three of her boys fought for it, and her two daughters worked for it. As they say, life moves on.

Boston Globe 10-8-1946 Joseph F Moore

# CHAPTER XIII
## Oldest State Prison

Months had passed since Bill's incarceration. Madeline and Christie had visited him many times in the state's antiquated prison. Ma had finally visited, but it wasn't an outing she looked forward to. What could she say to her son, who was once again in an institution, only now this institution had bars, regulated visiting hours, and time-limited visits?

When a visitor brought an item into the prison for an inmate, it was examined and then given to the inmate after the visitor had left, provided the item met the prison's restrictions. During visits, you were not separated physically, but numerous guards monitored you. Because of my age, I was not allowed to visit. I had to wait until I was eighteen. That was more than a year away. I did inquire about Bill's welfare. I asked what the prison was like, and asked many other questions, because the only things I knew about prison life were from the few Hollywood depictions that I had seen; that of Paul Muni, for one. I did read *Twenty Thousand Years in Sing Sing,* written by Lewis Lawes and published by Long and Smith in 1932, which was probably the only true account of prison life available to me at that time.

My association with Bill had met a big void. Nicholas and Gregory did not meet my expectations for the closeness I lacked and needed. Gregory and I got along quite well, but he was too busy with his own life to spend time with me. He displayed a lot of humor, which was entertaining, but not what I needed.

Nicholas, who was only three years older than me, was not one I got along with. When we were together, outside, before he went into the

Merchant Marines, he had a habit of belittling and bullying me in front of my friends. Nicholas outweighed me by seventy pounds, and he was at least four inches taller. If I challenged him, I knew it would be a lost cause. A couple of times when I did, I got the worst of it. One of his bad habits was his teasing, and he wouldn't give up this tormenting, so he would be the last person I could go to. Of course, Christie and I got along very well, but he lived in Copley Square, in the center of Boston, so I never had the opportunity to get as close as I wanted. When he did visit, it was mainly to see Ma and Madeline, have supper, and then go out with his friends. I must say, he did talk to me, and we would have lengthy conversation, but he was not a replacement for Bill. No one was.

As the days and weeks passed, I got more despondent. Bill was on my mind constantly. I had to figure out some way to go see him. Maybe I could try to go to the prison and lie about my name. If I could get my hands on a fake driver's license, it would prove my age. Okay, no fake identification available.

My head got out of sync so bad; I started thinking that I could just join him in prison. Gee, we could play music together, talk like old times, eat together, and maybe I could sleep right next to his cell. After all, we were related. The officials would want us to be together. I would be with him as much as I wanted.

I asked my friends in school; if you commit a certain kind of crime how long do they put you away? Of course, I got all kind of answers. Like me, my friends knew about as much as I did, but I listened and took mental notes. Okay, once I figured that out, what did I really know of prison life? Only what I read from one book. I thought there must also be a lot of tough bad guys. How would I handle that?

The other problem seemed to be what crime to commit. Of course, I would probably only have to commit one crime, but which one? Murder, that's an ugly thought. There are many types of robberies, bank, store, etcetera, but none appealed to me. How would I handle the arrest, waiting for the trial, and how would my family take this into account: two criminals in one family?

Family--as far as I was concerned I didn't have much of a family. I had little contact with my mother until I was fifteen. I left my father when I was fourteen, and I hadn't seen or heard from him until later in my life, so who did I have? Well, I had my one and only grandmother, who let me do whatever I wanted. I had four uncles: one in jail, two too distant, and the other friendly, but trying to figure out his life. I also had one aunt and a sister who were too occupied to spend time with me.

I couldn't think of any crime that I was willing to commit; it wasn't part of my makeup. In reality, it was self-effacing. Eventually I had to give up all my ideas and thoughts about any criminal action or that I was ever going to go to jail. I wanted to be with Bill, but I realized that I didn't have the courage. I also realized that there was no way I could be with him and be an honest person. How foolishly one thinks when one is a teenager! And so I went on with my life.

As I think back, Dorothea had given up on me as I wandered the streets. I had gone to Maine the previous two summers, and actually lived there for six months as an indentured servant (read *The Boy Who Was Shanghaied*) when I was fifteen. I had to leave that situation before I would be stifled to death, so guidance or sister-motherhood was nonexistent. No mentor, no parental guidance. I was on my own.

The day finally arrived when I turned eighteen. Six days after my birthday, I joined the Army, and I didn't need a signature from my parents. The recruiting sergeant said I was old enough to join. A week later, I was on a train heading to my basic training post. This would take all of eight weeks and then I had an assignment to the south Pacific. The Army gave me a seven-day leave of absence after basic training, so I returned to my grandmother's house. I wanted to see everyone, and I had planned to go see my uncle Bill. The state would now let me in, and I would go dressed in my class "A" uniform. Won't Bill be surprised--I hadn't seen him since I gave him that candy bar.

When the day arrived for me to see Bill, I got up, took a bath, shaved the few hairs off my face, the ones the Army made me shave off in basic training, and polished my belt's brass buckle and the brass buttons on my *Ike* jacket. This was a blouse style jacket that fit snugly around your waist. The patch on my sleeve was the screaming eagle, the 101st Airborne Infantry. The last item I polished was the US Army insignia on my visor hat.

Finding out from my aunt when visiting hours and visiting days were, I walked to the nearest streetcar and headed toward the prison located in

Charlestown. I had to change a few times from streetcar to train, and get off at City Square, but I finally arrived at the walled-up, barred institution. I was excited, but also had reservations about entering. I had never seen this prison up close, so I found it intriguing, mysterious, and secretive. Citizens have little knowledge of what transpires behind those granite walls. There are no daily reports; only an occasional, rare article in the newspapers or maybe on the radio, about the events taking place in the lives of the incarcerated. Unless you had, or have, a relative or a friend in a prison, it is an alien world.

Another factor to consider, is that if you did have a relative in prison, it wasn't something you were about to divulge freely; it was considered an embarrassment for any family. Of course, everyone in the neighborhood knew about Bill, but I can honestly say that no one ever said anything derogatory, or even mentioned anything about his crime, at least to our faces.

I arrived at the state's maximum, antiquated prison. It was called Charlestown State Prison. I say antiquated because it was a very, very old prison. It was built in 1804-1805. I believe it was the oldest one used in America at the time of Bill's confinement. I was informed that Charles Dickens, the famous English author of *David Copperfield*, *A Christmas Carol*, *Oliver Twist*, and *Great Expectations* and on and on, visited this prison on his first visit to the States, somewhere in the year of 1841-1842. Charles Dickens at the time, held slavery and what he thought of as persecution in America's society as "disdain and non-liberal."

How and why it came about I do not know, but I do know it was said by the inmates that Dickens visited the prison on one occasion. His comments about his visit were that he found the prison cruel in the sense of its amenities for its inhabitants; he thought the prison should be torn down, and that was over a hundred years before my first visit.

To enter the prison I went up a few stairs and entered through a metal door, it being the only one obvious from the street, but also one with a printed sign saying, "Visitor Entrance." A large section of the prison was adjacent to the sidewalk. You could see the evenly square-cut thick granite blocks which made the sides of the building. Visible windows were heavily barred, and the prison appeared impenetrable. It had the look of a fortress.

Nothing fancy or extravagant met my eyes as I walked toward a glassed-in office. There was an open window where I had to sign in and inform the guard, sitting behind a counter, which prisoner I wanted to visit. There was a document which I had to fill out, indicating my name, age, address, and relationship to the prisoner. I had to empty my pockets and put everything into a brown paper envelope. I was then told to go with a guard to a nearby room where I was thoroughly searched, and then instructed to sit in the waiting room next to the entrance.

After what seemed to be just a few minutes, they called me over to the window and told me to go through a thick metal locked door that had a very small thick-glassed window. As I stepped up to the door, I heard a loud click as the door unlocked and swung open automatically. I stepped through the opening, having to stand beyond a painted arched stripe on the floor to allow for the swing of the door to close. The door then closed automatically and then there was another loud click as it locked behind me. I was now locked inside the prison. I saw myself confined inside a barred cubicle large enough to hold about a dozen individuals. There were also a few people that went through with me. They had the look of experience about this event, like they knew the routine. No one spoke, as we all stood there briefly and a steel-barred door clicked loudly in front of us and then opened. We then entered a very large opening inside the prison. With all visitors inside the large room, the bars were closed and locked again. You could hear the lock latch go into place. The prison had barred walls on two sides, from floor to ceiling, two stories high; the other two walls were made of solid granite blocks.

Above the barred door, which we had just passed through, there was a small cubicle with two or three guards with a complete view of the interior and everything below, even directly below. In front of us and toward the left were wooden chairs that had spindled, high curved backs and arm rests all lined up in two rows: about twenty-four chairs, twelve facing twelve. These chairs were of a blonde color, and they were quite handsome and looked new. This surprised me greatly. The visitors automatically separated, and no one sat next to each other or said anything. Were we all embarrassed or was quietness the norm?

As I sat waiting and looking at the bars facing me, there were convicts moving about on the other side of those bars. Some of them would gaze over as they passed, make eye contact, and move beyond sight behind the solid wall connected to the bars. No one smiled. An eerie feeling crept over me.

This convict corridor was parallel to the chairs. I sat in a chair facing the corridor. To my left behind a two-story barred wall were two tiers that housed celled inmates. At the end of each tier, adjacent to me, there was a single water faucet, just a plain spigot of unheated water. The tier extended off to your left, so that you could only see the walkway, not the cells. I noticed no activity on either tier. I assumed everybody was at work or in their locked cells. There were other cells in another part of the prison that were not visible from the visitor's area.

In front of me, in the wall of bars, there was a locked door that matched the appearance of the wall. It was on the far right side, and if you didn't look closely it went unnoticed. Standing by the door, inside the room I was in, was a uniformed guard with a large key opening the door to allow a convict to enter the guest area one at a time, after the prisoner showed him a piece of paper, and then said his name out loud. The prisoner would then pass through the door and then the guard would re-lock the door. You could see a few inmates forming a line waiting to enter.

I watched Bill walk to this door, go through the procedure, and then the guard allowed him to enter the guest area. He looked over toward the visitors, but he made no recognition of my presence. I guess he didn't recognize me in my uniform. Of course, my hat was off and my hair was a crew cut, not my usual curly mop. He walked over, scanning the crowd. I smiled at him, and he immediately acknowledged with a return smile. I could see he was completely surprised and happy to see that it was me. He had no idea that I was home, although he knew I was in the Army.

He was dressed in a navy, light blue long-sleeved shirt, the same type the US Navy sailors wore when they are on work details. His pants were boxy-looking dungarees, and he wore black shoes. All the inmates wore the same clothes. Except for body shape and color of skin they all looked alike, similar to the same regimen that I was now attached to, only I was free. He came over and shook my hand as I stood up to greet him. We sat down beside each other and started to talk. We kept our voices low, but when you stopped talking you could hear the other conversations, unless they whispered in each other's ear.

Some inmates had lady visitors. They held hands, and even kissed. I watched one inmate fondle a lady's breast. No one said anything and this surprised me. In the movies they were always separated by glass, and no one ever touched. This visit was somewhat intimate.

We talked for about an hour discussing our health and welfare, and what prison life was like, but did not mention his crime. He pointed to a green door to our right on the far wall, and explained that was where the electric chair was housed. It sent a chill through me.

I missed him, but we both realized that this would be the state of affairs for years to come. I asked him if I could leave him some money, and how I could do that. Bill told me to leave it at the entrance as I was leaving, in his name. He said they were good about that, and he would have no trouble getting it, as it was put into some kind of an account in his name. Bill was in a good mood and laughed and smiled at some of our comments, although we didn't joke around. It was a pleasant meeting. It was good to see him again, even under those conditions.

Finally, a guard announced through a PA system that the visiting time was over. We shook hands, stood and said our good-byes, as did all the other people. The visitors sat back down, so I followed suit. The convicts headed toward the door that they entered, and one by one, as they crossed over to the other side, they were searched from top to bottom by two guards. They disappeared behind the solid wall, either to the left or to the right.

After all the prisoners had gone behind the bars and the door was secured, the visitors returned through the same doors through which we had entered. The prison was not going to open the visitor's door until all the prisoners were on the other side of the thick bars. The same loud clicks announced that you were being freed, but the convicts were being jailed. On my way out, I picked up my hat off the chair, took another look at the green door, where death took place, and I shuddered, went out and took a deep breath of fresh air.

I found my way home and felt relieved that I had seen Bill. I could now see him at any opportunity, although I was aware that it would be many months before I could make a return visit, and as it was, visiting procedures were restricted to only certain days, and being in the Army my own time had restrictions. I paralleled the two life styles and saw some similarities, but overall I had my freedom. No bars in my life, I could go out at night and look toward the heavens.

I left the old homestead and headed west for my new assignment overseas. The next time that I could see Bill again, or my family and friends, would be eighteen months away if all went as predicted. I never told my Army buddies about my uncle or my visit to the prison. In reality, I somewhat forgot about him as my new assignment took my energy in other directions. Of course, I was maturing and learning to deal with life on my own accord, as we all do after leaving home.

Fifteen months passed, and the Army decided they were going to ship us home and give us new assignments. I was also given a thirty-day leave of absence. It was the first time since I left home that I was given any time off except Sundays. I returned to my grandmother's home after a cross-country ride in a DC-6, American Airlines four-prop twin tail commuter airplane. It made two stops and took fourteen hours. They made an announcement over the Rocky Mountains that we were over fourteen thousand feet. The cabin was poorly pressurized, if at all, and I had an earache during the entire flight. It finally went away after my ears popped upon landing in New York City. From there I took a Greyhound bus to Boston. The plane ticket was a bargain at ninety-nine dollars, so they said. That was almost a month's pay for me.

My grandmother informed me that my mother was living a few houses away and she had lots of room. She said I should consider going there to stay with her. I contemplated her suggestion and said to myself, Why not? My mother was renting a second-floor apartment with five rooms. It was a cold-water flat, meaning that there wasn't any hot water until you lit a gas burner that heated a copper twenty-five gallon water tank. Maybe it was thirty gallons. The only good thing about this type of heater was you could heat as much water as you needed, and you didn't keep the water hot all day, thus not wasting a lot of energy, and it was a lot cheaper in the dollar sense. It would be nice to see my mother again, but also this would be another opportunity to see Bill.

After a few days seeing family and friends, I decided to go to the prison, as the visitor's day had approached. I repeated the same trip to the prison, and the same procedure to gain entry as my first visit, search and all. The routine had not changed, and it probably never would.

I sat in the wooden chair and watched for Bill to appear behind the wall of bars. He had been in jail over three years at the time of this visit. Watching Bill enter the visitor's area I noticed there was no smile. He stared at me and had a scowl on his face, his dark brown eyes were piercing, and you could feel the sharp edge of his glare. His stride was stiff and mechanical, not the smooth glide I was used to seeing. There was no smile of recognition of me, just flat recognition. It wasn't anger towards me; he was angry about his environment. Obviously prison life was taking a personal toll on him. After all, what was his future? If released, he would always be a cop killer!

We did shake hands, and he was glad to see me, but his demeanor hid his excitement about my return. When he talked, he kept his lips tight, and he talked out of the side of his mouth, and it seemed that his teeth were gnashing. He discussed his bad times in the prison, talking about how bad the food was, the space, the cliques, and the confinement. He talked of the homosexuals, and then pointed to an inmate that was sitting across the way with a lady, that Bill said was his wife, and said that he was having anal sex with other prisoners. This disgusted him. I had to look a few times at this man; this was all new to me. This subject did not come up during our last meeting. I wasn't shocked, but I didn't go there to discuss such events. It's not why I went. The visit hadn't gone as I planned. It turned out to be an unpleasant visit for me, maybe not for him, because he could vent his anger. I happened to be his sounding board. Lucky me!

I don't know if I expected the same demeanor from him as before, but I hadn't given it much thought. This visit wasn't going smoothly. I took it personally and felt that he didn't care that I even visited. I felt uncomfortable and squirmed in my chair, as I was put off-guard, and I didn't know how to react. I knew what I wanted to do, I wanted to *amscray* (leave), but I had to wait for the all-clear. That is, when all the prisoners leave the visiting area, and are behind bars, and then the visitors can be released. Until then I was imprisoned.

We sat and waited for the end of the visiting hour. Bill did most of the talking. In actuality, he could leave anytime he wanted. The guards by the prisoner's door were always there. I was the one that had to wait.

I knew deep down inside that he was glad to see me, and of course, I was also glad to see him, but I wasn't pleased to see him in this hardened state of mind. It weighed heavily upon me. We finally separated and went on our different paths. Once again, I left him some money and told him so. I must say that he was polite in his demeanor towards me, but I wouldn't want to have crossed him or have stepped on his toes. Look out! I wouldn't see him again for about twenty-nine months. Would he be mentally worse? I would find out when the time came.

# CHAPTER XIV
## Visit Inside the Prison

My Army enlistment finally ended after four long years, and five days after my discharge, I married my wife. We traveled to New York City for our honeymoon from Hamilton, Ohio. She was raised in the Appalachian Mountains of southeastern Kentucky, and it was the first time for her in the East. We stayed at the Hotel Chesterfield near Times Square, and went to Coney Island for rides on the giant Ferris wheel and on the parachute fall. We went to jazz clubs like Down Beat and Birdland. We ate at Horn and Hardart Cafeteria and at Italian and Chinese restaurants, and she rode the subways for the first time. We had the time of our lives. After a week in New York, we proceeded to Boston, the place of my birth, to meet my family and begin our new life together. Life now took on a new role. In the course of time, I explained to my wife that I had an uncle in prison, and I told her about the crime he had committed. She listened and accepted the facts without any disparaging remarks.

In the meantime, I wanted to see Bill, but for me this visit would have a different emotional aspect. Too much had happened to me in the previous four years. As it was, I still had no mentor, no father image or big brother. It wasn't that I didn't need one; I just didn't have one. Bill had been removed far too long from my life to fulfill those needs. There was little contact between us except when I visited, or in the few letters we exchanged, and those letters had been few in number in those four years. Now that I was married I had a new future to carve, and Bill could not be a part of that. I still loved him, but we were both on separate roads.

After settling about a month at home, I decided to see him in his new environment, a prison called Norfolk Colony, "Colony" for short. Today it is called MCI-Norfolk. It was a newer prison than the old Charlestown State Prison, and he was as happy as one can be when confined. Charlestown State Prison was torn down and inmates were housed in Norfolk, Massachusetts until a new prison was built.

Bill told me he was still in a jazz band, had his own room with a radio, and that he wasn't locked up for eighteen hours as in Charlestown. The visitor's room was smaller than Charlestown's and it wasn't lined with bars. There were two correctional officers in attendance, one standing next to the entrance, and the other one roaming around the room. Similar to Charlestown, you sat next to the inmate, and the clothing worn by the inmates was similar as in Charlestown. I left him some money and said I would return for another visit, but I didn't know when. I told him I was searching for a job and also a place to live with my wife, as we were staying with Dolly and her husband. Bill was now twenty-six, and I was twenty-two. We weren't kids anymore. He was in good spirits and not talking with stiff lips or radiating glares of meanness. Bill was as much his own self as confinement would allow. We parted with smiles on our faces, and he expressed his happiness for me.

I assumed Bill had adjusted to his confinement as best he could, but according to Christie, he was still going through mood swings. Christie said it was a guess as to how he would be on any given visit. In all our visits we never discussed the crime or his involvement, as we all knew what he had done. It was a terrible deed, but what could we do? We accepted the fact and went on with our lives.

Using his intellect, Bill studied his instrument, learned Spanish, and then taught Spanish to inmates. Eventually he became the leader of the jazz band, gave guitar lessons, and built a reputation as one of the country's leading guitar players, some claiming the best, but this was all in the joint (prison). Outside of the prison walls, no one ever heard of him, at least as a musician.

Bill was at Colony only until the new prison, MCI-Walpole located at Walpole, Massachusetts, was opened in 1956 (the name was changed to MCI-Cedar Junction in the 1980s). Security prisoners were transferred back to the high security prison. Bill worked in the prison's chapel with a priest assigned to the prison and with Richard Cardinal Cushing,

Archbishop of Boston, whenever he visited. By this time, Bill had been in prison over a decade. There was goodness in his heart, as before the crime, and his presence projected these vibrations again. As you will read later on, it was his savoir-faire.

I visited Bill, but not as often as the years rolled by. With my work and family it was difficult to find the time. Months would pass before a visit, but we both understood, and our relationship never changed. Even after all those years, I still didn't share this story with my friends, until I told it fifty years later. How could I?

Christie and I visited Bill at the new prison on numerous occasions together. We would make arrangements for a certain date, and either Christie or I would drive.

The formalities of entering the different prisons--having to go through body searches, emptying your pockets, putting your belongings into a manila envelope and depositing it with the authorities was tedious, so we would take our personal belongings and leave them under the car's seat so we could go in empty handed, except for money to give to Bill, and our driver's license for identification. Occasionally, we would bring packages of food or items that he was allowed to receive. Each package would be opened and searched, and if it met their criteria, he would be allowed to receive it. Of course, everyone knew what not to bring, so for us it never was a problem. We could visit Bill in pairs, but if there was a third visitor, they would have to wait in the visitor's room, and then someone would have to leave, so the third person could go in. The prison authorities were lenient in that respect. We never visited with more than three persons.

As in the other two prisons, the new state prison allowed you to sit aside the inmate. Prisoners were thoroughly searched upon leaving the visiting area. The search took place out of view of the visitors. Today, they probably use a metal detector along with the patting down approach. Some prisons do a naked search.

In the main building for visitors, there was a store that sold items the inmates made: jewelry, lamps, inlaid boxes, sailboats, paintings, and carvings. One inmate, Albert DeSalvo, who was confined for strangling women using silk stockings in the Boston area during the 1960s, made chokers using glass stones and a gold chain. Actually, they were quite charming. He was eventually killed in prison by another prisoner.

The new prison had facilities for stage plays with updated equipment for professional productions. The inmates would produce various shows for the inmates and officials. Christie informed me that the warden was allowing family members that were registered at the front office (everyone registered on their first visit) to enter the prison and view a special performance. Christie and I decided that we would attend and set foot into the depths of the prison to observe one of those programs. This sounded exciting and intriguing.

It was a summer evening as Christie and I entered the prison. We went through the usual search formalities, and then we were escorted by convicts and guards to the interior conclave of the prison. Prisoners and guards were everywhere in the hallways, either walking, standing around talking, or just looking. All the inmates were dressed in light blue work shirts, blue dungarees, and black polished shoes.

We reached our destination after passing through numerous locked doors, all with bars. On entering the auditorium, we were ushered to our seats by inmates dressed in white pressed shirts and sporting colorful ties. I looked around and my imagination wandered into prison situations that felt uncomfortable. I thought to myself that if they were to riot we'd be the hostages. What an advantage for the convicts, but if you think about it logically, most of the guests were either friends or relatives, so why would they do that? Also, I'm sure those prisoners were not the most violent ones. I dismissed those fantasies and settled back in my seat and relaxed.

The performance for this evening was *The Solid Gold Cadillac*. It was originally a Broadway play before it was made into a movie in 1956, starring Judy Holliday, a buxom blonde bombshell, and Paul Douglas, a middle-aged, slightly paunchy, big strapping fellow. The plot was about a former corporate chief who assists a lowly stockholder to make corporate waves. Judy was the stockholder. It was a comedy and it was well-received by the public when it played on Broadway and in the movies. I saw the movie with my wife.

The prisoners, wearing makeup, wigs, bras, civilian clothes, etcetera, played all the characters, and I must admit they did a marvelous job. Seated in the orchestra below the stage was the prison band, with Bill performing on his guitar. The musicians played the score that accompanied the play, but before the performance the band played jazz music. The music was excellent and it was great to see and hear Bill play his guitar. More than once he played some solo riffs. The actors and musicians received a well-deserved applause, demanding many curtain calls on its completion. As for me, I was relaxed and lost myself into the performance. When the final curtain went down, I wanted more. In fact, the band played a few more numbers because of the audience's demand. Bill gave another solo riff that was outstanding. I could really hear his improvement.

Christie and I didn't have a chance to talk with Bill, or even let him know that we were there, but he knew we were there, because he told us later that he spotted us in the crowd. Christie and I left and drove home, discussing the night's event and what a good time we had. That was the only time I ever ventured into the prison beyond the visitor's area.

Christie went inside the prison one time to witness a debate team. Bill was one of the debaters. Different colleges sent debating teams to the prison and challenged the inmates. Not all prisoners are uneducated; we are all well aware that intellectuals break the law also.

Christie visited Bill throughout his interment. He would go a couple times a month, and sometimes, depending where he was, what he was doing, he may miss one or two. He even brought his girlfriend, Dixie, but that was before he was married.

When Christie visited to witness the debate team agenda, he went in there without them knowing he was his brother and took pictures. Bill was on the debating team, and he told Christie one day this group was coming, a college group. Bill said Saint Anselm's College or UNH, or Dartmouth will be there. Anyway, it was a college.

Christie thought, he would see if he could get permission to get in, so he went to the debate and told them he was with this newspaper, and he wanted to take some photographs of this debate that was going on between some inmates and the college team. He showed them his press identification. They allowed him in, showed him around, and he went downstairs to where the men were (inmate debating team), and they were mingling right there in the hall. The other prisoners had just been let out of their rooms, and they were just standing around. Christie was walking with a guard, and it was a narrow hall and, there was Bill, they looked at each other, Bill didn't say anything, and Christie didn't say anything. This was underneath the auditorium.

The prison debating team went up to the balcony. The college debating team went to the stage. It is assumed the officials didn't want any confrontation to happen if it got out of hand, for whatever reason. Christie took pictures, and told the guard he needed to get closer. He remembered taking some close shots. The inmates attended the debate. As they go to everything.

Christie went there another time when Bill played the guitar. It was some kind of musical review. Bill eventually took over the musical group. Christie visited Bill more than anyone else in the family, like Madeline, Dorothea, my mother, and Ma. I can't speak of extended family members.

When Nicholas moved to the same town as the new state prison, Christie told him, 'You should be able to visit.' Nicholas firmly answered, 'Oh, I can't do that, those guards, all those guards over there, ah, they live in this town and I live in this town, and they know my name.' Christie thought what's that got to do with it?

Nicholas and his wife sold something belonging to Bill, but they didn't give him the money. It was in this credit union and the credit union went bust, and they told Christie the money was lost through bankruptcy of some sort, so Bill never got his money, but when he died Nicholas's wife paid for his grave marker, although it cost more than that money, so Christie let her do it. He let her pay for the marker.

# CHAPTER XV
## Paroled

In the twenty-five years that Bill spent in prison, he never worked at jobs that required physical labor. He was given all the easy jobs. The inmates knew that Bill had heart trouble, so he wasn't razzed about the easy jobs, at least from the main population.

Life in prison is devised on a system of rules and timed schedules. You eat only when it is time to eat. You work when you're scheduled. You relax when allowed. Your inner biological clock becomes fixed according to prison time. I believe those structured routines break your spirit, but they also developed those routines to effectively control the inmates, and a structured life is what some of these men need. Their life does become robotic, but robots have no spirit.

There is of course, another system internally apparent behind those concrete walls. Your social circles, your enemy circles: prison circles. There is hate and anger in that collected pile of humans. With this comes violent bursts of fights, riots, and, even more violent, death.

Bill had his friends, his associates, those he felt comfortable with. Many of Bill's friends were Afro-Americans. As I mentioned earlier, having the talent as a jazz musician, he was drawn to the black prison musicians, and they to him, but he had some white enemies because of that. Luckily, those whites never did anything physical with their hatred toward him.

Bill did have this one man, Joe Barboza, a white man that became his enemy. Neither Bill nor this individual ever fought it out, but Bill told me if they had the chance they would have fought to the death. They avoided each other like the plague, but that fight to the death never occurred. What a relief!

While researching information for this book, I found out more about Joseph Barboza. Joe "The Animal" Barboza was a killer for the Howie Winter Hill gang in Somerville. Joe got his nickname, "The Animal," for chewing the ear off a man that he got into a scuffle with for practically no reason while in a barroom. Barboza's number of kills was outnumbered in the Boston area by John "The Hitman" Martarano, who was a member of the Boston Mafia. John Martarano admitted that he killed twenty people. Barboza was killed in San Francisco by a shotgun by gang members.

One has to realize how the years of prison life can change personal attitudes. Bill was a peaceful youngster and now he was expressing the desire to kill an enemy, but we mustn't forget that he ended up in prison for taking a life. I never found out why he despised Joe Barboza, but when this man was released, his criminal activities were reported in the newspaper, including the fact that he was a bully and picked on peaceful individuals. A coward in the real sense!

Bill and Jake were incarcerated in the same prisons at the same time. In all the years that they were confined together, Bill and Jake were not friends. Bill told Christie and me that he didn't like Jake. Whether Jake liked him is anyone's guess, but I assumed if Bill had nothing to do with him, Jake would have resented the brush off. As it was, Jake was released much earlier than Bill. Jake received parole after ten to twelve years. He was part of the crime with Bill, but he didn't fire the shots at the officer. I supposed the parole board took this into consideration and his time in prison probably went well, without any misgivings. The other fact to also consider is that the officer's family probably didn't object to his release. Bill never saw Jake again as far as I knew, so I asked Christie about Jake, and he said that Bill never saw him again after Jake was released.

In the early 1960s, Bill went before the parole board for the first time. He had been confined for over twelve years. Of course, he was denied. He went before the parole board a year or two later. At this hearing, I appeared before the board, commented that I thought that he had paid for his crime, and I felt he was rehabilitated and he would not commit any more crimes. What else could one say? Deep down inside I felt this was true, but in reality I didn't know for sure. I also told the board that

I would have a place in my home for him. They asked questions, and you would reply with whatever you thought would be to his advantage. You were alone before the board, and everything was private, but it was recorded. Of course, the board had his prison records, which detailed his confining years. As with previous hearings, he was denied. When Christie attended Bill's parole board hearings, he contributed whatever he could for his release. Madeline and Ma also went to express their concern for his release once or twice.

The slain officer's family was always informed of Bill's parole board hearings. They were given the opportunity to express their position on his possible release. At all the hearings the officer's family objected to his release. I understand their position. I would probably take on the same attitude as this family. No parole!

Obtaining parole would not come easy for Bill. He obviously had to have a clean prison record, good prison work habits, and remorse for his crimes, but he would receive no sympathy from the victim's family.

At Bill's last parole board hearing, when his parole was finally approved, Christie informed the board that he would teach his brother his profession. Christie was a professional photographer, so the board approved wholeheartedly. They were cognizant that Bill was very accomplished at playing the guitar, but they didn't want Bill to pursue this activity for a living. They said it would require Bill to most likely play in clubs, and to the parole board this was most undesirable as a profession.

Christie did a lot with the parole board. I didn't know everything, but I was aware that he went before the board several times. The board didn't worry that Bill played the guitar so well, they worried that he didn't have another profession, and Christie didn't want to use the guitar playing for his living after he got out. Most of that is in nightclubs, and the board didn't want him in an environment, nightclubs and drinking. Christie knew better than to bring that up as an issue of work. He told them that he needed help in photography, because he was working for this company for his day job, but he also did a lot of work on his own. He did weddings and commercial work, and his commercial work helped him financially, and he also told them, he had to refuse a lot of work, because he just couldn't handle all of it. He told the board that he would teach him photography.

That was one of the issues that helped Bill get out. In fact, that was one of the main issues, the fact that he could be a photographer and be with Christie, but even a clean prison record and Christie's support was not enough for his release; something else was needed. That something else came from a recommendation from a spiritual leader, Richard Cardinal Cushing, Archbishop of Boston. Bill had worked directly with the Archbishop in Walpole's prison chapel, and also with the prison's chaplain. This spiritual leader carried a lot of clout. The parole board would take into consideration whatever this man offered. It wasn't every day that the Archbishop presented his thoughts in person, or through a letter recommending parole for a policeman's killer. In most cases, it would be considered impossible for this leader of the church, considered to be conservative, to express leniency: he usually only did so in death penalty cases. The parole board authorized Bill to move to Christie's home and work with him.

Parole for Bill materialized in 1969 after he had spent twenty-two (you will read of three more years) of his most productive years behind bars. Twenty-two years of lock-up! Twenty-two years of alienation from society! Twenty-two years of a formalized, regimented life. Never having to prepare your own meal, do your own laundries, buy your own clothes, or walk outside through city streets or parks. Life outside prison walls had changed: newer cars, larger stores, malls, and supermarkets. Also, having to work for money in order to survive would be a new challenge. He would not be alone in facing freedom after two decades, for others have met the same fate, but as an individual, he would be alone. The family would help, but the world was his to face and challenge. What would it be like for him and what would he be like?

Bill told me, after his release, that an infamous prisoner named Aggie, whom he had served time with in prison, had connections to the Boston underworld. The crime boss at the time of Bill's crime was Raymond Laredoa Salvatore Patriarca. He controlled Boston's Mafia out of Providence, Rhode Island. His replacement after his death was Gennemaro (Jerry) Angiulo, who was the boss from the 1960s to the 1880s. He ran the crime family from Francesco's Restaurant, located on North Washington Street, but had an office at 98 Prince Street, also in the North End.

Bill also told me that Aggie was one of the masterminds of the Boston Brink's robbery January 17, 1950 of 2.7 million dollars. Brink's location was 165 Prince Street, on the corner of Commercial Street, also in the north end. It is now a parking garage. Bill also told me that Aggie had some influence on his release. How this came about I don't know, and he would never tell me. Bill and I never discussed this subject any further. What happened, happened. Closed subject. The reality of it all was that he was freed.

When Bill was paroled, word of his release spread through the family like wildfire. I was home when my aunt Madeline called to tell me of his release. I was in shock and in utter disbelief. After such a long time, who could believe that his release was imminent? Especially after Bill's numerous appearances before the parole board, which had each ended in denial. The officer's family always opposed his release, and the board took this very seriously. Madeline confirmed her story to me very rigorously, as I kept saying it couldn't be true. Of course, I had no alternative but to believe her. To say the least, I was ecstatic, but numerous questions raced through my mind.

On the day of Bill's release, Christie went to the prison to pick him up. Bill's release was subject to his leaving Massachusetts, the state of the crime. It was also understood that Christie would take him into his home in New Hampshire, and Christie would use him in his photography business for work. I don't know what would have happened if no one lived out of state. New Hampshire was obliged to handle his case and to assign him to a local parole officer. This was the final order of the parole board.

# CHAPTER XVI
## After Paroled

The day of Bill's release was very interesting. When Bill got out, Christie went to the prison to take him to his home. He didn't use his car, he borrowed Rita's new husband's car. His name was Lou Foti. Christie related the following story to me.

Foti had a convertible, and Christie borrowed it. He left his car where Foti lived and drove the convertible, so they wouldn't recognize Christie's car, because he didn't know if the press was going to be there. Sometimes they know about this prisoner is going to be released, and it might be a notorious prisoner, and they might do a thing. You know like an article. As it was, there was nobody there, Christie was surprised. It worked out fine, and what he did was, he entered the prison, completed all the paperwork, and then Bill and Christie went outside. The plan was that Christie was going to go outside, get into the car, pull up to the door, and let him get in, so that there would be a short distance between the door and the car just in case, but they didn't have to do that. Christie told me; sometimes they use long lenses, because he knew all the tricks. Bill got into the car, and they were driving away when not very far on the highway all of a sudden Bill says, 'Pull over, pull over, I'm sick.'

He wasn't used to the fast motion of the car. When he went in, cars didn't do much more that 35 to50 mph on the roads, and here Christie is doing 55-60 mph, and Bill hadn't been in a car for a long time. It drove him crazy. Bill said, 'Holy mackerel.' Well, between television and cars, Bill was not tuned with the changes with the outside world.

Being outdoors and having that freedom, he couldn't believe how much the outside had changed, and, he said, 'Everything is fast, everything is so fast.'

So they started to drive back and Christie had to slow down. Bill was holding on to his seat, but by the time they got home, about half way home, he adjusted, and he seemed to acclimate pretty fast.

When they got home, Bill didn't have many clothes. He only had what he took with him, and that wasn't very much, so Christie took him shopping down to Bradley's that used to be on Oak Street. At that time, it was one of the new stores; a big open store. When Bill walked inside he said, 'Holy mackerel.'

He was shocked at the size of the store, and the way you shopped. Before he went into prison you went to a counter and you asked. Now you go and just grab them. You do your own shopping. Christie bought him a bunch of summertime shirts of several colors, and some pants and some shoes. I found out while writing this story that Christie still had a couple of those shirts even though Bill had passed.

An incident happened as Bill was looking around. Christie went wandering off. Of course, you go where you want to. The next thing that happened was Christie looked down the aisle and Bill was coming up to him and he was breathing hard, and he had this strange look on his face. Christie wanted to know what was wrong. Bill said, 'I didn't know where you were. Well, I panicked a minute. I looked around and you weren't there. I looked around and didn't know what to do.'

Christie thought a thing like that never dawned on him. Twenty-two years of everything done for you. All of a sudden he's in a store, and these stores are big now, and he's thinking, what do you do, what's all this. And of course, he didn't have money on top of that. So, he panicked when he didn't see Christie. Christie told him, 'Until you go on your own, you'll always know where I am.' He relied on Christie for a lot.

Bill finally adjusted to civilian life and went outside and took long walks. He wasn't as slow as Christie thought. He adjusted fairly fast. He eventually learned to drive. Once he learned to drive he zipped around. Christie's friend Fred gave him an automobile. Fred owned a garage down on Upton Street. Christie had told him about Bill.

The time Christie took Bill to New Orleans wasn't much longer after Bill was released. This would be a big adventure for Bill as he hadn't been anywhere in the country except for New York and that was twenty-three years ago.

Christie had a Buick Riviera. He wanted to go to a press convention down south and the Buick had no air condition. So he sold the Buick and bought a Dodge Polaris. It was, at that time, the biggest car on the road and it had air. He had to buy a larger car because he wanted to take his wife, Bill, and their two children to the convention in New Orleans. He sold the Buick to the guy that delivered his heating oil.

Christie drove all the way, because Bill couldn't drive then, and his wife wanted to see the scenery. They were going through Mississippi when Christie pulled into a gas station. I'm going to relate of what I remember of what Christie told me about the trip.

A bunch of men were sitting around, and naturally it was warm out; it was the fall of 1969. Bill went inside with Christie to get gas. There was an older guy sitting outside playing the guitar. The station was owned by a black man and there were some older black men sitting around and talking. It was a black neighborhood.

The owner went out to pump the gas and Bill and Christie were talking and getting cold drinks, and other snacks. Well, this other older man was playing his guitar, and after they went outside Bill went over to talk to him. The man was sitting, and he said something to Bill and about the guitar, so Bill opened the trunk, retrieved his guitar and showed it to the man, and then he started to play. Bill was playing on his classical (acoustic) guitar. He didn't have the one he used for jazz, because he used that one with an amplifier, and he didn't want to bring that with him. When he went anywhere, he always carried the classical. The reason he gave was to practice.

Bill put his foot on the back bumper and played. He played some jazz riffs, and then went into some classical stuff. His fingers slid up and down the keyboard so fast it was hard to follow. They just stared in disbelief. They said they never saw anyone play like that, or even heard anyone like that before. The older man said, 'Listen to how he plays.'

A young man was surprised and said something like, 'He knows how to play.' When Bill finished, the younger man sat down and took the older guy's guitar and he started playing, and he was showing them how he could play. When he finished Christie said something like, 'Why don't you get some recognition? Go to the radio station, go play on the radio station.'

Christie asked Bill later on when they were on the road, 'What did you think of his playing?'

Bill said, 'He's got nice clean fingers, I mean he works very well. He doesn't have a style. He's not distinctive in style. He needs to be taught styling.'

Before they left Christie told the young man again why don't you go someplace to try and get a radio station to play some of your music as background music or maybe play something and they can air it. The kid replied, 'The trouble around here is you got to be sponsored. I can't get any sponsors.' They got into the car and drove on.

Even though Bill had his guitar he didn't play in public again while in New Orleans. Bill had a good time there, met a lot of people, and just practiced. He always practiced, because his theory was you have to stretch your fingers, you have to keep your fingers, the left hand especially, you have to keep them limber, you have to keep stretching, otherwise they'll cramp.

As they were returning home from the convention they had a problem. They stopped at a place to get a cup of coffee. It was night time and the kids were asleep. Of course, in those days, before the interstate highways, there weren't many places open, especially that time of night; it was about two in the morning. Well, they finally found a place and they got their cup of coffee to keep awake and all that. They were driving along, and the next day Bill had to go to the bathroom.

So, Christie pulled into a garage and Bill goes running in, he had diarrhea. After that was over with, they were driving along and all of a sudden Christie's wife says, 'I got to go.' He stopped at a station and he runs in to get the keys. He guards the door to make sure she was all right. She almost felt like she was going to pass out. They got back in the car and then it happened to Christie.

It had to be the water. You'd think the coffee would have made a difference, but you know when you're traveling it's like being in a foreign country. Don't drink the water in strange places. Although the water is better these days, I've also driven through Mississippi, but that was a few years ago, well, probably twenty years ago, but I didn't get sick. I did get sick eating in a truck stop out West in 1997, but that can happen anywhere, but that's another story.

Bill told me about that trip. He said he wanted so much to get up and play in some of those clubs they all went to, but he knew if he did get up on stage and played, the musicians would ask him who or where have you played. What could he tell them? That I played for twenty-two years in prison. I was the leader of the prison band. I was in prison for killing a police officer. He told me he was too embarrassed. He said he had the greatest urge to go on stage, but he didn't want to be rejected. Life was difficult for him after released from prison, and the main reason was that his musical skills never got recognized. He could never go public. He never told Christie that. I guess he knew that Christie would be too upset, but I can see his point. What a shame!

# CHAPTER XVII
## Returned to Prison

Bill's return to society was not the most celebrated event of the day. His release wasn't covered by any of the news media, and family members, except Christie, went on with their usual daily routines. The family knew that Bill was going to live with Christie and his wife and two children. They also knew that Christie was going to pick him up at the prison. I waited a few days before I made a telephone call to talk to Bill. During our conversation we made plans to see each other the following weekend. Talking to Bill on the phone was as different as going to the moon. Seeing him in a home would have the same affect.

I left my family at home because I didn't want to overwhelm Bill on the first meeting. Also, I didn't know what to expect, or what his state of mind would be. As it turned out, he was very relaxed and his conduct was as if he never was in prison. The visit went quite well, and during our conversation he mentioned his trip home. Bill said that he didn't know how to open the car door, because on older cars, the door handle had to be turned downwards. He told me that he was taking lots of walks and exploring the neighborhood, and he found it extremely rewarding. Bill also told me he wanted to learn to drive and then get an automobile.

Bill and I talked occasionally on the phone, and on trips to his house I took some of my children to meet him. I never mentioned the fact that he was ever in prison. The children were told that he'd been living elsewhere and he just moved back. At the time of his release, my oldest daughter was sixteen, and she accepted this story. Over a period of visits, Bill met my wife and my seven children. In the course of time, except for those family members that dismissed Bill as a relative, he had the opportunity to meet all the children and relatives except Nicholas' and Gregory's families. His sister Madeline and her children visited whenever they could. The family acknowledged that a large reception or dinner for his release was out of the question. How do you make a declaration for an inmate that spent years in jail for murder? We didn't have to discuss this; it was just understood. Those of us that wanted to associate with Bill did it in our own way. My way was to visit, but for the first two years of his release it was sparingly.

Bill worked with Christie for two years in the photography business. Christie instructed Bill until he finally got to the point where he could do some jobs on his own, but he could see that he didn't have his heart in it, and also some of the customers weren't totally satisfied, for he had to repeat some of Bill's work.

Bill eventually learned to drive and received his license. This gave him the opportunity to be more independent, and allowed Bill to travel. One day he took the chance to drive to Massachusetts. This broke parole! Why he went back I don't know. I can only relate the event.

Bill drove back to Boston, to the city of his crime, and he was tooling around when he came across one of his fellow inmates. One of the rules of the parole board was that paroled cons were not to hang around together. Of course, after twenty-two years in prison who else do you know but ex-cons, so if you meet one by chance what are you supposed to do, ignore him? Anyhow, this ex-con asked Bill if he would take him to a courthouse. He obliged and drove to the courthouse. While parking his vehicle, Bill was spotted by a police official from a courthouse window. The officer, seeing Bill, said to another officer, "That's William Goudas." How this officer recognized Bill or the other convict after all those years is a mystery. Maybe he had been a guard in one of the prisons where Bill was confined.

The two officers went outside and arrested Bill on the spot. Either this one officer knew that Bill wasn't supposed to be in that state or he also knew that the other fellow was an inmate and they weren't supposed to be together. Whatever the case, Bill was put in the local jail and then transferred back to Walpole, to the prison where he was previously confined. It wasn't a serious violation, but nevertheless it was a violation. Bill spent two more years in jail before he was released. Once again,

Christie was instrumental in his parole. Bill had now spent twenty-four years behind bars. I didn't visit him during this confinement.

After Bill's second parole, he returned to Christie's home, promising Christie that he wouldn't do that again. Christie was disappointed in Bill, but he had to accept his promise. Bill went back to work with Christie doing photography jobs, but he also got jobs playing his guitar in Greek clubs. Christie realized that Bill needed to play his guitar and there was little he could do to stop him. Christie also realized that if he played in the area, he could keep an eye on him. What else could Christie do? Bill was forty-seven years old and a free man.

Bill, while playing in Manchester's Pericles Club one night, he met his future wife. Her name was Bonnie. When I met Bonnie I liked her from the get-go. Christie told me the story of how Bill met Bonnie.

She used to go to this club (Pericles) a lot, and he played a lot in a band. He played in another Greek band too. That club was almost across the street.

Bonnie used to go in there with girlfriends, and they would go in there, drink and pick up guys, and that's how they met. She was in there all the time. She was in the business (prostitution) at the time. Somebody else told Christie the same thing.

She had this beautiful long hair, and she was very good looking. She had a good build, and the other girls were beautiful too. So Christie made some reference to somebody: 'Boy, they're a couple of good-looking girls.' This man said to Christie, 'You don't want to go around with them, they're expensive. I don't want to have anything to do with them.' Christie only mentioned to him how good they looked.

Even Bill told Christie, 'You don't want to do much with them, and they're pretty expensive.' Bill ended up with her, and then eventually he moved in with her, and then they got married. They got married more or less for protection. It was a convenient thing for him, and it got him independence. It was more like an order to leave Christie. Not to stay under his control, but the marriage didn't work out that good after a length of time.

But Bill was adjusting to civilian life pretty well. He didn't have any problems adjusting to his wife's activities.

I met Bonnie for the first time when Christie told me that Bill had moved out and was living with this woman. Christie didn't elaborate about Bonnie's profession to me, only that she was very pretty. Christie gave me the directions to Bill's house on Bridge Street, after making a telephone call to make sure Bill was home. I then drove to the other side of town to see Bill's new home and to meet his girlfriend.

Their home was a single-family two-story building. They were only using the first floor, as the second floor was unfurnished. Bill was in good spirits, and he seemed as happy as I have ever seen him. He was very bubbly.

Bill introduced me to Bonnie. She was 5' 7", of slender build, but very well-proportioned. She had brown wavy hair resting below her shoulders, brown eyes to match, perfectly shaped lips, and a face that belonged in Hollywood. I was taken back by her beauty, but she also had the personality to match. What a find for Bill! I could see why he was so happy, at least for now. I enjoyed this visit, and especially the opportunity to spend time with Bonnie. She was an interesting lady and she was pretty to look at.

It wasn't long after I met Bonnie that she and Bill got married. It didn't surprise me that Bill wanted her, but I was a little surprised they got married. Bonnie was about ten years his junior, but she looked ten years younger than her age. On one of my visits, Bill told me what Bonnie did for money, although I already knew by then, I acted as if I didn't know.

A couple of months after they were married, I drove one weekend to see them. Bonnie was very excited about her new place of employment. She immediately took me upstairs in their house. On entering the upstairs hallway, she switched on the lights and the place lit up with red lights. She then took me to four bedrooms that were all furnished with beds, fake flowers and knickknacks sitting on end tables, but no bureaus. Each room had its own color scheme with dimmed lights. Bonnie was now in full swing. She was now the madam of a brothel, her brothel!

When I got the chance, I asked them separately how her prostitution affected their relationship. Bill said he didn't care, and that she made good money. After all, she wasn't doing it for love. Bonnie expressed the fact that it was just business and it was only for the money, and when she got home (she did outside jobs too), or she was finished upstairs, she would take a bath and make love to Bill, because he was the man she loved. I thought that it was a little bizarre, but I just shrugged it off.

I don't know how much money she made, but she did tell me that some of her clients were professional men, such as lawyers, judges, and business people. And then it happened!

The police raided the place and closed it down, but they didn't indict Bill for the crime, but that broke them up. He was arrested because of what she was doing, even though she did all the promotional work. After all he lived in the same house where the prostitution took place. Bonnie had to pay a fine, but no jail time. Maybe her high clientele helped her, but they shipped Bill back to prison again,

This caused Christie some concern once again. Christie kept Bill's history a secret to all but his closest friends, and that was only a couple or so. A friend of his visited and said something like, 'I don't know, I want to ask you something, but I don't know how to ask you. I really want to know. Well, I saw a guy, you know, I saw this thing about Bill Goudas's release. Is he your brother?' Christie replied, 'Yes.' He replied like, 'I kinda thought so.' He found out on his own, otherwise nobody else knew, of course, he could have told somebody, but the name is unique. Another fact about the name is that Christie's wife with the same last name was horrified of anybody finding out. It really bothered her. Christie told his children about Bill when he thought it was important for them to know. Christie's attitude was if you want to go into politics, you don't want to be off-guard when the name is used.

Christie had to go before the parole board again. That time he went in with Bonnie. Maybe it was about a year later, but it wasn't right away, but it wasn't as long as the time he got busted for being with that ex-con. The two of them were in a little private hearing. No formal thing or anything like before; just the board, Bonnie and Christie. Christie was telling them (board) what he thought the problem was.

The board wanted to know what was he doing in a place like that. Christie told them that Bill's wife was doing that and Bill had nothing to do with it. He also was telling them that he tried to teach him photography. The trouble was he wasn't as good in photography as he was. People would rather have Christie and not have him. He didn't want to do pictures. He just wasn't catching on. He didn't have an artistic view with a camera, although he was artistic with his hands and his music.

The parole board knew he was playing music in clubs. Christie didn't know what they knew and he didn't want to ask. He also didn't want to act like Bill didn't go in them either, because then it would look like Christie was lying, and then they wouldn't trust him. Christie wanted to show them that he was honest. He told them that he went to places where he was playing. Bill was making pretty good money, and everybody enjoyed him. The meeting went pretty well. They released him soon after that, back to his wife! The paroled board meeting took place before they got divorced. Bill and Bonnie separated because they both realized it was only a convenient marriage, and it was mostly Bill that wanted out. It turned out that it wasn't a love relationship for Bill.

So, he was in for about another year. That would have made it twenty-five years in jail.

Bill left the state after he and Bonnie got their divorce and he moved to Boston. He couldn't express himself musically in those little clubs. He wasn't satisfied, for him it was small-time. He probably could have adjusted, but he didn't seem to have the natural drive. Maybe he just wasn't interested.

Christie had this recorder and he could have recorded him and give it to somebody, but he was afraid to admit to people what he had done, and that it would have come out.

If Bill ever became too prominent, it probably would have come out to the public, and who knows what would have happened, especially in those days. Maybe even today, but people seem to be more tolerant today, especially if you have a craft they want to hear, but I'm sure that was a big factor for him.

When he was paroled, Christie told him, 'Anythng you do I can only help you after the fact.' They took it easy on him at the local probation office. The parole officer at the office said they knew of him, and they knew he was here, but they never told the police. As far as Christie knew, he thought nobody knew until he got arrested, because they stayed away from him. He never had to report. Even after all the years he was there and even after two or three years of marriage, even the Massachusetts parole officers never checked on him. He was on his own.

Christie told him, 'You know you got a deal, because of my photography.' Christie was more worried about his wife's feelings. She was freaked out about Bill living with them. She was an innocent person, and she was very sensitive to it.

Her mother and father knew nothing about anything. No one in that family knew anything, even when he got arrested with Bonnie. I don't know what they told the mother and father or the family.

Bill finally decided to go back to Boston on his own, but you never knew where. He didn't divulge a lot. He never told Christie where he was living, but he did visit Christie a couple of times. Christie never pried into people's affairs. His attitude was, if they want me to know, they will tell me. He never asked Bill what he was doing in Massachusetts. He only found out what Bill would tell him.

The car Bill had was given to him by Christie's friend who owned that garage on Upton Street. Christie had bought a lot of cars from him, and Christie also bought some cars for him that had damage; a little wrecked. Christie would foot the bill for a few of them and they would split the profits. It would give the garage work and then they could sell them. He also gave a car to Christie's son.

Getting back to Bill and Bonnie, they were together maybe three or four years, but they remained friends after their divorce. They visited each other all the time. In fact, she moved after he left. She didn't live too far from where he had moved to. That's what he told Christie.

I did see Bill just before they got raided, and after the raid I didn't see him for a long time. Then one day he showed up at my house and told me he is working in a music store. I was working so much and traveling, and this was a few years after my wife died. I lost contact with him and I was surprised when he told me he had moved back. He just didn't care. He told me Bonnie had three girls with her. They still operated, but under different conditions.

Christie told me that another girl with Bonnie came up to visit him; because he remembered one time they came in a convertible. Bill was also with them. One of Christie's friends who was visiting said, 'Hey, hey, what's this?' Bill fixed him up.

I remember Bill telling me that Bonnie was still in the prostitution business, and she was living a few towns away from him. Bill told me she went on welfare. She had kids, and she didn't have any other kind of work she wanted to do. Of course, she had these kids before meeting Bill, and I guess she had just left them. She was from Michigan and her sister from Michigan moved here and lived here for a while with her two young children. She was hiding from her boyfriend or husband. I don't remember much about that, but the sister moved back to Michigan. Bonnie's children moved to live with her after she left Bill, but as I mentioned, near Bill.

Once Bill left Christie they had little connections, but he called Christie once in a while, and he would ask how things were. A few times after he called he would go to their house. Christie told me that he never said much about what he was doing, but one time he was showing them how to play the guitar. I think he was teaching them because he was teaching at John Peeron's place for a while. I forgot about that as I was writing this, but I forget the name of the store. I went there a few times to visit Bill at that music store. It was either in Medford, Malden or Melrose, but anyhow, the classes were held in back of the music store. It was not an elaborate situation. It's interesting how you forget about things until you start thinking or talking about those years.

I think Bill was still playing in clubs somewhere and teaching, but I know he wasn't too happy with Peeron. First of all, I guess the pay wasn't that good, Peeron had restrictions on him, and he couldn't teach as he wanted whatever the case may be; Bill didn't get along that good with Peeron. He wanted Bill to teach a certain way.

Bill had told Christie that he was teaching somebody to play a certain way, and some people maybe complained, because Bill wanted them to do something, and they wanted to do something else, I think Peeron said, 'If that's what they want and they are paying for it, then you do what they want.'

Bill probably said, 'That's okay if you want to be their teacher, but if you want me to be their teacher I'm going to teach them the right way, because if they don't learn the right way, and they want to learn that other way, then why come for lessons?'

So he had that kind of conflict. You have to have patience. You have to be a very patient person just to make an ordinary living and to climb slowly or whatever. I don't think Bill looked and acted like he had the patience, but I don't think he had the patience to what we thought he did, because he couldn't wait to get money that slow. He could have got a job as a clerk or a lot of medium jobs that don't call for a great deal of schooling, because he was smart. He had enough education to do a good office job. They don't pay a great deal like some offices pay now, but he would have got subsistence pay, and that was too slow to make decent money. Whereas you go to where some people who have a lot of money, it's always corporations or big places like that that you rob. I think the people in that vein think, well you're not hitting the small person, you're hitting people making money faster than anybody else, so you're taking some of their money and you get it in a hurry. I think that's the vein that they lived in, that Bill lived in.

Thinking about Bill as a young kid, he never really tried to get a job. He never asked his brothers if there was a job where they were working. Did I think that was his first job (robbing)? Christie and I talked about that. Both of us thought that when he got into that MacEachern gang, they had him making money for them. They were making a bit more than either one of us, evidently. What they would do was robbing, then live, then rob, then live. Maybe Bill was doing that on a steady basis, and he would make much more money quickly, and money went further than like today. Let's say he made in one robbery five times as much as we made. Well, all right then, he can go along without working, because we were still living on a smaller amount. They were living on a larger amount, and then spending time to rob again. Maybe Bill was robbing before he met MacEachern, on a smaller scale, but we're sure he didn't have a gun until he met Jake. Maybe he was just breaking into homes or small stores. Who knows?

His buddy, Swenson, used to come to the house, and none of us liked him. He had that tight kind of face; a cleft mouth. Swenson had just got out of reform school or jail, or whatever, and he acted like a wise guy. He acted like a cheap punk. We wondered how they really met. Like how did they start to talk to each other? We knew they met in some club somewhere, but what prompted them to meet?

We had no idea how they met, but once you go in with them, you go their way, and all of a sudden, look at this; I got myself several hundred dollars, as compared to anyone in the family. Maybe we had fifteen or twenty bucks, and he (Bill) had a few hundred.

Bill never ever showed anyone a lot of money. Bill did have insurance to pay for his funeral and all that, because Christie was his beneficiary. Christie thought that he made him the beneficiary, because probably he felt really obligated, because Christie helped him the most out of the family. Christie also helped him by giving him money, but Christie gave him much more, and I don't only mean money. Christie was there for him all the way. Bill was very fortunate to have Christie.

When Bill got arrested in New Hampshire the local police department had no knowledge of Bill being paroled to their city; they didn't know he was out (prison). They didn't even know he was in their state. They didn't know anything at all until that arrest came, and of course, they (Bonnie and Bill) were in their hands.

When Bill was arrested on Bridge Street, Christie knew the neighbors and they told him about the arrest. I think the neighbors were Greek. Christie told me about visiting the police chief after Bill was arrested.

The police chief and the assistant chief, they all knew Christie because he was always taking pictures of different subjects. Bill called Christie, because they allowed him to make a call within a day or two. Bill told Christie that they weren't treating him well. He didn't like something they were doing or whatever.

Christie went to the police chief to see if Bill was being mistreated. The chief responded to Christie's question, 'What do you mean?' Maybe somebody was needling him or some police was threatening him.

The chief told Christie that he was being treated very well. They walked to the section where he was. Christie asked Bill if everything was okay or whatever. Bill told his brother 'Everything was all right.' Maybe with the chief right there he decided not to say too much.

From there they shipped him back to prison, because he broke parole again, but neither the chief nor any of the other police ever said anything about it to Christie again. I guess they respected Christie and they knew he had nothing to do with the crime. The other thing I should like to mention is that everybody liked Bill. He had lots of friends.

Christie told me of this one fellow, who was a representative for photography supplies, worked for a New York dealer, who at the time was the distributors in the U.S. for Nikon and Mamiya flex cameras. This man attended all the National Press Photographer's conventions.

He would show up and put on demonstrations, bring in new equipment that they were working on, and join photographers when they went out to clubs. His first name was Peter. Peter lived in the Queens, New York. He had a place in New Hampshire also, up in the mountains. He would drop by and visit Christie on his way up north. He loved northern New England. Well, he and Bill became good friends, and he would call up, and he and his wife would drop by, because of Bill. He didn't know anything about Bill.

This other fellow who was the Associated Press's main photographer in the New England office, who hung around with Peter, knew the name and he knew all about Bill, because he covered that kind of news, but he never said anything. He became friends with Bill also. The only thing he ever said to Christie, 'What a nice guy.'

That's not to take away of the fact that he killed a policeman, because he did make a stupid and terrible mistake. And he can never be forgiven for that act, but he spent many years in prison, and he was a model prisoner, but it also showed that he did have a nice side about him. For whatever that is worth to the reader!

Christie and I wanted to talk about Bill's friend from prison, Aggie. He was the one that helped him get out. I mean, he really helped. I think he was a Greek. He made a lamp that Christie owned made of cypress while in prison. It's a signed piece. Aggie got out a lot sooner for it was for a lesser crime than Bill's.

Christie told me that Aggie got in touch with him, and that Christie went to his house once, because Bill asked him to. It was something Bill wanted him to do. They couldn't go and visit, because they were felons, but Aggie also built a ship while in prison that Christie now owned. It's a cargo ship (a sailboat). He was not in for robbery. I think it was the numbers racket. He actually worked on that ship. It was decommissioned in 1935. It sure is beautiful and very detailed. It must be worth lots of money. You see those in museum.

When Aggie got out he eventually went to New Jersey. Bill had said he was operating a tugboat or he owned one.

Aggie, as I wrote earlier, had connections, and somehow he was instrumental in Bill's release. Bill told me personally that he was one of the masterminds of that big job (Boston's Brink's robbery, January, 17,

1950, in the North End, over 2.7 million dollars), and that he was the one who pulled strings to get him out, besides the Cardinal.

Bill also told me one day that Richard James Cardinal Cushing helped him to get out, but I wondered how Aggie had connections with the parole board. It's anyone's guess. I wasn't going to say anything about the Cardinal in this story, but why not? The Cardinal was very instrumental in Bill's release; anyhow it is been over forty years. Who cares now?

Of course, Christie knew all about the Cardinal. He certainly never got any help from the Greek priest. Bill had said they were more into--the Greek priest, you got to be saved. You got to change your life over, and pray for the things that are bad. Well, that was fine, and that is what he should have done, but it didn't help him to get out. But what do I know. Maybe he did pray for God's help.

# CHAPTER XVIII
## Meeting Bracy

Since Bill's trial, I can't recall meeting or knowing any person that had been institutionalized in the old state prison, except Bill. Of course, I didn't pursue that endeavor either. I was busy raising a family, working, and spending time traveling throughout the Midwest and the Northeast with my wife and children. Also, my vocation and my friends were far removed from prison circles, but it's not that we went out of our way to avoid it. The fact of the matter is that it never materialized, and if someone I knew hid that secret identity, I wasn't aware of it.

That all changed about twenty-four years later, at a chance introduction when I was with some of my friends. We visited the black section of the Boston area. I was working in Cambridge when I had this brief encounter with this particular black man who was about fifty years old. A handshake ensued between us; a handshake I'll never forget. It was not overpowering, although he had strong hands and it was firm. What I remember most was the human warmth emanating from it. I immediately liked this individual.

A few months later, I met him again through a mutual friend that said to me, "You should meet this one good dude." My friend, David (Dave) Brown, and I set a date to go see this man, who owned a second-hand furniture store. Dave said that he had many interesting articles, and I might be interested in purchasing something.

It was springtime, the days were warm, and the new leaves on the trees enveloped the city with greenery. Dave and I traveled to Shawmut Avenue in Roxbury that had rows of multi-family units that were three or four stories. All the surrounding blocks were similar, and all the buildings edged on sidewalks with alleyways adjacent in the rear. The alleyways were used to pick up trash and to park a few cars where possible and as short cuts to avoid traffic. They were not paved. What I noticed the most was the lack of greenery. No grass, no trees.

In this one city block, there were small business establishments at street level along the length of a red brick building. Dave's friend's store was located in this one block, and over the store there were three floors of apartments. It was an area of struggling, poor black people. We approached the premises after parking our vehicle across from the store, and entered this shop of merchandise.

I was taken aback somewhat by what I observed inside this store. There were pieces of second-hand furniture, yes, but there were also some beautiful antique pieces for sale. There were the usual household items --irons, toasters, ashtrays, and etcetera, but placed on top of tables, dressers, and commodes were beautiful items of value: colored glass pieces, decorative lamps, various artworks, porcelain pieces, and collectable knickknacks. It seemed unlikely that all this quality merchandise would be housed in what we call the ghetto, but here it was. It all reverberated back to its owner.

Inside the store there were a couple of prospective customers. Even with the crowding of merchandise, the place was consumed with tranquility. Standing next to one of the customers, having a dialogue over an item of interest, was the same individual that I had met in that brief encounter a few months ago. An exchange of words passed between them and then the couple left without buying anything, but they said they would return. Dave then approached the owner with a greeting and introduced me. His name was Almont, but he announced that everyone called him Bracy, so Bracy it was; we recognized each other from that previous encounter.

This man had a beautiful smile that glowed on his entire face with happiness. I had to smile back; it was catchy. Bracy shook my hand firmly with compassion, and I immediately felt the same warmth. Little did I know at the time that we would become friends. We small-talked for about a half-hour, and in the meantime, I selected an Aladdin antique kerosene lantern that had a tanned colored glass globe with Byzantine designs etched on the rim of the glass. Bracy informed me that it came from the South End of Boston, an area in the city where Greeks and Middle-Easterners had lived. The asking price was fifteen dollars. I paid for it gladly. We said our good-byes, promising that Dave and I would make a return visit. I walked out carrying my prized possession.

I returned with David, or sometimes alone, many times, and most times I purchased an item. I must admit that I purchased many kerosene lanterns and many other items from him over the years. As I mentioned, we became friends and began to have personal conversations. About a year went by, and Bracy decided to move his business to Kilmarnock Street, in the Fens area of Boston, that had larger apartment buildings housing mostly students, transients, and permanent residents. This area would increase his sales and also give him more opportunity to replace his sold merchandise. The area was also greener, an added pleasantness.

The new store was larger, and its basement was used for storage and for temporary housing for Bracy, although the city would not have approved. This place became not only one for purchasing house furnishings, but a place for neighborhood people to lounge, chat, and drink coffee. I went there many times after work, and I met many individuals. Some I would interpret as real characters. It was a place for people watching, and everybody loved Bracy.

During one of our conversations, the fact came out that Bracy knew Bill. Bracy had spent seven years behind bars, and some of that time was at the old State Prison, before they built a new modern maximum-security institution. Bracy told me that when he was younger, he committed armed robbery, paid for his crime, went straight, and that was the last time he had anything to do with the law. Bracy was extremely trustworthy and honest, he gave people good deals in his shop, and he in return was respected by the community. I loved this man very much and I believe you would, too.

Bracy had a personality that reached out to you. It was smooth as honey. His voice was an octave lower than most males. He wasn't a tall man, actually he was shorter than me, but he carried his sturdy frame with authority. Bracy's color reminded you of dark chocolate, skin clear of any blemishes or wrinkles, and his head was clean-shaven and reflected lights and the sun. If you needed to move a refrigerator or a piano, Bracy was the one to ask. He was as strong as two men; believe me.

Bracy and I spent a lot of time together, either at the store or for a dinner engagement, or at friendly gatherings. Nothing was ever mentioned of his past illegality. Actually, I don't think anyone would have cared, for this man had proven himself as a great individual. Through Bracy, I met a few of his associates that had spent time behind bars with him. On one occasion, a group of us were in Bracy's basement living quarters having coffee, beer or some other drink. There were about six or seven of us, including Bracy. One man was an ex-bank robber, one was an ex-safe cracker, and one was this and one was that. I was the only one that hadn't spent time behind bars, and you know what? I had a great time! I thought about it when I left this group; here I am, a so-called professional, mixing with ex-cons (prisoners) and actually enjoying it. I was much younger then, and I don't know if it would have the same effect on me today, but at the time, I thought, "Who cares?"

# CHAPTER XIX
## Interview with Two Ex-Convicts

### May 5, 1999

When I planned on writing this story, I called Bracy and told him about my story idea and about the research I was doing. I asked if he would be interested in helping me contact some of Bill's friends from prison, and if he himself would agree to be interviewed. He immediately acquiesced to my proposal and said he would love to sit for an interview. Bracy delivered a dozen names and only a couple of possible addresses. They were all musicians that played with Bill in the can (prison). Bracy said he would also try to arrange a meeting with one of his friends who got Bill interested in playing jazz in the prison's band at the old State Prison. I was thrilled by the events about to take place.

A meeting was arranged for Bracy and me to go to this friend's apartment. I knew the area very well, as I was born around the corner on Walnut Park Avenue, and I had lived at 60 Seaver Street, Roxbury, during 1952-54 with my new bride. This man to be interviewed lived on the same street, but a few blocks away. Although the building this man lived in was not there back then.

Bracy and I decided to take public transportation to Robert's (Bob) house. For medical reasons, I couldn't drive at the time, and Bracy did have use of a car, but he opted for public transportation and let the driver take us there, so we could relax and talk and eliminate driving anxieties.

The apartment complex that Bob lived in was a round building ten stories high. It was designed to house senior citizens, but it was incorporating poor young families now, and this interrupted the solace of the building. Bob later revealed that there were many problems from the younger individuals: drugs, gangs, dirty hallways, loud music, and other infractions were now normal.

Pressing one of the many doorbells, Bracy spoke into the intercom and said that we had arrived; it was around noontime. We had to take an elevator to Bob's floor. I followed Bracy to Bob's door, and after a knock, the metal door opened and there was Bob. Bracy told me that Bob was almost eighty, but he didn't look a day over sixty-five. He was small in stature, but his muscle tone was very evident. Bob had a handsome face, graying hair, and was three shades lighter than Bracy. He motioned us in, locked the door, and brought us into his living room. We all sat down after introductions.

After some discussion between Bracy and Bob, the conversation was directed towards me. Bob inquired about me, asking the general inquisitive questions that are usually posed when meeting a person for the first time. I answered them openly, for I was about to ask this man some personal questions myself. I described my project and told about how Bracy offered to help. I also told Bob that I appreciated his offer of assistance, and apologized in advance, should an inquiry hit a sore spot. Bob informed me then, that Bracy had given me a decent characterization, and he would be happy to assist in any way possible.

For my first question, I asked about the electric chair, for I had this fascination about the chair. "Did either of you ever see the chair or know of anyone electrocuted?"

Bob spoke first, "I saw it once."

Then Bracy said, "I saw it once and I sat in it."

Bob continued, "There were three electrocutions together. The first man was a black man, the first. He tried to escape and he killed a guard. One of the men was cooked and was stuck in the chair. The lights would dim. They generated their own power."

Bracy commented, "I volunteered to clean up after the electrocution. It was a mess. Part of his skin was burnt onto the chair, and a section of his skull was still there."

I became uncomfortable with the direction of this conversation, as my fascination for the chair had disappeared. I changed the subject and asked about prison life.

The following words are free-flowing with little input from me. Bob talked about what happened when they moved all the prisoners into separate prisons when they were going to build a new prison and tear down the old one. Bracy, Bob, and Bill all went to the same place about the same time. It was not a maximum-security prison, and was referred to as the "Colony."

Bob said, "The Colony had tunnels, and the cons (prisoners) used to make liquor. A fellow named 'Bootleg Jack,' made liquor out of mush melons. You cut the top off, add brown sugar, and put it back in the ground. They think of everything for necessities. Now Bill liked his salads. At the Colony, cons were given a small plot for a garden. Thinking of those days, some are comical, some are sad, the chair behind the 'Green Door' (old State Prison) for one. A religious screw (guard), named Gomerly had prayer beads in one hand, he thought it was inhuman. It smelled. For the last mile they are escorted around the prison. They are housed in a separate section (a building called Cherry Hill), then behind the Green Door. In the tunnels (Colony) they stored food. A guy named Blimp used to send up a lot of food. Blimp sent up a whole block of American cheese and Bill ate the whole block. He didn't go to supper that night. Also, Bill didn't drink any mush melons. Bill had his garden and he grew salad ingredients. He liked his salads. I grew mush melons."

As Bob continued, I just sat there and listened. I let him vent in any direction he wanted.

"There were those two big black men, Dansberry and Junior Cooper, a Geechy, a salt water Geechy from South Carolina, off the coast."

I interrupted, "What's a Geechy?"

Bob replied, "Something to do with Portuguese. A group of Africans stranded on an island off the coast. They gradually moved inland. Well, these two men had a fight and it was the dumbest fight. They were both huge. They fought, but no one hurt the other, and they ended up laughing. Junior Cooper told this saying, 'Don't move him, let him slept.' They had their own dialect."

The conversation moved in another direction. Bob started talking about the music band that they had. "Now this man named Ollie played piano," Bob said, thinking back to his days in prison after they moved from the Colony to the new State Prison.

"I was the leader of the band. Bill took over later. I had as many as fifteen members or down to seven, always a rhythm section. Peter played base, Sammy played base. They burned him up (Sammy). They threw some substance in his cell and burnt him up. He tried to be slick and that's no place to be slick. They had a firebug (arsonist) in the prison. They kept him in the foundry. He was a good artist. They had quite a few lifers."

Bob went on, "I was lost when I got out. I was paroled to Connecticut. I used to stare across the street at a traffic light, and big Buicks driving by and traffic. I took my bad ass and went across the street and go to this place to buy a couple T-shirts. I'm standing there waiting for someone to wait on me. I didn't know you could pick them up and bring them to a cashier, because before I went to prison, I put my hands on them things, the floor walker would walk up to you and ask, 'Can you pay for those things?' Then I see people picking up things and putting them in a basket. It's sad but true, I was afraid to touch anything. I'm standing there looking like a fool. I was afraid to touch anything in that damn store. The parole officer up in Connecticut told my sister, 'Let him do everything for himself. Don't do anything for him.' Once you lose your freedom, especially over twenty years of it, God damn, a hellava long time. It takes a long time to get used to everyone and everything. You don't have a chip on your shoulder, but it takes time to trust anyone. If someone comes up to you and treats you decently, you wonder, what's his game?"

Bracy, during Bob's spiel, sat and nodded his head in acknowledgment, and occasionally uttered a "yeah."

Bracy inserted, "At the Colony, there were eight men per house, grouped into three houses per unit. You could walk around from your room, not like the State Prison or even in the new one that was being built. It had a nice library, woodworking, vocational things, and support from it, so your mind is not on the devastating thing of doing time. Not just there, jerking off!"

Bracy went on to tell this one story that had nothing to do with prison life. They were reminiscing about life, so I thought. Why not let's hear what he has to say?

"I was living on Washington Street, in the southwest section of Roxbury. Bob came by in a Rambler. He said he had a turtle outside in the back of his Rambler. He got it out of a city park. It was three o'clock in the morning, with this big-ass turtle. Take that thing back. It was in the back seat trying to get to the front. His nephew told him it was a landmark. So he took it back. He really wanted to eat it."

Bob went on to say that his daughter was eighteen months when he went to prison and the child's mother died while he was away. She (the daughter) grew up in New York.

Bracy commented, "My son was born six months after I was in. He (the son) died when he was nineteen, and the mother died seven months after the son. It really hurts, it's tough."

I listened with compassion, but what can one do? I asked Bob, "When did you go to jail?"

"I was there in 1942. Bill was there a few years after me. I called it the Bastille. I put out a paper and my column was called, 'Walleddorf Astoria.' The paper at the Colony was called, 'The Mentor.'"

Bracy interjected, "I went there in 1944. At the old State Prison we had a pitcher of water and a slop bucket. We got our water at the end of the tier. You dipped the slop bucket in sulfur naphtha. We get in line and file down carrying the bucket to the bucket deposit center, and one windy day it blew on this guy, and there was a rumble (chuckle). We had earphones for a radio and the prison played what they wanted. It went off sharp at ten p.m., all lights out; locked up for eighteen hours a day. Mornings out for work--two hours, lunchtime, file back to your cell and eat in the cell. No cellmate. No mess hall. You could touch both sides of the cell, and the cot's head and foot rested against the walls. The walls and floors used to get wet, solid granite needed a mop to wipe it down. The length was about seven feet. That was the west wing. It was well over a hundred years old when they tore it down. It was the oldest prison in use in the United States; Charles Dickens visited it. In the north wing, the walls were taken down, so you took two cells and made it into one. Bob used to play his horn and disturb the cons, so the warden moved him to the block that housed the condemned prisoners. That was where the library was. The cells there were for two and three people, and it held women at one time."

There was a long pause in the conversation and then Bob said, "Bill wanted to play football, but he was restricted, heart. His work wasn't physical. He did library work. He put himself into a position where he would have a soft touch, maybe license plates, or a runner passing out books, papers, messenger in a tier. The west wing was cold and a blanket cover over the cell entrance would help. The others were warm. Bill was in the north wing, but they moved the cons around. Rise, eat, go to work, yard time, a half-hour. No smoking in the yard, only in the cell, but they had a gathering in the auditorium with the warden. It was a blood-donors set up with the Red Cross. The warden announced that smoking was allowed in the yard. They smoked reefer. It was growing everywhere (chuckle). Everyone was sucking in air and getting high. I worked in the foundry. They got high while working. I was seven years making sewer covers. Mold them one day, fire them the next, then dip them in tar, and they were removed."

Bracy said, "I worked making socks."

Bob interjected, "I worked making pants for the Russian army during World War II. They had a clothing shop making underwear."

"A paint shop," Bracy added, "I was there about three years plus, then I went to the Colony."

Bob gave an account of his first day there, "March 26th, 1942, I'll never forget the day. You had to file in and stand in line to get your cell. This guy walked up to me and put a knife to me and I said, 'I will.' But you had to prove yourself. You don't voluntary get into it, it just is automatic."

Bracy said, "Ghetto black guys would help you out, except this one black Muslim (Malcolm X). They put, whipped him, on him, so he was mad at everyone especially white skin."

Then Bob said, "I'll tell you something about Bill. The only white guy Malcolm would talk to was Bill. William Goudas, he hung more with blacks than he did with white guys, in the band and outside."

Bracy spurted, "He got protection (chuckle)."

Bob replied, "He was a great guy. He associated, you know. He got along with everybody. Everyone liked him. Bill didn't have a reputation, like a bad-ass, or don't mess with him, nothing like that. He was an easygoing guy."

Bracy then said, "You know, very few people in there in their right mind would mess with a guy doing book."

"Doing book?" I interrupted.

Bracy responded, "Doing life. The action is that, ah, lifers don't have anything to lose. If you're doing two and a half, or three, or three to five, so you don't do anything foolish, cause you're going home. By going up a guy doing book, you're doing something very foolish. That's what Bill was doing, book."

Bob said, "Even so, he wasn't that type. He wasn't an aggressive person. He was well-toned, a musician and a good musician."

I said, "Bill told me he had trouble with this one prisoner. They were enemies. His name was Joe Barboza. Bill said that they had a standing order if either one could get at each other they would kill each other. I have no idea why Bill didn't like him, as he wouldn't tell me when I asked him."

Bob said, "I worked with Barboza when he was sixteen in the prison cement shop, and at another time in the bakery. He was a prizefighter when he got older. He was heavy when he beat Lope's; I think that was his name. The next time I seen him coming in (returned to prison), he was taking off weight, but most of the time he was big, but he wasn't too tall, anyhow, when he returned to prison he would pick on the younger and weaker prisoners. He was a bully. Yes, A vicious bastard."

"Thanks Bob for telling me more about Barboza, I can see why Bill didn't like him, but I wonder if Barboza tried to mess with Bill one time. I guess we will never know. I do know that Barboza is still alive as I read his name in the paper recently, maybe something to do with the Winter Hill Gang or the Mafia."

I wanted to return the conversation back to Bill's time in prison and about his music. I asked Bob, "When did he start playing music in a group?"

The reply from Bob, "As he was going to go into prison he said, 'I'm not going over there unless my guitar goes with me.' I had to laugh at that, but at least the guitar came with him."

Bracy blurted, "And, ah, he wasn't aggressive."

Bob responded, "Most of the time, he just sat in his cell playing--"

Bracy interrupted, "Playing drums."

"Liked to play brushes on the floor," Bob said.

"Magazine!" Bracy retorted.

"He could really play. As the years went by he got better, especially when Rudy (guitar player) came to the joint; he was rated about twenty-seventh," Bob replied,

I asked Bob, "Did they have a band in the old State Prison?"

"Yeah, an orchestra," Bob answered. "He played in the rhythm section. Bill had a group himself. We had a good rhythm section."

I asked Bob, "You played horn?"

"I played sax."

"All you played was jazz?"

"Yeah, jazz and on holidays, like Easter Sunday, we played, 'Put On Your Easter Bonnet,' or something like that."

Bracy said, "Arthur Fiedler came in and we did a number with him. That was in the Colony. At the State, they played in an auditorium, and they also showed movies up there."

Bob filled in, "The best place, like for stage, was the Colony. Bill played in the band the whole time he was in there. We went to the Colony when they tore down the old prison. There we had our own radios. At the State, if you had your own radio they would tear out the speaker, so you wouldn't disturb anyone. It was ancient. The paint on the walls was so thick, if there was fire in there, they had to go around and unlock every door, and at the Colony, they would press a button and each door would unlock. At the State, they would have a job getting the guys out, having to unlock each door with a turnkey."

After a pause to sip water that Bob brought to us, we continued. I had more inquiries, but I was enjoying this discourse. I didn't know how this interview was going to terminate. To tell you the truth, I didn't care.

I asked Bob if Bill wrote any music.

His reply was, "He made some music arrangements, he wrote too. He wrote some good things. He wrote a song, 'Let Freedom Ring.' That was good. He liked the blues. We all collaborated, you know."

I inquired about the screws, also known as guards. Did he get along with them or did they ever bother him?

Bob replied to this inquiry. "No, but we had a few assholes up there. I had a few run-ins with a couple. Like I say, there were a few assholes. One was an ex-marine. He was bad strutting around there."

Bob continued, "We had a riot, you know, where they housed the condemned (Cherry Hill). That was when a famous bank robber tried to get away. His name was Theodore (Teddy) Green. He was a Greek. They held this screw (an ex-marine) hostage, ha, ha. When he got out, he never came back, ha, ha. Oh man! Swat, and all them guys, they treated him like a woman, ha, ha. He thought he was a tough marine."

Bracy laughed, "Yeah, yeah, when I think about that place, ah, the prison and the street. It was eight feet separating them."

Bob spoke up and said, "Yeah, I went to band practice and was looking out a window onto the street in Charlestown."

Bracy joined in, "You could look right out, thick walls, yeah, the impression was, ha, ha, its funny man!"

I asked if they ever put on plays or concerts at State.

Bob said, "We put on plays, put on wigs, and dresses, and put nightclub stuff on."

Bracy added, "We had a guy named Bow. He was a nightclub comedian. He did some writing and arranging plays, skits, you know. I remember one of them was called, 'I Got The Number.' Remember that one? Gibby was in it. I was in it. It was great. It was something to break up the monotony of the Colony."

Bob said, "Most of that stuff went down at the Colony. Up at State we didn't have too much of that."

"Not too much at State?" I asked.

Bob answered, "Eighteen hours at State you were locked up. At least at Colony you had your house to walk around. When I first went down there, after doing twelve years in State, we went to the movie one night, or something. That was something; it was the first time I was out at night, and I looked up and saw the stars. It was something else, (laugh); first time in twelve years."

Bracy and I both laughed.

Bob said, "It was like being in the street."

Bracy responded, "Yeah, like different colors, huh?"

"Out in the stars--like being out, being in the street. Twelve years of State! I did a year and a half at Colony, bounced back to State for old movies," Bob lamented.

Bracy said, "To the tunnel?"

Bob replied, "Yeah."

Bracy thinking back to those days said, "All the pipes are in the tunnel. It stayed hot in the tunnel, and whatever you brewed would cook faster (home brew)."

Bob continued, "It took a couple of days of whatever you cooked to brew. One guy took some up to his cell and put it on his bed. And one night it popped. Man what a smell! It stunk the whole place."

I asked Bob, "Did you end up at the new facility, the new maximum?"

His reply was, "Yeah, yeah."

I then asked him, "Was Bill there when you got there?"

"I think so. It was so long ago I forget," Bob answered.

Bracy retorted, "I was gone by then, yeah. It was a whole different kind of prison."

Bob said, "It was maximum security, no bars, you lived in dorms."

Bracy asked Bob, "Colony?"

Bob answered, "Yeah, oh, the new State?"

Bracy interrupted, "You were in a cell again by yourself!"

"Oh yeah, by yourself. I think Bill was already there," Bob said.

I asked Bob, "Did Bill work in the chapel?" I knew this already, but I wanted to get his response on this subject.

Bob replied, "Yeah, I think he did by then. As I say, he always did those soft touches. I guess they knew his condition, but he let them know of his condition. He was sarcastic as hell about it."

I continued with Bob. "Didn't Bill become leader of the band?"

Bob replied, "Yeah, well, I was the leader the whole time I was in there, but I got out in 1962, and Bill took over. He was the most capable. He was my right-hand man. He also taught Spanish. He used to talk to this one musician and they always spoke Spanish."

My next question had to do with solitary confinement. "Did Bill ever do solitary?"

Bob said, "Not that I was aware of. Oh, when you first went in, you did solitary."

Bracy said, "It was probationary, everyone does it. It was the process."

Bob interjected, "Before you go out into the community!"

Bracy continued, "Yeah, but people that go into solitary are certain kinds of persons, because somebody pushes somebody wrong and he's got to snap, and a person comes by and causes him to snap. He'll go down the hole. It's not his fault, you know. It happens that way when doing time."

I asked about the cells in the new State. "Were they a decent size?"

Bob answered in quick responses. "Oh yeah, bigger, better, running water, toilet."

"Metal?"

"No, regular porcelain."

"Running water? That's different than the old State," I replied.

"Yeah, running hot, running cold," Bob replied with a smile on his face.

"Could you have a radio?"

"Yeah. By the time I got out you could have a TV."

"What about noise from all the radios and TVs?"

"We had doors that were solid."

"Was there a window in it?"

"A big window. You had a radio, TV, and when you went in, you could tell the guard to lock you in. Once you closed the door, nobody could hear you."

"Okay, that sounds like it was better conditions, but did you spend eighteen hours in the cell?"

Bob was quick to respond, "Oh, no, you could lock up when you wanted to get locked up. When I was writing the column or arranging music, I would tell the guard to lock me in. In the morning, after you got out, it was like a city. Guys going to work here, going to work there, at certain times. In the new State, you weren't locked up that long. File into the cafeteria dining room, eat dinner and file out again."

Bracy added, "I know they had a library too, a beautiful library."

I inquired, "How did the food compare from one prison to the other?"

Bracy responded first, "I'd say it was better at Colony."

Bob said, "At both state prisons the food wasn't that great."

I asked, "Any seconds?"

Bob said, "No, that's why I got a job in the kitchen, I could cook that food for myself."

Bracy said, "He used to send me down some."

Laughs from Bob and Bracy.

I asked, "Did the cons discuss their crimes?"

Bob interrupted and said, "No-o-o."

Bracy added, "Most people didn't want anyone to know what they did."

Bob said, "If they did ask, they would say I didn't do anything. They were all innocent. I didn't do it!"

"Just talking about this stuff brings back memories more and more," Bob said. "As you guys are talking I'm thinking too, about Colony. Remembering something Bracy said, I remember one time me and Brian were sitting out back of the cement shop. You had to work there, (Colony) when you first went in. That was the heaviest thing, the cement shop. We made cement poles, those three-sided poles you see on the edge of highways. Yeah, that's what we made. That's one of the poles we made (pointing out the window)."

Bob continued his story, "Well, we could rest outside in the back and some of them farm horses would come in the back, it was Duke! It wasn't me, it was Travis; he was funny."

Bracy laughing, "Yeah, he was funny."

After laughs by Bob and Bracy, Bob continued, "Duke the horse, remember that horse? Duke came through there and took a shit, and each day it would dry up and dry and dry. Travis rolled up some cigarettes (using the dry manure), ha, ha, and give to all the guys."

Bracy started to chuckle.

Bob continued "There was a nut (Brian) and he took two drags. He was flying, oh, man"

Now the three of us are cracking up laughing.

"That's so funny," Bracy said.

Bob added, "So, what's his name said (Brian). 'That's some good shit in it.' " By this time the three of us are really cracking up and there are tears in our eyes.

Bracy said, after we quieted down some, "Yeah, that place had a lot of humor flying around, lots of charisma. I guess it had to in order to survive."

Bob said, "You didn't have too much room in the old times (old State), like a good day like today. You'd be locked up, oh man! But down there (Colony), it was solid, that's why everyone would grab a paper and read my column, because I used to write all kind of stuff."

Bracy inserted, "It was a mentor."

Bob said, "That was the name of the paper. I wrote it for a long time. When I was ready to getting out, my lawyer had all the papers. My column the Walleddorf Astoria and things like that. It kinda helped me to get out."

"Yeah, the Mentor," Bracy thinking out loud.

Bob continued, "When I wanted to quit, they didn't want me to, because nobody was kicking my ass for what I wrote."

Bracy affirming, "Yeah, right."

Bob said, "Some guys couldn't write like that, because a lot of them would get mad at me too, gangsters."

Bracy said, "Yeah, a lot of wannabes. The real ones kept to themselves."

Bob added, "They were real gentlemen, the nicest guys in there. I had a real Mafia come by and see me (after Bob's release) and left me fifty dollars, yeah. They tried to get me a job, 'Can you drive a diesel?' I said, 'I don't even know what a diesel is.'"

We all laughed at that one.

"Now Gibby would have taken a chance." Bracy said, "Yeah, he drove tractor trailer. Yeah, remember when he was driving and he pulled over and this guy smashes into the rear of his truck and decapitated himself? Gibby had some funny experiences. He turned one over and they canned him."

Bob added, "Gibby was something else."

"Yeah, he was," Bracy replied.

I met Gibby at Bracy's store and he always had some scheme or new idea that he was going to try and get going. The outcome was how he could make an income from it. I must admit that he wasn't very successful, but he sure was an interesting character. I asked Bob and Bracy about sports in the prison.

Bob was first to reply, "Yeah, baseball, football. They played some good teams too. Played some semi-pros. McGill, etcetera, North Oxford, England came in here."

Bracy said, "We had some great guys in there, some heavies."

After this brief talk on sports, I asked if they ever saw Bill after he was released.

Bob replied, "No, I never saw him."

Bracy informed us, "I saw him twice."

Bob then spoke up, "He knew where I was living, but I never seen him. Yeah, I think I did see him, because I think he told me someone was looking for me. I was living in Corregidor Court. I think I did see him. It was so long ago."

Bracy thinking hard, "I haven't sat down and talked about that in years, little excerpts now and then. You know, little things run by your mind, but to sit down."

Bob said, "Yeah! Yeah, sometimes I think, not too many people alive have done time in the oldest prison in the United States. You wonder how many people are alive at this time that did time in that prison. I think about that."

Bracy asked, "Do you remember this? Where they had this big iron ring where the boats used to come in. Yeah, that used to be surrounded by water and boats used to come in."

Bob added, "I worked in the foundry and this great green ring was way up on the wall. You could see them mussels. What do you call them?"

I said, "Carbuncles?"

Bob said, "Yeah, carbuncles, yeah, it was an ancient prison."

Bracy finished, "Those granite pieces, they were big!"

While we were sitting, I told them about how when I was young I wanted to be with Bill in prison. Bob commented about an inmate, Parker, and his brother, who also ended up in the same prison, and how his brother had to take care of him. "The worst thing you could do," Bob ended.

I never asked Bob what his crime was. I felt it wasn't necessary at the time, but because of his long internment, I knew it was a serious offense. I was informed later that he was in for killing another black man. Bracy's opinion was that if it were a white man he would have received the death penalty. I don't know all the circumstances, so I have no opinion on the matter. After Bob's release, he did menial jobs, one of which was serving as a security guard for a private company. He was married, and his wife was in a wheelchair at the time of our visit. I never saw her, because she remained in her bedroom. I would have never known from his demeanor that he spent twenty years in prison for killing a man. Like good wine, he improved with age.

# CHAPTER XX
## American Friends Service

March 13, 1999

W hen I first went to the American Friends Service Committee organization to meet someone who might remember Bill, I met Phyllis C, who was housing him at the time of his death. I entered the office and spoke to this friendly smiling receptionist and introduced myself. I asked if there was anyone there who had been working there in the years prior to Bill's death or during that event. Bill passed away September 1982. He was fifty-six years old.

The receptionist recalled that there was a lady working there at that time and she was in her office, and she would call her and inform her of my presence. After a few moments, this middle-aged woman came into the reception area and introduced herself, shaking my hand firmly.

Her hair was dark brown with streaks of gray and she had the stature of a mature woman, about five foot five. Her eyes were dark brown, and along with her smile they expressed warmth. She became very interested when I expressed my desire to write this story about Bill, whom she recalled after I mentioned his name. She told me of this man, John, who was working at the Justice Department in their building. She said that he might be a good resource for information about what Bill was doing, and about his death.

Phyllis stated that we should make a date when she would be free to spend the time for an interview. She asked me why I wanted to pursue this project and what relationship I was to Bill. I told her that I was his nephew, but almost four years younger than him. I thought that it would be an interesting story for the family and maybe for the public. It had been a secret among the family for all these years, but now most of the older generation had died, and Bill's crime would not have any effect on the younger generation. I know it didn't affect mine, and I was living with him at the time of this crime. I had gotten over the personal guilt of his crime years ago and could now freely discuss it. Not that I went out of my way to tell friends or acquaintances, but now I knew I could, because I felt that I had led a productive and honest life. Phyllis and I agreed on a set date a few months ahead, as I was going to be away for a while and she would be busy for the next few weeks. We shook hands and said our salutations. I left the building, looking forward to this interview.

After the first meeting with Phyllis, I got hold of John by calling an office in Central Square, Cambridge. From that office, he was doing some legal work for prisoners and writing a column for a peace and justice periodical. It took a few phone calls to reach him, as he was only there a couple times a week. Finally, we set a date, and I ventured into this office building and found the office, where John was sitting behind this cluttered desk of papers.

I was expecting an older man. I don't know why--but John was in his early sixties. He had a full head of salt and pepper hair, and he had skin that was light brown. He was somewhat youthful-looking, with what looked like a firm body with a slight paunch. John stood about five feet ten and carried about one hundred and eighty pounds. He had a great smile and a firm handshake. I liked him immediately, for his aura was one of kindness and warmth.

I made my introduction and told him that I appreciated his thoughtfulness in helping me to establish some information about Bill. I also told John that he was the fourth person that I was going to interview. We felt comfortable with each other, as one can tell when the dialogue is not strained, and this one started with ease.

"John, when did you meet Bill Goudas?"

"I met Bill at the Peace and Justice program where Phyllis works."

"So, that was in 1980-1981?"

"Yes, I believe it was 1981."

"How did Bill end up at that place?"

John said, "It was David Collins. David and Bill were tight. They knew each other in the new State Prison, the one that Bill was finally released from."

"So, you didn't know Bill from prison life?"

"No, I had been in the Colony, but after Bill had left there. We talked about our prison time, like where we were and when. Bill was a lot older than me, well not much older, maybe fifteen to twenty years. What I mean, I guess, is that Bill went to prison long before I did. We never crossed path in the can."

"Did you know of his crime?"

John answered, "I think someone told me that he was in a robbery and a cop was shot, but I never knew who the shooter was. I suspected it was Bill, but I never asked him. I believe David told me something about it."

"If you knew he had shot the cop, would that have made any difference in your relationship with him?"

"Oh no, I knew some bad guys much meaner than him. You knew that he made one bad mistake, but he had no meanness in him. He was a good man."

"You worked with Bill, or I should restate that, and say that Bill worked with you in the Justice Department, in the basement where he was living. What did he do there?"

John said, "Well, he would run errands, get files, and stuff envelopes. Sometimes he would make telephone calls or answer the phone. I guess you would call it secretary work, although we didn't tell him that. He was very helpful, and he could be with David. As I said, they were tight and he needed David at that time of his life. You could see that something was bothering him. Not only his health, which seemed to decline the longer he was there, but something psychologically. He was pretty closed-mouthed. A lot of guys get that way, especially when life isn't going good for them. One could see that he wasn't, at that time of his life, in the best space for whatever reason."

"He never opened up to you or said anything to give you a clue what was going on?"

"No, but you knew he was depressed, and he kept very quiet about it, especially towards me. I'm sure David knew what was going on, and there was this lady who worked at the office. Her name was Priscilla. She doesn't work there anymore, but she lives in the area. I believe only a few miles from here. Phyllis C can give you her telephone number."

I called Priscilla several times after my second visit with Phyllis, but each time she was either too busy or she acted vague about being interviewed. The reality of the situation was she didn't want to be interviewed. I told her I understood her position, and I apologized for my intrusions and thanked her anyhow.

"So, what was your job there at the Justice Department?"

"Well, I wrote this column for this paper, and I worked with ex-cons. I guess you would say I was a counselor. I helped them in any way I could to adjust to the outside world. Sometimes it would work out, and sometimes the same individual you thought was doing okay, and then before you know it, he would get into trouble and land up in the clink again. Some guys just have a hard time doing the right thing. Their heads are all screwed up. They never adjust, and when they do, life had passed them by, and they are now on their deathbeds or almost there, and that's when it don't make any difference. It's too late, life has fled by. Of course, there are those cons that lose their families. I mean, their families don't want anything to do with them for whatever reason. When you lose your right to be with your family, what have you got? Nothing! I've seen big tough guys break down and cry because they lost their wives, children, and etcetera. It can be tough on you, but for the most part, they have to take the blame. You did what you did, and you're responsible for your actions."

"Yes, I agree with you, but it must be awful lonesome to have no one."

John said, "Let me say this. Prison reform was vague and Bill could have taken advantage of it, but he kept it to himself. You can't let people get to you. It don't matter what they say, you got to get over with it. Don't let it get to you. You have to find something. Apply yourself. There are guys out there that have done horrible stuff, but you wouldn't know it, and if you do, they don't care."

"I suppose you're right, but Bill always carried too much, obviously."

"Right, that is why he was so depressed. He let it get in the way of what he really wanted to do in life."

I said, "And that would be to play the guitar for a living. He was a great musician and he never gave himself the opportunity to express that avenue of himself to the public. When some people recognized his talent, I guess he just shrugged it off, or changed his venue."

John said, "Yeah, that's too bad. I heard him play a few times and I was really impressed, but you could see that he was hiding himself in a closet, when it came to his playing. I remember saying something at one time, but he just buzzed me off and went on like I didn't say a word. I didn't pursue it, for it was up to him, not me."

"Yes, he played jazz and classical extremely well. He had a guitar for each style."

"Yeah, I know. He gave me his electric guitar just before he passed away. He knew how sick he was. When he gave it to me, he just said that he wasn't playing it anymore. He was only playing his classical, and he knew I admired the electric. I still have it."

I was surprised that Bill gave him his guitar, but it was his to give. John would put it to good use, and it showed me how much Bill liked John. I cannot think of anyone in the family who would use it. For Bill, John was the most likely choice.

John said he would try to get a hold of David Collins for me, because he knew where Bill's head was. Also, he was probably full of stories about Bill.

I asked John if he was there the day that Bill died. He gave me this account: "Kim, Lynn, and I went to the Justice office. Someone told us that Bill had died during the night. We went down the stairs and went to where Bill was living. Kim, she was praying on entering Bill's room. She was doing this Asian ritual, standing with her arms folded across her bosom, and she was mumbling something. I just looked down at Bill. It was quite obvious that he was dead. One side of body was all blue where the blood settled. He was naked. Some other people came, paid their respects, and then we called the coroner. We left him as he was, because we know they would want to see just how he died. No one touched anything. Then of course, the police came, the coroner and the ambulance. We just lost one of our friends and worker. It was very hard on the personnel on the building. Everyone liked Bill, yeah, we all liked Bill."

# CHAPTER XXI
## Peace and Justice

### December 29, 2002

My research led me back to the American Friends Service Committee building on Massachusetts Avenue in Cambridge. This artery eventually flowed into Boston, the place of Bill's birth, and was now his last place on earth. This building housed the American Friends Service Committee, a Quaker affiliation. It is an organization that is sympathetic to the underprivileged citizens of the world. Some of the constituents they assisted were ex-convicts.

I didn't know how this move materialized or why Bill moved there, as our association had been diminishing prior to the time of his move. He had found his way there and stayed until his death. He used to visit me in an apartment that I occupied that was no more than six blocks away.

This closeness was of course by pure chance, not one he pursued on purpose. I was somewhat taken aback by his arrival in Cambridge, knowing that he did not have the approval of the parole authorities or of Massachusetts state officials to move back. He wasn't even supposed to visit this state where he was now living on a permanent basis. I questioned him later about this, and his attitude was of no concern whatsoever. He simply shrugged it off as a non-entity. I did on two occasions visit him, as he wanted me to see where and how his situation was. I found his quarters clean and sparse, but adequate for someone that had little in the sense of material objects. His prized possessions were of course his guitars, one electric, and the other acoustic. These were the only objects that were dear to him throughout his life.

On the set date, I returned to interview Phyllis C. The receptionist informed Phyllis that I had arrived. Phyllis came out front and led me to her office. After sitting down and completing our hellos, the interview commenced. Phyllis reminded me that it had been almost twenty years since Bill had lived there, but since my last visit, she had taken some moments to consider the events which might interest me.

My first question: "How did Bill arrive here to stay?"

Phyllis said, "If I recall, he was here all of a sudden, and he was hanging out with the Criminal Justice Program, which was housed in our basement. Like a lot of other folks around here, he was here and he'd be helping out downstairs with the Criminal Justice staff. I know he was a friend of David's. David Collins. I don't know if you know him."

"I have become aware of David, but I have not been able to locate him, or get in touch with him. No one seems to know where he is."

"He does not have a happy history. I know he's had his alcoholic problems. It contributed to his landing in prison in the first place, which is not atypical. I don't know if that was true for Bill or not. I don't remember Bill drinking."

"No, Bill was not a drinker. No one in the family is a drinker; maybe a glass or two of beer or wine."

Phyllis said, "Anyway, suddenly he was here and he'd be helping out."

"With his help with the Justice Department, was he a counselor, legal avenues?"

"No, no, just like helping to get the envelopes stuffed, you know, get that kind of work done. Odd jobs, which is volunteer kind of work around here."

"When did he come here, approximately?"

"Counting backwards you're going to need to help me. He was here for a couple of years. He wasn't living here all that time, but intermittently he stayed here. Probably for a year or two, about a year and a half to two years before he died."

"That was in 1982, in the fall."

Phyllis said, "I figure it was about fifteen to twenty years ago. I'm trying to remember. He wound up doing a stint. He ended up doing odd jobs more broadly outside of the Justice Department, and then, ah, the receptionist was out on leave, and I can't remember if she was out on maternity leave or she had jury duty for a long time, but Bill wound up, ah, answering the phone (pause) for us. We wound up paying him eventually for that, so he went from just helping out to, ah, to a paying gig. He was getting sicker and sicker in that period. At one point, I went to the doctor with him, and I was not particular happy with the treatment he was receiving."

"Was that the gentleman on Cambridge Street in this city?"

"Yes, yeah."

"That's the same doctor that I took him to."

Phyllis said, "I don't know what kind of impression you had, but I had the impression that this guy was not paying attention, ah, it was kind of difficult to figure how to help Bill. I was not family. I had no right to intrude on his life, certainly not in medical areas. At the same time, I was really disturbed at the fact that he seemed not to be getting the care that he needed."

"Our family doesn't have any evidence of malpractice, but we're sure he was not treated correctly."

"Yeah."

"He should have gone to a hospital."

"Yeah."

"We didn't know, or at least I didn't, of the seriousness of his condition until it was too late. When Bill first came here, he wasn't staying here?"

Phyllis said, "No. I have no idea where he was staying at that point."

"When did Bill start staying here, sleeping?"

"About the last six months."

"Any reason why he stayed here?"

"I think he needed a place to stay, and at that point we had a number of break-ins, so it was okay to have someone in the building. You know, it might not have been a bad idea."

I said, "Right, and you trusted him?"

"And we trusted him. We totally trusted him."

"And Bill never faulted that trust?"

"No."

"That's good."

Phyllis said, "I had no idea what he was in jail for, and my general policy is, if people want to tell me they'll tell me, and if they don't want to tell me---"

"And he never related?"

"No, he never related it, ah, but I, I didn't figure he was in for a violent crime."

I said, "A very violent crime."

Phyllis surprisingly said, "A very violent crime would have come as a totally---if other people had committed crimes and then later grow up, changed their lives, mellowed out, whatever it is that people do to become different people, I would have been really shocked, because Bill was the gentlest guy."

"He was a gentle person. He just did that one violent crime. He panicked and killed the person."

"I could see him panicking. He was certainly not a calculating guy, ah; I could see him not knowing what to do especially in youth."

"When Bill was here, I'm sure no one monitored his situation, but did he take off for a day or two sometimes?"

Phyllis answered, "Ah, I think in the beginning more, but I think later, when he got sicker, like you know, just like laying low. We'd keep an eye on him."

"When Bill came here, did he mention family or talk about family?"

"Not that I recall, you know, we are going back a long time, not that I recall."

I asked, "He never related that he had a nephew around the corner? He used to visit me."

"You know I do, no, I'm remembering if I heard that from you, or I heard that long ago. I'm not remembering it directly."

"He didn't talk about his mother?"

"Mmmmmm."

"Or his brother?"

"Mmmmmmm."

"So he really didn't discuss family members?"

Phyllis said, "He was very quiet."

"Very quiet?"

"A very quiet guy. It was sometime before I realized he played music."

"He didn't have his instruments here?"

"He did, yeah, he did. Every once in a while you could coax him into playing, but mostly it was a very private thing."

"You had to coax Bill into playing? That's surprising!"

Phyllis said, "Yeah, yeah, we coaxed him once to play at a party. We had a Christmas party or something and he played."

"I didn't realize he sheltered himself from his music."

"He sheltered himself period."

"That's really surprising."

"Yeah. Every once in a while, we could encourage him to play."

"When he played, did he play jazz, classical?"

Phyllis said, "He played classical. Yeah, he was wonderful, and he protested how rusty he was, but he was wonderful."

I said, "So he didn't practice a lot here then?"

"No, no. He would play by himself, when he was by himself, and every once in a while he played for us."

"He had just his acoustical guitar here or an electric?"

"I didn't realize he played electric."

"Oh yeah, Bill played electric."

"It was just classical. I don't remember hearing him playing jazz, just classical."

"No jazz?"

Phyllis said, "So, he was a jazz guitarist also?"

"All the convicts arriving into prison would tell him, and say, 'Bill if you were outside, you're the greatest.' He played with a lot of musicians; a lot of guys would go in for short stints. Yeah, he played with a lot of good musicians. He was an excellent guitarist."

"Did he play before he went in?"

"Oh yeah. That's why he went in. He was trying to get money to go to the New England Conservatory of Music. There were no funds; we came from a poor family, especially his. There was no money there for him. He got into the wrong business to get money."

Phyllis answered with a moan.

I asked, "Did he confide in you how he was feeling?"

"Physically, emotionally?"

I answered, "Emotionally, before he died, did he divulge anything you can remember?"

"No, no, he really was a very private guy."

"Did he eat here?"

Phyllis replied, "Yeah."

"Did he go out to eat?"

"Sometimes we'd often have meetings here and there would be food around, and we tried to make sure that we offered him what we could, but he would take care of himself."

"Did he have facilities to wash here?"

"Oh yeah, there's showers here. We had them filled them up with storage, but there is showers here, yup."

"What kind of possessions did he have?"

Phyllis answered, "Well, ah, like most prisoners, I think they learn to live in a very confined space, and only what is most precious to them. They learn to live in six square feet you know, ah, and I think that is what he did. His guitar was his most private possession."

"So, he was living a confined life, like he was in prison, but he had freedom."

"Yeah."

"And his room wasn't all that large?"

"No."

"So, he was comfortable in that small room?"

"Yeah."

"Because that's probably what he knew the best?"

"Yeah."

"It doesn't sound like the time he was out, for the years he was out, that he changed his habits, his prison habits?"

Phyllis said, "No, no. As I said, I thought he got out much more recently. I didn't realize that he had been out that many years. I do remember of hearing about the state he was paroled in, or should I say paroled to."

"Yeah, well he was in for twenty-two years, and then two years more, and then another year. He was forty-two years old when he first got out, and he died when he was fifty-six. Bill was four years older than me."

Phyllis said, "He was born in 1927? No, that was the year my mom was married."

"No, 1926. That was the same year my mother got married. I was born in 1930. What do you think his state of mind was while he was here? Do you have any impression?"

Phyllis said, "He was happy to be in a place that accepted him, and I think giving responsibility, and giving trust here was a positive thing. He was, as I said, he was a quiet guy. Ummm, I think he liked to be present, but sit back. I think he felt comfortable here or he wouldn't have been here."

"Do you think Bill was comfortable in his position and where he was in his life? Did you get any feeling on that?"

"Mmmmmm."

I asked, "Did he joke around?"

"Yeah."

"Tease? A little bit?"

"Yeah, he did stuff like that, yeah. He gave the impression that he was a gentle person. He had this laugh, giggle, brown melting eyes, you know."

"Did you find him to be intelligent?"

Phyllis said, "Oh, (a sigh) hard to say. I was thinking of that before, actually, ummm, I think he was probably a philosopher. I don't think he was an academic, ah, but I think he thought a lot. He didn't necessarily show it at all. We got the impression that he was thinking a lot."

"Did he use his Spanish here?"

"No."

I asked, "He never did?"

"Not that I remember, again, he spent a lot of time down in the Justice Department where Spanish must have come in handy there."

"Bill taught Spanish in prison."

Phyllis said, "I didn't know that. All I knew was that he practiced his music in prison. I knew that at the time. Where was he in prison?"

"Bill was in three different ones. He was originally in the Charlestown State Prison, and then they were going to tear down that one, so they sent him out to Norfolk Colony, which was like a country club, especially after old State. And then, after they built the new maximum state prison, he was moved there and spent his last remaining years in prison there. Even when he returned for two more stints, that's where he went."

"I think that he must have been in prison with David Rollins there."

"Yeah."

Phyllis said, "I think that's how he got here."

I said, "The people that I've talked to all know David Rollins, but no one knows where he is, and they all tried to contact him for me. There are a couple of more persons I would like to get a hold of, but my contacts don't know where they are, and I don't know how to get in touch with them. These contacts are old and they say, 'I don't know where he is or where they are.'"

"Have you spoken to John at all?"

"I interviewed John over in Central Square."

Phyllis said, "Okay, okay. He actually has moved to the ocean recently. He was just recently here being interviewed for something else."

"I had a good session with him."

"Yes, he was a good guy, so they served time together?"

"No, he talked about working with him here, in the Justice Department Center."

Phyllis said, "A-huh, a-huh, okay."

"Yes, I did get a few things from him, now I'm trying to get his last days and what went on in his state of mind, and if you could share anything—."

"It was--in spite of his physical state, because he was really kind of floating in his last period of time. He was operating in slow motion."

"So, he was showing signs of physical sickness?"

"Oh yeah! Oh yeah!"

"In which way?"

Phyllis said, "There would be longer and longer losses in speech, so you know, you ask a question and you get a very slow answer."

"Really!"

Phyllis said, "And his movements were really slowing down."

"So, you noticed that he was slowing down?"

"Yeah, he was by himself when he died, and my guess it was pretty peaceful. I had the feeling he was just slowing down. Ummm, there was no indication it was difficult in any way. I think he felt being cared for, being here."

"So, Bill felt like people liked him, and being cared for?"

Phyllis said, "Yeah, yeah, I think that was important to him, like it's not important to the rest of us."

"I wonder why he didn't share any of that with his family. Well, he did somewhat, but not much, and not too many of us."

Phyllis said, "So, he was seeing you right up to the end?"

"Yeah somewhat. He was seeing his sister, who is still alive, and we did discuss to him about that doctor, but it was towards the latter part of his illness when we found out that we thought he wasn't treated all that great. Bill didn't last much longer after that."

"So, you, you weren't--I'm trying to remember, like the funeral was well attended, and I knew there was family there."

"Uh-huh, uh-huh."

Phyllis said, "And I guess David knew how to go find people?"

"I don't remember who contacted me, but it had to be someone in the family. David wouldn't have contacted me, because I don't have the same last name."

Phyllis said, "Mmmmmm. I attended the funeral. I remember a gentleman here, but I don't remember his name, and he said he had a lot of Bill's possessions, and if anyone wanted them, 'Come and pick them up,' I just assumed that his brother or his sister was most qualified to come and get it. Yeah, I don't remember who did. Somebody came and got his personal stuff. I know we just didn't dump stuff."

I said, "I don't know who came, but I'll probably find out as my research goes on."

"Somebody must of taken his guitar."

"John has his guitar (his electric guitar)."

Phyllis said, "Okay, okay."

"Bill gave it to him. Not long before he died. Maybe he just knew his outcome."

Phyllis said, "That would make sense."

"I didn't come. I don't know what was here. I just felt it wasn't my position, and then I found out that no one from the family came and took his personal items, but his brother did acquire his most prized possession the acoustical guitar. He gave it to his daughter. She still has it."

"Okay."

I said, "That's what I was told."

"Okay."

"I felt bad about that, like everybody just forgot about him. Maybe some of the family felt like he was still a burden on their guilt, and now that he was gone, that part of the family history was buried. Really buried!"

Phyllis said, "Well, people did show up for the funeral."

"Oh, yeah, but it wasn't a typical show. There were many that never went. More than you realize."

Phyllis said, "People didn't forget about him."

"Oh no, not in that sense, but once he was gone, no one cared for his possessions."

"I realize that, but---"

"The guitar was the most critical. I guess all his other possessions probably didn't amount to much, a few clothes and such. Maybe that's what his brother meant when he told me that nobody got his things, just the guitar. Like you said, it was a long time ago, and individuals' remembrance of incidences become obscure sometimes."

Phyllis said, "Well, there weren't a whole lot of possessions that I can remember. Well, at least John got one of his guitars. Yes, well, that would make sense."

"I guess."

"Yeah, that would make sense, yeah. Bill was a gentle spirit. Also, it would have made sense that they would have bonded."

"When Bill passed away he was discovered in the morning. Who discovered him?"

Phyllis replied "I think David Collins did."

"David Collins?"

"Yeah, I think David did."

"And then they called the police and an ambulance?"

"Yeah."

I asked, "And they went from there?"

"Yes."

"I was told that he was nude. Do you recall that?"

"That was what I was told. I was not actually down there in the basement."

"And Bill regurgitated?"

Phyllis replied, "That's what I heard."

"Which is typical of a heart attack; a myocardial infarction, and he was on his stomach?"

"I don't know."

"Oh. Did he have a television in his room?"

Phyllis said, "No."

"Radio?"

"Just a radio. There are a lot of radios around the building."

"Did he have a sink in his room?"

Phyllis said, "There is a bathroom down there. I'm trying to remember at what point when we renovated the kitchen. The kitchen was upstairs, a full kitchen. We renovated the building more recently to make it wheelchair accessible. Basically this is a house."

"Originally this was once a house?"

"Yes, it was a doctor's residence and practice."

"What was the sense of the workers when they found out?"

Phyllis said, "A lot of sadness. Yes, there was a lot of sadness."

"They liked him!"

Phyllis said, "It was a shock, obviously, that someone died in the building, and, ah, that someone was downstairs, and he wasn't there for long, and you see I think he died at night. He was discovered in the morning, ah, but it still was a sense of shock, and that people were coming in the building, not knowing what was going on with one of our colleagues below us."

"It must have been strange and hard?"

"It was strange and hard. He was well liked, he was very well liked!"

I said, "It's nice to hear that."

"He was helpful. I really think he wanted to be helpful."

"Did Bill ever show any anger?"

Phyllis said, "Not that I ever saw."

"Bill didn't joke around that much?"

"He joked around. He wasn't like a practical joker. He certainly had a sense of humor, ah, yeah, he wanted to be helpful. I think that he felt like the organization was helpful to him. He had been accepted, and he wanted to be helpful."

"Right, but, I think I've already asked, but he never gave a sense or opened up and talked to you about anything, like on his own? Did he ever say he had remorse for his crime?"

"No, we didn't discuss it."

"Did Bill mention how much time he had done?"

Phyllis said, "I knew he had done a lot of time, but didn't know how much. I knew he had a gun, but I didn't know if he was the shooter, or it was, ah, with the shooter."

"Right."

Phyllis said, "In fact, I had the impression he was with the shooter, but I don't know if that was what I told myself, ah, to somewhat account for myself, that he was this gentle guy, or whether I been told that, or whether, or you know, why I thought that."

"Mmmm, so he never related that, as you mentioned?"

"No."

"If you hadn't known of his past, would you have thought he was in prison?"

Phyllis said, "Well again, the kind of things that I've come to, ah, to know how people lived as tightly as they do, and as tightly lipped as they are, and all that, so I might, but you know what I don't recall about him, which has been my experience with a lot of folks who end up in prison, is this tendency to, of a whole lot folks, blame a lot of people for their actions. To blame other people for what happened to them. I didn't get that from him."

"So, he never said, 'I didn't do it?'"

"No, no it's not even that. I mean life in general, you know, where there is this tendency to, ah, something bad happened, but 'it wasn't my fault' or, or whatever. I didn't get that with him. I didn't get excuses. I didn't get, ah; I didn't get that from him."

I asked, "Bill never gave you that tight lipped kinda sneer talk, some of them get?"

"Naw."

"I used to visit him, 'oh my God, my uncle is changing.' That's what I would see when I saw those expressions. So, you would say that he was basically, or least he seemed to be content?"

Phyllis said, "I don't know whether he wanted to do other things in his life. Yeah, I don't know, but, ah, did he want to be living in the basement of an organization, you know? Probably not, but did he want to be in a place where people liked him and appreciated the help they gave him? Yeah, he probably liked that."

"What about holidays. Did he stay here?"

"By the end he did. Earlier on, I had the feeling he would go to his brother's from time to time. It's hard to remember back that many years ago."

I asked, "And he had a car while he was here?"

"He had a car for part of that time."

"So, there were times that he would just disappear for a day, or maybe for a few days, but never explained where he went or what he had done?"

Phyllis answered, "Yes, there would be those times, but I don't remember them being that often, especially towards the end. He was generally a slow mover. It was only when he got sick that he slowed down. It became almost a character of itself, but generally he was a slow mover."

"So, you would say he was always fairly calm?"

"Yes, he was, he was. You got this sense he was internalizing a lot. You did get the sense he was slow moving, slow speaking. You asked me before, if I did think he was smart, and again, I think that slow moving, ah, kind of masked I think, what was more brightness underneath. You got the sense that he was philosophizing inwardly, but he wasn't flashy with his intelligence."

"Do you think he might have shared his thoughts with his friend David Collins?"

Phyllis said, "Or maybe with John. I don't know what you got from John. He certainly liked to talk, but Bill did not share a whole lot about himself, which is not a big surprise. Again, I think people in prison tend to mask a whole lot. If they showed their softness, which proceeds to be softness."

"Right, you can't do that or they'll all be on top of you. Is there anything you can think of that you can share, or any incidences, any particular situation?"

Phyllis said, "I wish not so much time has gone by. I wish I could remember better or wish I was not getting older, or having difficulty remembering things."

"I understand. I forget a lot of things, and I was somewhat implicated at the beginning of this crime. I had to go to the Boston Public Library and research all the newspapers and step back and try to remember everything I could. After I read all the papers, all that material, then a lot of memory came back to me. Then of course, talking to those three individuals who were incarcerated helped a lot. One of those convicts, Bob, was in prison for twenty years or something like that. I never asked him what he did to get such a long sentence, but I thought it couldn't have been anything too cool."

Phyllis laughing, "Yeah, right."

"When you do five years, seven years, well it is long, but when compared to twenty or more straight years, oh boy. It's a lot different if you do five, get out, do six more, get out, do some more etcetera, but twenty years straight, that's really something, so many changes on the outside world. How do you catch up? All those missing years."

"Exactly."

I continued, "You know how some guys go in for a short stint and get out, but Bob's straight concurrent years. I said to myself, oh boy, that's violence, but I'm not asking. But this guy is in his early eighties and he seems okay. It is interesting material."

"Have you tried to interview his former wife (referring to Bill's)?"

"I just found out that she's still alive and where she is living. I had no idea. I just found that out about two weeks ago."

"So, you're going to try and find her?"

"Yes. She lives near me about fifty miles from my home. I can't believe that."

Phyllis said, "So, that has to be a treasure trove of information there."

"Oh yeah. Oh yeah. Not only that, she is now a Jehovah Witness, so that should make it easier to find her. I don't have the address, but maybe I can get it. I'm trying."

"Okay, okay."

"Yeah, I'll find her, but I can't believe she did a complete turnaround, but that's okay with me. Yeah, she'll be a lot of information."

"Do you know her well enough?"

"Oh yeah, I used to visit her when they had a whorehouse. When they set it all up, she said to me, 'Come upstairs and see all these rooms.' And I said, 'What is all this?' I was freaking out. I, ah, like totally different than my life, but---"

Phyllis asked, "Was Bill the only person in your family that took that path?"

"Oh yeah. He was the only one who got into trouble. I had much older relatives that did not come to this country who were thieves, my, ah, let's see, that would be my great grandfather's wife's relatives. They were known as thieves in the area of Northern Epirus. It was a part of Greece at that time, but now it is part of Albania. Yeah, they were well-known, and now there are some of their descendants living in Clinton, Massachusetts. I really don't know that side of the family, so we have it in our background (laughter). At least some of us do."

"So, everyone else took the straight and narrow?"

"Yes."

Phyllis said, "I grew up in a rough neighborhood of Brooklyn, and they'd be the kids, despite all the conditions around them, they would take the straight and narrow, and there would be the ones who wind up, you know, dying on a rooftop with a needle in their arm. Why do some go in one direction and some in the other? How do you bottle it?"

I answered, "I don't know, I can only speak for myself."

# CHAPTER XXII
## Stew's Interview

October 3, 2002

Bill had this friend, Stew, who he hung out with at old State Prison. After Bill was released, they had a chance meeting in a jazz club in Boston, where Bill was not supposed to be as part of his parole arrangement. As most prisoners broke the law anyway, this one rule, was obviously not important to Bill, It wasn't like committing a felony. Going to a jazz club in a city full of clubs seemed like the thing to do, so Bill and his wife Bonnie went one night to have fun and to listen to the sounds of the night. It so happened that the one convict that was close to Bill in prison during his early years had the same idea; a night of jazz.

A couple of weeks after their chance meeting, I drove to Bill's home in New Hampshire and met this individual. We met many times at Bill's home, and again a few years later at Bracy's store. Stewart and Bracy had also been in prison at old State. Visits between Bracy and Stewart ended about the time of Bill's death. Actually, it was a few months before his death.

During the latter part of writing this story, my friend, Dave Brown, ran into Stewart (Stew) while visiting Bracy. Dave had moved to Florida, was in business for himself, and decided to visit some of his old haunts and see friends he hadn't seen in years. Stewart had recently returned to the area from his native home in Philadelphia, and was reconnecting with old friends, and of course, one of them was Bracy. Dave, as you know, introduced me to Bracy, so it wasn't much of a surprise to Dave that he ran into Stew. Dave was aware that Stew and Bracy hadn't seen each other in twenty years or so, although they had been in touch, but not on a regular basis, and there was a period when no contact at all transpired.

Dave traveled to my home in Maine after visiting Bracy during his summer vacation, and stayed for a few days. He knew I was writing about Bill and couldn't wait to tell me about Stew's return to the area. Dave told me that he saw Bracy and Stew together, and they talked about the book and me. Bracy told Stew that I had interviewed him and Bob together a few months earlier. Stew got all excited and said that he had a lot to say about Bill, and he would love to see me and tell me all what he knew. Of course, I was well aware of Bill and Stew's association, but I didn't know all the details about their prison involvements. Knowing that they were in prison at the same time is one thing, but how they related to one another is something else.

Because Stew wanted me to interview him, he told Dave for me to get a hold of him for a meeting. As for me, I was more excited about interviewing Stew, and of course, seeing him, probably more than he was. Dave gave me Stew's address and I immediately wrote him and set a date for a get-together. Before I could gather all the information I needed from Stew, we had to have three meetings.

The first meeting, about three months after Dave's visit, ended quickly and briefly after Stew became overwhelmed relating past events between him and Bill. Stew was also not feeling well. He had been ill for a few months and he was trying to recover. I hadn't seen him in about twenty years, and we were both very excited. Talking about Bill and the past obviously had an effect on him that his body couldn't handle. He was relating an incident about Bill when he became emotional. I immediately ended the interview and told him that we could do it at another time, and that I would be back in the area in a couple of months. I said I would call and we could get together. He felt better about that arrangement. Stew apologized, but I told him, "Don't worry about it, it's okay."

Two months later, I returned for that second interview. Stew and I met at his studio apartment, located in a senior residential building on Norway Street near Symphony Hall in Boston. He looked more rested, and he claimed that he felt much better. Twenty years ago Stew weighed about two hundred or more pounds. In those early days, he stood about 5'11" and had a muscular build, a handsome face and two rows of perfectly white teeth. His black hair had been cropped close, but now his hair is pure white, but still cropped close. His weight had dropped to one hundred and fifty pounds, and it looked like he had lost about two inches in height. Some of those perfect white teeth are missing also, but he still had a great smile, and his personality hadn't changed a bit. Age and sickness have taken a toll on his body, but not on his mind.

One subject Stew told me, at one of the meetings, was a total shock for me. Not in a bad sense, but something I never realized, nor had even given any thought. It had to do with Bill's outlook towards me, but that subject did not materialize until our third interview.

I asked Stew, "How did you meet Bill?"

"Well—you really have to understand that I'm Stew, seventy-one years old. We're sitting here in apartment 202, and ah, we're discussing William Goudas, my deep wonderful friend, who I met in the old State Prison in the year 1953."

"How old were you?"

Stew replied, "God. You have to count it from 1931 to 53."

I answered immediately, "Twenty-two!"

"Wow," he sighed heavily, "Teachers, you have to watch them guys (laughing)."

I was laughing also.

Stew said, "Watch what you say in front of them."

Now I'm giggling.

Stew said, "Worse than the FBI."

"I'm sorry, man."

"So, ah, it was, ah, our meeting was--I had no knowledge of Bill at that time. I didn't even know he was in prison, but there was just this aura around him. When you saw him in the quadrangle with his guitar, people used to do strange things when you would wave to him or say something, but he would always be there by himself, and sometimes he would sit there with a sneer or a funny way of---"

I asked, "Excuse me, but is the quadrangle outside, in the yard?

Stew said, "The yard, but inside the prison, that's outside the prison there. It's called the quadrangle. It was like a rectangular area where you could dump your shit bucket there. The candy store was there. It was where all the guys hung out when they come out of their cells, for that period of time, during that period of the day."

"Okay."

"And everybody would segregate themselves in little sections. Those guys would hung out with this guy group, or they hung with that group, but---"

"Right."

Stew continued, "How it happened was, Bill and I was one of them guys that never knew an organization or any group. I just was there, and ah, it was amazing, because I shouldn't of been there anyway, but anyway I—But the day it happened with Bill, he was playing this song, ah, 'Stella by Starlight.' He was picking it out on his guitar. That was my, my favorite piece of music, and I fell in love of it years ago. So, anyway, I says, 'Hey man, I like that you know.' I say, 'blah, blah, blah.' I said some things I don't remember now exactly, but we started up a rapport, you know. And then every once in a while, it seemed like, it seemed like our position unbeknownst to me would move closer and closer to the spot where we would hang out, and suddenly him and I were sitting together talking. It was amazing to me. I never knew how that happened."

"What were you sitting on? Benches?"

"No, we were sitting on concrete, up against the wall, in the quadrangle."

"Oh."

Stew said, "There were no benches or seats, or anything? No, there were no benches."

"So, you either sat on the ground or on the wall."

Stew said, "Real comfort! Your back was against the wall."

"I hear you."

"Above your head was all those guys with the guns."

"Oh yeah, right."

Stew continued, "Yeah, and ah, and you look around and see this clique hanging with this clique, but I never noticed that Bill hanged with any particular clique, but they always gave him respect. I never understood that. Now I do."

I said, "But not at that time?"

"Not at that time, it was his charisma, it was his charisma. He just had that kind of magnet. He's a person, now that I reflect back on it, he's a person I would call a very quiet gentleman, and a gentleman is the most dangerous person I ever met in my life, because he gives and takes, but you never want to cross him, a gentleman, because he'll give more than his share, but never cross him. So, anyway we started talking, and ah, I told him I used to sing with a group. I don't know how long the conversation got into writing songs, but he sang a note and he said, 'Sing a note.' And I sang a note and we started talking and he'd pick and I'd sing some more, and he'd pick. Then suddenly he put his guitar down and we just started talking, and having the story that we used to talk about I don't know what they were about, but they carried a lot of power, because when I went back to my cell, it seemed like I was at a library, and I could go and pick out what we talked about. I would pick this book and study that, just because of a conversation that would just happen that Bill and I had. So, then we, ah, got to a point when our discussions, our meeting, because we just knew. We didn't make any promises that we would meet there the next day or anything. We just sort of knew when one would be out, because I didn't come out every day, and he didn't come out every day. I did notice though, that after a while we start hanging out together, other people start coming up to get his attention, and I didn't have the slightest idea why. I think it was Bob Jeffries who told me about that."

Stew said, "Man, you know, Bob said, 'Man, you know Goudas was one of those guys that he's respected in here, because of just who he is.' Bob says, 'And when they see you sitting down talking with him, they want to find out if he is open for conversation or not.' And I never understand that, but anyway."

"But prior to that time he never hung around with anyone?"

"No, no."

"He was—"

Stew interrupted, "No."

"—solitary?"

"He was solitary. Confinement man, that's how he took it, so they respected him."

"Oh."

"Ultimately the main powerhouse, Teddy Green, and that cat from Watertown that was with the Winter Hill gang, used to come up to talk to him. Ah, and I never knew any these guys and what their caliber was until later on, until I went to the Colony, but anyway our conversation got into that—Bill said, 'Do you ever learn anything?' I said, 'Yeah.'"

I asked, "Musically?"

Stew replied, "Musically!"

Bill asked, "Did you write any songs?"

Stew said, "I said, 'Yeah, you don't want to hear what I write.' So, Bill says, 'Man, write something down.'"

"So, I wrote down this song, 'Magic Mirror,' which I had started to write in Philadelphia."

Stew sang his song: "Magic mirror on the wall. Prince of beauty who hates all. Lend a helping hand to a lonely man. Find me someone to love."

Stew said, "So, we started with that. So then, one day I came out, and I said, 'Man, you know last night I was in the cell, and this blues came up, because it reminded me of you.' Bill said, 'What?'"

Stew said, "And he had a funny way of laughing. He never really laughed. I don't know what it was. A smirk, but he'd move his mouth, and he do a funny way of--I never knew him to laugh. I never saw him laugh, ah, never! Except later on in years when we got out into the streets, I made him laugh a couple of times, ha, ha, ha. But, anyway we started talking and ah, I said, 'Man, I started writing this blues,' cause he was a blues lover. Man, he loved B-L-U-E-S. He loved blues, man. A blues lover. Bill said, 'Man, write some blues.'"

Stew said, "Well, I said, I did. 'Remember what you said the other day about blues? I came up with this song you want to hear it?' Ha, ha. Bill picked a couple notes on the box (guitar). I'll never forget this morning, it was like---"

Stew recited this song: "Falling leaves, falling gently to the ground, falling leaves, watch them as they drifting down, they look so lonely, so very lonely as they fall silently to the ground."

Stew said, "This is the song."

I responded with a "Wow!"

"We wrote the whole song out to blues, ah, three, two, eight. We wrote it all out. He made me sit there with him and sing it, and get it all correct, and I hadn't the slightest idea of the function of music. Believe me, but anyway, he was tuning me into it, and then we got into it. Long conversations about life, and how he was railroaded (I wonder if Bill even said this), and it was deep. It was hurting, cause he had these things that he would say, and a lot of them I can't remember. I can only feel a lot that, ah, that ah, even bother me to this day, because somewhere inside, I felt that they had stolen some of his soul and stripped off some of his life. Ah, ah, that, like he was paying the penance for somebody else's wrong, and he could never get over that. He didn't understand why he didn't see it, so it went like this for some years. Yeah, and most generally, somehow, we had some kind of guilt rapport, knowing who would be in the yard at that time, or that day, we would be out in the yard of course, and we would never hook up. We would never sit together, but it wasn't because we couldn't, it just was the way it happened. We could always feel each other across that quadrangle. Until one day we sat down to talk, Bill says, 'Man, you know, I talked to a guard about, ah, our music, to see if we could get something working.'"

Stew said, "And he meant about recording. This guy that was working in one of the shops said he wanted to record, so anyway, ah, ah, we sat down and I said, 'Listen, you know I wrote this song, a blues song to Rowena,' my girlfriend at the time, and ah, and she wanted to sing it, and she had somebody that would record it for her. I said, 'W-h-o-a---that is where's it is at,' so ah, we finished, ah, finished capping the song off. Taking the loose ends out, taking it out. Bill wanted me to sing the song, but we couldn't get to where we could record it then."

While Stew and I were sitting and talking about other matters, Bracy arrived, which put the mood into another perspective. We ended the conversation. This man is ill right now, so another day will have to suffice.

Bracy's visit benefited Stew. Stew was having a hard time reminiscing when Bracy arrived, but he got his composure, and Bracy never suspected a thing. The mood swung over to laughter, and it became a joyous occasion.

Stew served us some collards, black-eyed peas, rice, bread, cheese and crackers, red wine, and fruit. We talked about the old times, Bill, and what we were doing now in our lives. The three of us hadn't been together like this in twenty years, so it seemed like old times, but we were younger men then; now we were three older dudes reminiscing. The time seemed to pass quickly, until suddenly Bracy and I had to leave. Bracy and I said our goodbyes to Stew, and walked together to Bracy's bus stop, then went our separate ways. I had my car. It was nice being with those guys once again.

I'll get back to another conversation with Stew to finish my interview.

# CHAPTER XXIII
## Stew's Last Comments

**December 4, 2002**

The next interview took place two months later at Stew's apartment. This time Bracy wasn't coming over, so it was just the two of us. Stew was feeling much better physically, and his emotions were stronger, and he was up for this rendezvous. I started the conversation after settling down with a fresh cup of coffee, and Stew sat opposite me at his kitchen table. Stew was drinking a glass of fruit juice.

I started the interview with the following question: "I'd like to know about the time, and when you went into what prison."

"Oh, that came about in 1952, ah, I went to, ah. I went into the old, the massive dungeon of old State Prison. Oh my God! It was in the time where prisons like Charlestown had lost all of their good. It really was a dungeon. The worst place you'd want to be. That's where I met Bill. He always stood, on, on the sunshine side of the quadrangle against the wall. It was the one spot he always liked, and he sit there. First, he'd stand for a long while and just look around the yard, and most days he'd have his guitar with him."

"He'd take his guitar outside?"

"Yeah, outside. Cause he didn't come out that much. He didn't associate too much, really didn't, but the people would come around to him. He never went to anyone, but the people would come over to him. 'Hi Bill,' or whatever they said to him, but they'd give him their greetings."

"Let me ask you this. Why did you go in?"

Stew said, "I went in for armed robbery."

"Armed robbery?"

"Yeah."

"What was your sentence?"

"My sentence was, ah, ah, seven to ten years."

"You didn't do the full ten?"

"No."

"Did you do seven?"

"I did five."

"You did five, so you got out on good behavior?"

Stew said, "Ah, yeah, cause I finished a counting course there."

"What kind of course?"

"Accounting course."

"Accounting, oh, so that helped you?"

"Yeah. Two years off."

"And you received that course from where?"

Stew explained, "From Boston University extension school. They had an extension school at the time. They had, ah, O'Leary who was superintendent of schools, ah, had a petition for, ah, for the colleges to send courses in the prison. It was attended at the academic center, at the prison at that time. Yeah, classes were held in rooms, and new teachers."

"Were there a lot of prisoners taking advantage of that?"

Stew said, "Yeah, at first. At first it was very few, and you could always tell which few it was, because there was always those guys that had that, that had that high I.Q. In prison for some of the most stupid offenses you could think of, but they were beautiful people."

"Nice people?"

"Yeah, they were. They just did something stupid. They just didn't see something."

"Right, did you go to another prison after that? The only time you were in?"

Stew answered, "Well, after that, well, I was transferred, but no."

"No?"

Stew said, "No. Prior to that it was different."

"You had some other---"

"All my life, I came in and out of boys' homes."

"Since you were what, fourteen?"

"Eleven."

"You were in---"

Stew interrupted, "New Jersey."

"Well, it doesn't matter where, but you never were---"

Stew again, "In boys' home."

"You were in boys' homes. Reformatory schools is what they called them then."

"Yeah, reformatory."

"Then you did more jails?"

"Yeah."

"In and out?"

Stew continued, "Yeah. It's funny how you do time. Short or long, but it was long to me."

"Of course, but you had a rap sheet, as they say?"

"I have a serious---I had at that time."

"Right."

Stew said, "This was fifty years ago."

"I understand. Okay, so after you did your time, you said the hell with it?"

"Yeah!"

"You said I had enough of this shit?"

"Yeah that was it."

"I see."

Stew said, "See, I had enough. I had a different sense of education value, and ah, when I got out, it was a strange thing, ah, I sort of knew where I was going. What I was going to do. I didn't, ah, I ah, I just felt that way, so I moved around the world for a while (Stew meant the USA)."

"You got out in 1957?"

"1957, yeah."

"Did you stay in the Boston area where you were prisoned?"

Stew said, "Yeah, I did about a year."

"And what kind of work did you do when you got out?"

Stew said, "I started to work in a bakery, a Jewish bakery."

"A Jewish bakery. Friedman's?"

"No, Kassanoff's."

"Oh Kassanoff's. Up on Blue Hill Avenue near Grove Hall, oh sure."

Stew said, "And I found it to be a very interesting thing, and I enjoyed it, so I went to become a Jewish baker. It wasn't easy to become a Jewish baker. You couldn't put your hands on that table if you wasn't ready. Kosher, man!"

"You had to be Kosher?"

"Yeah man. It was a real Jewish bakery bro!"

I said, "I hear you."

"When you got up on that table to touch that bread, you had to scrape so many floors, clean so many dough pots, and scrub so many pans, before you ready to bake, ha."

"Yeah right. That's beautiful."

Stew said, "Yeah, yeah! Yes! So then, after work, that one day I was at Wally's Café on Mass Ave."

I said, "Oh yeah, Wally's (Wally's Café was located at 427 Massachusetts Avenue in Roxbury)."

"I ran into one of the fellows, (one of the fellows are the following four cons) Jeff, Bracy, Bob, MacPherson, he was a sax player that was heavy with Bill. One of them told me that Bill was out. I says w-h-o-a-h! So, I get this message he was up north."

I said, "That was in the sixties? No, it had to be in the seventies."

Stew said, "Yeah, so, ah, we met at Wally's. Somehow or another, the message got through, and we hooked up this particular night at Wally's. You know, the old thing man, you know."

"Bill came down from up north?"

"Yeah. He came down."

"To Wally's Café?"

"To Wally's. Yeah, unbeknownst to me he had been coming into town all that time, and I mean, you know, but we didn't hook up."

"But you didn't know each other were around?"

"No, we didn't know that."

I said, "Right! So, Bill had been down a lot?"

"Yeah, he had been."

"He wasn't supposed to."

"Well, I don't know."

"No, he wasn't supposed to!"

Stew said, "Well, that was Bill."

"I know, but you see when he got out on parole, his parole was that he was supposed to stay out of this state and never come back."

"W-h-o-a!"

"And he used to do it all the time."

"Yeah, he did."

"That's why he got busted, because he came into the city and they caught him one time."

Stew said, "O-h-h. That's right, I remember that. I forgot about that."

"Anyhow, you met up with him in Wally's, so now you knew where he lived."

"Yeah."

"Let's go back to how did you actually meet him in old State?"

"Old State?"

I asked, "Yes. How did that come about? We covered this the first time we got together, but I want to get all the facts. Do you remember how?"

"Y-E-A-H! Sometimes there were this group of guys that were real musicians. Bob, ah, Jump, Bracy, there were guys that really played instruments, and they would get together and talk about music, and one day it happened to-- we happened to be, all of us, and Bill was there. This was a strange thing. Somehow or another, the group formed and we were sitting over against the wall, all of us. That's how I met Goudas, but I used to see him sitting there; I was in the can for about year until that meeting. It was Jump, Bracy."

"Bob?"

"Yeah."

"Ollie?"

"I forgot some of their names."

"MacPherson?"

Stew said, "MacPherson. We didn't meet until we got to the Colony."

"Oh, that was later?"

"Oh yeah. Well, it was a different period, Oh no, MacPherson was there."

"So, MacPherson was there?"

"Yeah. So anyway, that's how I, ah, then suddenly we start talking, and at that time I was singing in a group I had, so I started singing out there that day talking about songs, and Goudas said, 'W-o-w man.' He said, I don't remember exactly what he said to tell you the truth. We just felt something, and from that day on, we started meeting in that little spot. Just him and I."

"Oh, just you and him? You connected!"

"I had status. I had prison status, but I never realized, because I was sitting with William Goudas, man."

"O-h-h!"

Stew said, "You know, you know William Goudas hung by himself."

"So, why did he have status, because he was a cop killer?"

"No, no, because he, no man, that had nothing to do with it."

"That had nothing to do with it?"

Stew said, "No. The crime had nothing to do with that status of how you get in, in the penitentiary. Some of the greatest killers, man, were dead up pussies, so you can't, you don't know which status you're going to get in the prison. I don't care how many you kill. You here now man!"

I said, "I see."

"But, but Bill had a charisma. He had a thing, and on top of that, he was known as the baddest guitar player that there was, or came through the joint. He was that bad."

"I know he was good. Yeah!"

"Right."

I said, "So, his guitar playing and plus his ah, charisma---"

Stew interrupted, "Gave him a status, and when I came around, I hadn't the slightest idea of it, but later on, when I think about it, I say w-h-e-w. You know, it was like you hung out with, ah, a Whitey Bulger."

"I hear ya."

"Or a Teddy Green."

I said, "Oh yeah, Teddy Green. So, the fact that you and him hooked up, gave you a status?"

"Yeah. It gave me a status, ah, but I had, had no idea of it at that time. It is only a reflection."

I said, "Oh, I understand. You realized it later?"

"Oh yeah! Later."

"I can see that."

Stew said, "Cause that the, the, the last thing I worried about. I already had mine."

"Okay."

Stew laughing, "Ha, ha. See, so, ha, ha, so, ha, ha, Bill and I would sit down. We just started sitting down and, and we started—I don't understand how that happened, but how was it that Bill started bringing his ax (guitar) out, and he started to play, and what was it between him and you, you know, but you have to know what everything is happening. Changes you know. Whose hanging with who."

"That I guess, is information that goes around the prison."

"Yeah, you had to know what's going on."

I said, "The cons want to know what's going on."

"Correct. Bill, Bill never, never--it's almost like he'd sit there, and you could look out at the whole bunch, at one time, and read everything out there. That's what he always showed me. He was always philosophying (Stew's version of philosophizing). He was there, babe. He started talking about Neishy, Neishy."

"Who?"

"Neishy."

"Who's Neishy?"

"The ah, the, the poet, the German poet, the writer. The German, you know, he wrote. You know these heavy things that he---"

"You mean Friedrich Nietzsche the philosopher?"

Stew said, "Yeah. He was a philosopher, poet right? Ah, ah, he's quite a person. Wow, man, yeah, and ah, we'd talk about that, and he was very educated (Nietzsche). He was seriously educated."

"Yes, Nietzsche was an educated German. He lived during the middle 1800's to the beginning of the 1900's. Bill wasn't educated in the schools, but he did do a lot of reading. He was self-educated. Of course, he had all the time in the world to read. Bill also read a lot at home."

"Well, but you see when I speak of education---"

I said, "But, I'm just saying he got it from reading, not from academia."

Stew said, "It wasn't an academic system (prison)."

"Exactly."

Stew said, "Oh, okay. I see. He did a lot of reading."

"Right. Bill and I used to have all kinds of conversations, when we were younger."

"Okay."

"I was going to high school, Boston English. I was in a very good high school."

"Bill was telling me about that."

"It was one of the best in the city of Boston. It was a boys' school, about 4,000 went there. You had to have excellent grades to be accepted."

Stew said, "Boy, he talked about you, man, with a praise and emulation."

"Oh yeah! I love hearing that."

"You know, the first day, ah, he had me sit up there all day long, that evening, waiting for to meet you. That was the first time I met you."

"Correct."

"Bill said, 'Man, you got to meet.' He said, 'You got to.' And Goudas was wise. See, anyone else would introduce the opposite. He wouldn't bring them kind of spirits together."

"No?"

Stew said, "If he thought some explosion would come out of it, you'd never see each other."

"Bring those kind of spirits together. that's---"

Stew interrupting, "Right."

"--beautiful---"

Stew interrupting again, "Yeah."

"--phrasing."

Stew said, "Yeah, and, and that's how, that's how he played music. That's how he got into music. To him everything, everything a catch. He could, he could go from blues to jazz, to jazz to blues, and you'd never know it. You know what I'm saying? You'd hear it."

"Okay."

"But you wouldn't know how he got there, and, and you'd blend the same way, the music blends. You'd begin to blend that way, you'd begin to move in and out of jazz, blues intrusion, and flow the whole system. That's how he'd play."

I said, "And his life was like that."

"That's why he never went into big time."

"What's the big time?"

"Out there on the stage, with Barney Kessel."

"Oh!"

Stew said, "Ah, Grant Green. Out there with them cats."

I said, "I know musically he was there."

"When he played the ax. Did you ever hear him?"

"Yes, of course. We used to play together, and I heard him, one time, at Walpole."

"Hear them chords he could hit?"

"Yes, He was great."

"And when he went to picking, he got lost, you know, that ti-ti-ti-ti. That thing."

"Yes, he was outstanding."

Stew said, "Yeah, so anyway, that ah, you got to remember it's like a volcano. All it is, it's beginning to mash at old State Prison, and it continued to boil and boil. We wrote a couple of songs."

"You and him together?"

"Him and I together. Ah, we wrote 'Magic Mirror,' 'Falling Leaves.' Yeah."

"That was two songs."

Stew said, "Yeah."

"Were they jazz or blues?"

Stew answered, "Ah, ah, ballads. Two ballads. Yeah, two serious ballads."

"Whatever happened to them?"

Stew said, "One of them went out on the market. Which, I don't know anything about. Ah, I don't know what happened to the other."

"You don't have them?"

"No."

"You don't remember them?"

"Not really."

I said, "It's been a long time."

Stew continued, "And the blues, the last piece he wrote. I wish, I wish I could remember. It took us two weeks for him to come with a name. He was going to name this blues. Oh boy! As I think of it. It was, it was, he come with names, and he would scratch it out. No, not that. He would come up with another name, not that, but one day, he says, wha-wha-wha, and it, ah. I can't remember the name that he named. It was (pause), it was crushing, ah (pause), ah, ah (pause). Sorry (softly)."

"That's okay."

Stew got a little emotional. There was a moment of pause.

"So, you guys became friends. You interwove your lives around music. Did you do the same---"

Stew interrupted. "No, it wasn't around music (loudly interrupting)."

"But part of your life---"

Stew said emotionally, "Yeah, right (loudly interrupting again)."

"As I was saying, part of your life---"

Stew said, "Well, yeah (interrupting, but softly)."

I said, "It was the basis. Okay, what kind of work did you do in the prison?"

"I was in the foundry."

"Bill didn't do foundry work, did he?"

Stew said, "Oh yeah, he was at that time. He didn't do any work, but he was supposed to be---"

"A messenger guy or something?"

"No man, he was a trainer. Ha, ha."

"A trainer?"

"He was teaching people how to grind in the grinder, ha, ha."

"So, he was teaching people how to grind?"

Stew said, "As I was saying, the, the sewer covers come out of the mold, they cool down, and go to, you know, the grinder. They have to be refinished. All things have to be refinished."

"Yes, of course."

"And he would be the grinder who would bring it to perfection, ha, ha, ha."

I said, "So he would---"

Stew, not controlling his laughing, said, "Ha, ha, I got to, ha, ha, ha." Stew had to relieve himself. He returned and we started up again.

I asked, "Let's go back to he was a grinder. So he was a grinder?"

Stew laughing, "Ha, ha, ha, ha. Those guys, those guys become, ha, ha, ha, who he was teaching them in the, in the foundry, in the grinding. I said, 'Man, what are you doing in the grinding?' I told him, ha, ha, ha, and he come out wearing this fucking mask thing."

"Oh, he was a schemer."

"And all of them guys, actually he was a teacher."

"Yeah, but he knew how to keep out of---"

Stew said, "He was a hustler."

I said, "Yes, that's what I meant. He schemed his way, so he didn't do all that real heavy bullshit."

Stew said, "It just happened. He doesn't scheme, you know, ah, with him it just happens. You know what I'm saying?"

"Yes."

"Yeah, he's a hustler, man. It's, it's a whole different ball game, you know, man. It's like the blending of the Democrats and the Republicans, you know man. Yeah. He could bring people together. Get things."

Stew went into his kitchen, just a few feet away from where I was sitting, and said, "Oh, that's right (pause), I forgot about them things. I really did. You got to hear this one."

I said, "Okay, I know as you talk, things will come to you."

"Do you want any coffee?"

"No, thank you."

Stew said, "I have some colored bread in here too, if you want any."

"No." I was wondering what colored bread was, but I didn't ask. "Are you ready to continue this story?"

"No. I'm going to wait for the coffee, and I'd like to get my bag straightened out (colonoscopy bag)."

"Okay."

"You don't mind?"

"No, no."

Stew apologetically said, "Thank you."

I said, "Do your thing, man."

A pause, with the bathroom door ajar. Stew started talking after a few minutes, after going into the bathroom. I could hear him flushing and washing his hands. I made a comment about Bracy. "I guess Bracy is in no man's land, out there somewhere." Little did I know that a rift had opened between Bracy and Stew.

Stew returned to the kitchen and said, "So, anyway, you know, Goudas and I were ready to deal with a plumbing company."

"Plumbing? What plumbing company?"

"After Bill and I make contact, I used to go to his house every weekend (New Hampshire). Spend the weekends with him and Bonnie. Ah, we talked, we'd sit around, just talk, man, and run our mouth. Have good food and eat, and ah, we'd spend--we, liked each other's company. We could spend time together in the house, man, and be, be there man, and never say a word, but we knew each other was there, man. I may be laying in the bed, he may be sitting up writing, doing something, but it was nice, so I'd spend the weekend or some weeks there, and ah, it was enjoyable, because at the time, ah, I was working, running a plumbing construction company in Eliot Square. This dude, F. K. Blakey, and ah, Bill had known something about plumbing. Bill said that someone in the family, or something, was a plumber, or he knew something about plumbing."

"I don't know anyone in the family that was a plumber."

Stew said, "Okay, but anyway, ah, I had told Bill that we could take some of the action of this plumbing company. I said if we could find somebody that could back it with some money, but he knew Jerry and Julio at that time. He also knew Teddy, and a few other people who could help with the financing, so, ah, and Abe Sochet. He knew big Abe. He knew Abe, so, man, but I said, 'That's a good idea, but we don't want that kind of cash, you know.' I got the impression that Jerry, Julio, Teddy, and Abe did illegal things."

"So, that kind of cash was underground money?"

"Right, but ah, we started to, ah, become partners in the F. K. Blakely Plumbing Company, and, ah, Blakely and Bill really started liking each other. He was a powerful man, F. K. Blakely, and then ah, Bonnie, ah, they would come to the city and go out for jazz and food and talk about things. Then suddenly he (Bill), ah, moved. He moved somewhere else, ah, no, he met up with another bunch of friends. A group of acts he knew, and he started hanging with them. Dominic Edwards. Dominic Edwards was one of his main men, man. Dominic was a heavy, Dominic and Black Sam. He started hanging with them, and they got involved with moving different things. They had a little clique going, but they were cool cats, man. They were very cool, so, ah, I bought this house up on Centre Street (Roxbury), and that's where we used to meet, Bill, Dominic, ah, some others, Black Sam. They'd discuss, you know, that procedure they wanted to do, man, to make some money. It was a nice little move they were doing, but it wasn't, you know, legit."

"Really."

Stew said, "I tried to get him to play music, but the only place he would play music was in the Greek place."

"Right."

"And I'd try to get him to come to Wally's and sit in and, ah."

"He wouldn't do that."

Stew continued, "Because, ah, Bill could play the, the box (guitar), man. He was a hellava ax (guitar) man."

I said, "But, you see he wasn't supposed to be in that city."

"Oh, that might be one of the reasons, you know. You're probably right, so after that, we started drifting apart (coughing). Excuse me. So, anyway, we started drifting (coughing) apart. Excuse me. We didn't see each other again. I went my different direction, cause I left town for a while. I had to go into my family, and, ah, I, I lost my company. A dry wall company at that time, and ah, you know, it was kind of tough, and, ah, I went into my bag, and that's how, how we drifted apart."

"And you never saw him much after that?"

"Ah, no. I didn't see him much after that."

"Tell me about the time I was going to drive to Bill's place. When we met."

Stew replied, "Oh, when you were coming?"

"Yes."

"The first day we met?"

"Yes."

"Oh, well, I had been up at his house (Manchester). I forget what day it was, but anyway, he had, he had been talking to me for quite a while about you. 'You got to meet. You got to meet Angelo.'"

"Did he say my nephew?"

Stew said, "Yeah, yeah, he went into that, but guys like him, when they say you got to meet so and so, they mean what they say, cause they know what they are doing. They know human nature, so evidently he saw something very compatible with you and I, so he introduced us, and that first night you walked in and we started talking, you came in, and, ah, went into the living room, and we're sitting on the couch talking about things, and you, ah, ah, you were real cool. Cause you asked me questions. You know what I mean, we just blended into a feeling. We didn't get into nothing heavy. We just blended, and you just start talking, and we were laughing and joking, and you said, 'You want to see something strange, man?' I said, 'Yeah.' You said, 'This is a kazoo!' Ha, ha, ha, ha, ha. I said, 'W-h-a-t?' You went and got those clothes plastic bags from Bill, and you got a tub of water. Put it between and under this door threshold, and hung that up."

"I braided it."

"You braided it into strips."

"Right."

"And you lit--ha ha."

"I lit that mother. I lit that sucker up!"

Stew responded, "Y-E-A-H! I saw the fire jump from the plastic. I thought, 'He's crazy!' It was nice, Angelo."

I said, "Wasn't it pretty?"

"Yeah, yeah. Cause all the lights were out. Remember?"

"Yes."

Stew said, "Put the lights out, and this sucker was there dancing-aw-little drops at a time."

"Ha, ha, ha. What a light show!"

Stew said, "Yeah, it was weird how it would hit those knots at different times."

"I know it."

"Oh, wow. What you called it? A kazoo?"

"Yeah! Ha, ha, ha."

Stew laughing, "Ha, ha, ha, ha."

"I haven't done that in a while, ha, ha, ha."

Stew laughing, "Ha, ha, ha, and you know what, something? It broke a strange ice, because we all were in a happy feeling, man. It was nice, Angelo. It was really nice, man. That time was good times, yeah!"

"Yes, it was."

"And, ah, I didn't know it, know how it happened, we just blended together again, ah, over at Bracy's."

"Yeah, with Bracy."

Stew said, "Right, we started, yeah right, we started waiting for you. You come around, he (Bracy) always somehow got the message that, ah, Angelo was coming by."

I said, "I don't remember."

"For I'd shoot over, cause, ah, ah, you know. Ah, for it was good conversation. We'd have nice conversations. You know!"

"Yes we did."

Stew continued, "And in the middle of the day, Bracy and I were talking about it when we met, ah, over in front of Bracy's, and Jerry had the record shop on the corner, and we'd all pile in there, and, and I said, 'Bracy,' I says, you know everybody was there that day, and a lot don't even remember it. We were all in there and Jerry put these sounds on, and Bracy picked the bongos up. Gibby was there, David Brown was there."

"Really, you're remembering an event."

"Yeah. All of us were there, man. It was just one of those days, ah, Angelo, ah, I often think about that day!"

"Did I show up?"

Stew said, "Yeah, you were there, cause you had this, ah, this thing on, this serape, ha, ha."

"Serape?"

"Serape, yeah, you had your jewelry on."

"Oh yeah?"

Stew said, "You had beautiful turquoise, yeah, so, ah, after those days we started to see each other man, whenever we can, you know."

"Yeah, right."

"Then ah, you, you, made your move to Maine. I made my move to New Haven, and, ah, oh, you know it changed around."

"Yes, it changed. Getting back to our interview, you went to the Colony when they shut down old State. You all went to the Colony?"

"Yeah."

"What did you do up there?"

"Ah, ah, I was a presser and I went to school."

"Oh, that's where you went to school?"

Stew said, "Yeah, well, yeah, I continued. That's when I got into accounting. They had this, ah, new principal that came in. His name was Robert O'Leary. I'll never forget it. He said to me, he says one day, 'Man, you know what, you're sharp. I want you. You don't have any education, but you're sharp. Look, I'm going to start you upstairs in accounting; I'm going to put you in this.' So, ah, over the years I went to school and studied. Got my first thing in, ah, ah, certification ah, bookkeeper. Finished such and such, ah, accounting and things."

"That was good."

Stew continued, "Anyway, you know, so I went on it, and then he says, 'Listen, how would you like to work as a bookkeeper in the, ha, ha, in the accounting?' I say I'd like it, so he hooked me up with that, ah, I took the job. It was an excellent job. It followed the educational system. People were kind of nice, man. They were very nice people, and, ah, O'Leary, I saw him the next time he came down to visit me. We talked, and that was the last time I saw him. I went on with my life, you know!"

"When you got out, was it from Norfolk Colony?"

"Yeah."

"So you never went to the new prison?"

"No."

I asked, "Was Bill---"

Stew interrupted, "He never went to the Colony."

"Yeah, he was in the Colony. I used to visit him there."

"Not at the time, not at the time I was there."

"Oh, he wasn't there at the time you were there?"

"Yeah, well, he came afterwards. That's why I forgot. He came after."

"Bill was in old State and you went to the Colony?"

Stew said, "Yeah, he stayed. I went two years before."

"How long were you in old State?"

"A year or so, maybe."

"You were there for only a year, and then they shipped you to the Colony?"

Stew said, "Yeah, a year and a half, somewhere like that"

"The officials saw that you were okay and---"

Stew said, "Right, that's the way they work that phase of it."

"Okay."

"That's the type of prison, they bargain."

I said, "So, you didn't see Bill for a while?"

"Not for a while, until he moved back to the Colony."

"You had to have been surprised when he went to the Colony?"

Stew said, "Yeah, yeah, cause he was a different. A different person."

"He changed?"

"Yeah."

I asked, "How did he change?"

"Ah."

"Did he get more reclusive?"

Stew said, "In a way, but he always had this front, like he was jovial, but inside he was being eaten up."

"You think he was being eaten up inside?"

"Yeah, but inside he was bitter."

I said, "Outward he acted---"

Stew interrupted, "You wouldn't know it."

"He acted okay."

"A normal person."

"But he was bitter inside?"

Stew said, "You could tell it. I could."

"Really?"

"Cause a man like Goudas on the street, would never carry around that complacent attitude. I mean, you knew, you never talked like people, but you knew, but that hardness was there."

"So, what you mean is, the longer he was in, the harder he got."

"Yeah, bitter!"

"Yeah, I saw that too."

Stew said, "And he, and it was covered. He covered it well, and once in a while it come out."

"Well, I guess he had to cover it, but sometimes he had to release it."

"Yes, sometimes we'd be sitting in the house, in the living room, and ah, he'd start walking. You know that funny walk he had. You know that Goudas walk. He'd start doing that, and I knew he was going through them changes, man."

"Oh yeah?"

Stew said, "But, I knew he handled it well. I think Bonnie was a great help to him."

"Oh sure, she helped him a lot."

"Right, she really did."

"Did he ever talk about his crime to you?"

Stew answered, "Yeah, but I don't, I don't remember it in an exclusive sense. All I remember is, feeling that it would dominate at the time he'd be telling me. How he felt about it and stuff, you know."

"Yeah, but how did he feel about it?"

"In my, in my, estimate, ah, it hurt him deeply. It's almost like it was something that he always say to himself, 'Did I do that? Was I like that?' It, it, wasn't his character."

"No it wasn't."

Stew loudly, "Let me tell you!"

"We were all shocked because that wasn't---"

"No man (very loudly)! He came, and, and that character that tried to take over, I saw him fight that. He, he in a sense wanted to become hard and bitter, because he was hurt! Somehow in there, he saw a man, like his former fucking self, disappear in front of his fucking eyes!"

"Ah, I see. He saw it disappear and he didn't know how to handle that."

Stew said, "How do you handle that? M-A-N!!!"

"Good point. How do you handle that?"

"It hurts, man (said with sadness in his voice)!"

While writing this passage on my typewriter from my notes, sadness overcame me and I broke down and cried. Remembering how jovial Bill was as a young man, and now this. Bringing it back, I guess, was more than I could handle. This was a man that I loved very deeply. He messed up his life, and he was paying deeply for his crime. He could never wipe those images away, nor all the years spent behind bars. He was a doomed individual!

I replied, "He was hurt, man!"

Stew said, "He lost everything. He lost most of his family."

I said, "He's hurting, but he never denied the crime? You know, how some of them say, I didn't do that. N-O-O-O, he---"

Stew interrupted, "He never denied it. No, cause to him, to him it seemed like another person that did it. That he wasn't evil. It wasn't him that did it. It was an evil thing, you know. He, he, he just couldn't believe."

"Like where did this come from, out of me?"

"He couldn't believe it."

I said, " 'This is not me.'"

"No bro. No bro."

"I know he wasn't, he wasn't a hardened person before."

Stew responded, "No bro."

"But, he must have panicked. That's the only thing I can figure, because you know as I'm writing this story, I'm going, oh boy, that's the only thing I can see, because I knew him all my life. I lived with him and I used to talk with him, used to play music with him, we discussed philosophy, we discussed---"

Stew interrupted. "It was a shock!"

"He must have just panicked!"

Stew said, "Something shocked him, and he panicked."

"Yes, because he didn't fire just one, you know."

"No, no. It's like something took over. It was like--you know something man? It was like it, it, like suddenly you're at a window and a face jumps up, in a threatening sense, and you don't run or don't be scared of it, but you stand there panicked and something else takes over. It was like a compulsion, psh, psh, psh, psh, psh, you know."

"Exactly."

Stew said, "It wasn't him. You had to have a thought behind each shot. I don't give a fuck how fast they come. Something else had to be there, you know, boom, boom, boom, boom, boom. He wasn't like that. It didn't work like that with him, man."

"Okay."

"I don't understand it."

I said, "To put it mildly, he was upset at himself. Looking at the life he put himself into it, when that wasn't really him."

"Right bro."

"And that made him bitter, because he fucked his life up."

Stew agreed, "He got bitter."

"Yeah, I know. I saw that, oh yeah! There were times when I couldn't deal with him."

Stew said, "He would always wear his clothes a certain way, like he didn't care. You could look at the way he'd dress, and you would know he didn't care. I mean, right there I knew, but I kept feeling something in him when we would sit down, ah, I was learning. You know what he was teaching me? About things that he would of like to have done or become, and it was capable of him doing it, cause it was inside him, and I think they started coming out with me, and I think he sort-a, like, put them there, and I grabbed them, because I can see how he was instrumental in a lot of decisions that I made in the later years in my life, you know, and the joy I felt coming through all that period, because I got stronger. I, I, spread out more. I, I didn't get trapped, ah, you know. Those visits I used to take at his house freed me to a hell-of-a-degree, and it saved me a degree (sigh), and I'm, ah, thankful for that."

"That's interesting. It's an interesting life. You know what's interesting about it? Everybody I have talked to about him, no one has ever expressed what you just expressed about him. I wanted to get that from somebody. What was in his head?"

"Yeah, man."

"And no one said, 'Hey, you want to know something about Bill?'"

"Yeah."

"But, you have expressed it. I had some thoughts, but they would be only my assumptions."

"Yeah right."

"But now here it is. Coming out finally."

Stew said, "Yeah, so it was that close."

"Yes, it's come out finally."

"Yeah."

"It is so nice to hear where he was at in his life. Although it is sad, especially for me."

Stew admitted, "I never got that close with anyone else in the penitentiary, yeah never."

"Inside he was the closest person you had?"

"Yeah."

"Not even with Bracy?"

"Oh, we were never tight in the penitentiary. On the street."

"Oh, you got tight with Bracy after you got out, on the street?"

Stew replied, "Yeah. The first day I got out, Bracy was the first person I went to visit, you know."

"Oh yeah!"

"Cause we had struck something, you know. It was like Bill, man. Well, actually we all had that feeling about Bill, Jump, Bracy, Bob, a lot of people. A lot of people had that feeling."

"Okay, but getting back to you getting to see Bill again, under a strange incident, or should I say one of those strange meetings that happen throughout this world. Wasn't it strange that you were at Wally's Café, and all of a sudden Bill walks in, and there you guys are?"

Stew answered, "Yeah, there we are, man. After all those years."

"And you hadn't seen him since you got out, and you never went to visit him?"

"No man, that was some years."

"A lot of years?"

Stew confirmed, "Yeah, about ten years. Yeah man, and it was almost like we never parted when we met. It, it was sort-a, just, just like we were back again, ha, ha, ha."

"Isn't that one of those funny things that happens? You and everybody else had to have been surprised, and he must have been surprised---"

Stew interrupted, "Ha, oh yeah, man."

"---when he saw all those people?"

Stew said, "Really bro. It was like, Bonnie was there. She was there from the beginning. She was always a beautiful lady."

"Yes, she was a beautiful lady."

"I enjoyed, I enjoyed how she cared about Bill. She loved that guy. She sort-a looked, I, I don't know how, she was not a foolish woman. She was very intelligent."

"Yes, she was a beautiful woman."

Stew said, "Y-E-A-H! She would look out for that Bill, man. She loved that man. Yeah, I think that she gave him a stature that he needed at that time."

"Well, he never had a woman before."

"Right! Never did, and she gave him that stat, because he'd used to talk about it. We got down, man."

"Women liked him, you know, but he never had a girlfriend when he was younger. Imagine, he never had a girlfriend until he met up with Bonnie."

Stew said, "That's Bonnie, and he's still inviting these chicks around the house for me. I says, man, you can't fix me up, ha, ha."

"Oh really?"

"But, it was sweet the way we used to hang out together. We'd go eat at Chinatown or some restaurant, and we'd have a dinner. A nice dinner, and we'd go to an engagement. I forget some engagement we went to one night. It was quite a success, caused he got all dolled up. Cause you notice how he started to dressing different after he come with Bonnie."

"Really!"

Stew said, "He became, he became another kind of Goudas, ha."

"Yeah, a dapper."

"Ha, ha, a dapper Goudas, man. I used to laugh. I said you're the biggest gangster out here, ha, ha."

"He was a character."

Stew said, "He was, and he had a status even then. Oh, this was Bill."

"Yeah, did he ever talk about his brother Christie? His family?"

"N-O-O, ah, yeah, but I never really got into it. You, you're the only one that I can remember that he r-e-a-l-l-y talked about a lot, and I never got into hearing that until we got into his home, you know, so, ah, I don't know about anyone else."

"I see."

"Sometime his mother, he used to talk about her."

"Well, Bill and I were on the same level when I was a kid, and we talked about different subjects."

Stew said, "Really?"

"Yes, like music."

"Really?"

I said, "Yes, because I played the violin, he'd play the guitar. I could read music and I played in the high school orchestra."

"Oh!"

"We used to play together. Classical and some pop tunes. I couldn't play jazz, or let's say I never tried."

"This is before?"

I said, "This is before he got into trouble. Yes, we used to talk about the same subjects."

"That must of fucked you up when he got busted?"

"Oh, yeah! Oh, boy, I was torn up, man."

"Bad?"

"I wanted to go in. I was figuring how can I go there? I did!"

Stew understanding, "I don't blame you."

"I went, 'How can I get in there?'"

"Yeah. You couldn't part from Goudas."

"No, he was like my brother, my father."

Stew said, "Yeah, it was like ripping a piece of you up."

"Yes, but the thing is, like you said, it changed. I was like his father, his brother."

"Yeah, yeah. It was like that."

"Isn't that strange? It is for me."

Stew said, "Ah, it's the attitude. His relationship to you was never on uncle basis. It was higher than that. It was a reverence he had for you."

"I never knew that!"

"I don't think you did."

"No, I didn't."

"I don't know how you could have. He would never show it."

"No, he never showed it."

Stew said, "And I don't know if he told anyone else."

"He told you though!"

"Yeah, he told me."

"WOW!"

Stew said, "I remember him talking about it. He made me wait there at the time to meet you, and, ah, and so many things he talked about you that I, I really, I thought I knew you."

"Really!"

"In that sense, but when you did that, I think you know. When you did that kazoo, it was almost like a ritual, a tribal ritual. Wasn't it?"

I said, "I suppose."

"It was like a tribal ritual. You know, like we were a tribe, and we're thinking blessings that we were there at that time. That's what I thought of."

"Oh really?"

Stew said, "Yeah. Why else would, ah, we weren't into jokesters. It was no joke, ha, ha."

"No, no."

Stew talking seriously, "It wasn't no act, ha, you know. It wasn't emulation. It had a meaning. No one does a thing like that unless it has a meaning. You know who used to talk about that? Ah, this guy that just died, ah. This great historian I been reading, ah, ah, I can't remember his name, ah, ah. He wrote about these tribes, civilizations and things, but he, ah I forget. He talked about the existence of auras and feelings like that that have generated over the years, and ah, for some reason they don't go anywhere. There're out there! Some reasons, he says, happens to come together, and a tribe is formed, and a tribe never comes from the womb. They already existed out there from other places, then they become a tribe."

I asked, "They then become a tribe?"

"Yeah, yeah, you know, man. After they became a tribe, birth had a meaning. You know what I mean, man?"

I said, "I'm trying to understand."

"Otherwise man, you're just out there."

"I see what you mean."

"Yeah, man, you know---"

I interrupted, "Once you are a group, birth does have a meaning."

Stew affirmed, "Yeah, it has a meaning man, and, ah, he said, always out there something happens at that time, that goes into the ritual and then you don't know it, but you suddenly you're on that level, you're that tribe. He said it always is denoted out of something out of the ordinary. He said it wasn't planned, and it was planned, but in a different sense. It just happened, and you got to be able to deduce from that, what was real and what wasn't, you know. He said then you arrive at a station where you begin to understand the blessing of human nature. I said --w-h-o-a--, and exactly what Bill and my life represented, because its blending, like we did, at that time, in that place, from the points of life where we came from. It wasn't a coincidence that we met up, and started talking and sitting together. I can't remember ever sitting with a group of people ah, after Bill and I started hanging out together. I don't remember me ever sit out among a group of prisoners. It was usually only him and I just sitting there. I don't even remember half the time what we talked about or discussed. Just high points in there---"

"Yup."

"But it happened you know, and, ah, ah, when he changed. When he went into the gangster concept, I remember the day that ah, he said, man, he said, 'I'm going to go out and be something different. I'm going to start moving herb,' and he starting moving herb."

"I remember that."

Stew continued, "And, ah, he used to meet at my place with Hank with two or three pounds. Came to my house one day and wanted to give me a couple of pounds. I said, 'Man, p-l-e-a-s-e don't do that, you know. I don't want you and I to get that way, you know. I don't want what might happen, you know, so I don't want to be responsible, because if, if, we put ourselves on the line like that, something gonna happen, and we'll never in our mind adjust to it. We'll never have it like it was. The devil will come in and do some shit, man.'"

"Yup."

"'You know, I'll lose all the shit, and you out there to make money. You ain't out there to make friendship, and then you won't know whether I used it, fucked it up, or lying to you. What? Cause it will come in there just like that. You're on a different plane,' and I'll never forget we ended that day. Probably was the last time we met cause---"

I moaned, "A-h-h!"

Stew sadly said, "Yeah, it was, ah, yeah, it was the last time we met. I'll never forget that day."

"So, that's how it ended? I never knew."

"That's how it ended. Over that, ah, but it ended on Centre Street. Not on, ah, not at Hancock Street. It ended on Centre Street. Bill said, 'Stew,' he said, 'We got a phone in here. We can work from here.' I said, 'No, man.' But, he called Hank, and told them all to meet me here, cause he says I got a couple of pounds, kilo or whatever for Hank."

Stew continued, "I says, 'Bill, I says man, I'm not into this.' Hank came up the stairs and he started talking, and he says, 'I can help you get back into construction, I can help.'"

Stew said, "I says, 'Man, I don't want to.' Then Bill asked me if I wanna Betamax. I said no. I said I don't want nothing. And that was the last time I saw Bill. I didn't want anything, ah, ah, cause he changed into the gangster type of person at that time. I mean r-e-a-l-l-y. It was almost like, it was something that, that ah, made him feel comfortable, but it was eating him up still, you know. After he got out there, I think I found out that there is no such thing as gangsterism among these cats as you see it. It's just a bunch of mother fucking ghetto cats, man, trying to be. I told Bill, 'Leave them the fuck alone, man. Don't start blending and shit. Fuck that. Be real, man, but, but when you start playing it that way, you're going to stand out and you're going to fuck yourself.'"

"This is all after Bonnie and he split up."

Stew said, "Yeah man, it's after. This is when he got on that kick, man. Playing that gangster game, and shit. Whatever broke him, broke him down. Something broke him hard, cause then after a while everybody started saying, you know, 'What happened to Bill? What happened to Bill?' And then it started happening. And I know something bad had happened. This cat lost his aura. He lost it! He lost his aura, man."

"His aura disappeared!"

"His aura disappeared, man, and I would hear stories. The last story I heard, man, was in the barbershop. I said, 'Man, has anyone heard from Bill?' They said, 'Man, Billy's dead.' I said, 'What do you mean? What did he die from?' They told me he got an infected tooth, and he got blood poison, and he died from that."

"That's right!"

Stew said, "You know, that's the story I got."

"That's what happened as far as we know. He got, ah, he had bad teeth and the bacteria went down into his heart, and the doctor didn't treat him properly to get rid of the bacterial infection in his heart."

"So he was poisoned?"

I said, "Sort of, it was the bacterial infection. It then settled in his heart, and it killed him."

"Oh, I didn't really know that. See what I mean? What he'd been going through all these years, and nobody knew. He was suffering from a lot of things, man."

"I went to the doctor with him, and I told Bill that, 'This doctor is not treating you properly. Go see another doctor or go to a hospital.'"

Stew said, "You did?"

"Yes."

"What did he say, like he didn't care?"

"He just passed it on. Didn't want to do anything!"

"No shit!"

"Yes, and even this one woman I interviewed, she went to the doctor's with him, and she said the same thing. He didn't pay attention to her either. I think he wanted out!"

Stew said, "He did!"

"Life wasn't good to him."

"He called it on."

"You know, he thought when he got out, maybe music would be his thing, but he couldn't do it, because when he played with certain people, when he went on a trip to New Orleans, and when he got down there, he told me afterwards, he said, 'I would have got up there and played with all them dudes, but what are they going to say to me. Who have you played with?' What's he going to say? 'I just spent over twenty years in jail. I've been playing with convicts.'"

Stew said, "That, that would have been the greatest thing he could of done."

"But he was embarrassed to do it, and he didn't want to let anybody know, so he said, 'How am I going to get around that?' They're going to say, 'You can't be that good and not played with somebody. You play too good.'"

Stew said, "You know what? He told me the same thing, but in a different manner. See that! That's what been blowing my mind of what happened? Why? And every time I asked him that."

"He was afraid to do it, he couldn't hide it. It was too brutal!"

"Oh my God! That would down him."

"That would down him, and it would have, in those times."

Stew affirmed, "It could have, it could have, brother."

I said, "You know those days are different than these days. People today are quick to forget and forgive for past events. Especially if you have something to offer that they like. You know how celebrities can do almost anything and get away with it. Actually, they monopolize on it. They become a hero."

"Yeah, yeah."

"But it never materialized, so that ate him up."

Stew said, "Yeah, that did it."

"So, that's why he said, 'I can't make it in the Greek clubs. I can't make it playing anywhere.'"

"Yeah, he said he couldn't make it in these clubs, man."

"You know that was boring to him."

Stew affirmed.

"'So where can I go? I'm not supposed to go to the state where I committed the crime.'"

"He said that to me, man."

I said, "Where can I go? I guess the only way---"

Stew moaned, "O-h-h-h."

"--he turned into---"

Stew interrupted, "W-H-O-A!"

"--a gangster again."

"M-A-N!"

"He started telling me stuff that he was---"

Stew angrily, "I could kill, man, when I hear something like that."

"Exactly!"

"Its, its, its, o-o-o-h!"

"So---"

Stew interrupted, "That must of fucked him up!"

"Yes, he was depressed."

Stew said, "I kept saying to Billy, why not? Billy, don't you know, get on the stage and hit that bad boy (guitar), man, and watch what happens, Billy. Cause he could go, di-di-di-da, di-di-da. He could do some things, man, and make you stand there and say, 'WHAT? What?' I understand what he meant. That he'd go right there to the front, and they'd want to know everything. Then he's exposed. Now, he's got to talk about himself, the whole story."

I said, "Yes, and as I said, he was afraid of that."

"Yeah, and, ah, and ah, when he used to go into those Greek clubs, and I'd be parking, he hated going in there."

"He liked it at first, but then afterwards! I used to go to those clubs, but the thing is you're talking about the sixties and seventies. It's a different period today. If they had found out, oh, he killed a cop. It wasn't like he killed a regular person."

"He killed a cop!"

"Right!"

Stew said, "He'd been blackballed!"

"Yes."

"He'd been blackballed! And a police sergeant at that."

I said, "Definitely blackballed, and the sergeant was a hero in his department."

Stew continued, "It, it was a wonder he's on the street. Yes, it was a wonder that he was on the street, bro. That was some serious shit!"

"Oh, yeah! That was the second sergeant in the history of the Boston Police Department and the eighteenth cop since 1912 and the seventh since 1926 in Boston to be killed by gunfire, but see, for some reason, with Bill, it's almost like, when I look at it and it's like completely like another person came out of him. That wasn't the man I knew! You know what I mean?"

Stew said, "Yes, that wasn't my Bill!"

"No, and it wasn't mine either!"

Stew said, "You know what I'm saying?"

"Oh, yeah!"

"That must have been the way he felt."

I said, "Oh, yeah! Getting back to those gangster days, Bill used to come to my house, 'I got this reefer, and maybe you can do something with it.' I said, 'No way Bill.' He said, 'Well, I'm pushing pounds.' I went, 'oh!'"

"Really, man?"

"I told him, 'I want nothing to do with it! Yeah, I want nothing to do with it.'"

Stew asked, "He came to you too?"

"Yes! I asked Bill where he was getting the money to buy pounds. He told me that he was going to New Jersey and robbing gas stations. I said, 'Are you kidding?' Bill replied, 'Well, you asked.' I told no one in the family."

"See man, you're right, man, I think it's all of this. I think that Bonnie, you, and maybe myself, were the deepest people that ever went with Bill."

"I guess."

"You know what I'm saying? He accepted people, but he didn't get too deep."

"No."

"He didn't take you there. He'll never take you there, man, you know, cause he was a bad mother fucker."

"Right."

Stew said, "You don't want to see what was there, you know. What was there would blow most people's mind. You know what I mean? In a sense, and ah, and I, and ah, I got a great elation out of having known him, and you know what I'm proud of? That what was brought back to me, cause I had lost it. It was gone, man, you know. There was no way, once in a while figments of, of, of that old yesterday would cross my mind, but, but it wouldn't have the impact on me as it is today. As I, I reissued, I relived it, you know, and only things like that are worthwhile in your life. That's what saves people. When somebody comes around and brings the yesterday out of, ah, for them, cause what they're seeing today isn't for shit, ha, ha. Remember this, remember that shit, but now you, you got something to balance your day today with, man, and it's not easy for a lot of people. That's why I'm hoping that, ah, Bracy can be brought back to one of those yesterdays, you know, cause that's what he needs, something like that, to sit down and talk about Bill. Did you see in that picture how Bracy looked sitting at the table when we were talking about Bill? Did you see the expression of his face, man? You all went into a conversation at the time, and you could see that in the photograph. Y'all were into something there, man, and it was about Bill."

"Yeah, right."

Stew went on, "You know, I said, 'Wow. Look at these emotions come out, man,' and they were good emotions, cause after that we talked for days about your coming here. The event and we're sitting here and looking at the, the pictures after they were developed, and we talked about that. It was nice having you here, man, but you haven't got in touch with Bracy? Huh?"

"No, I haven't called him."

"Well, I don't know, but I'm not going to call him. I'm going to leave it like it is. I think if he wanted to reach out he would."

I said, "Probably, you know, but that's your thing, that's not mine."

"Right, that's different."

"Correct, but I've mainly been dealing with my family, my children, and---"

Stew said, "And finishing your book!"

"Yes, yes. I'm going out to New Mexico next week."

"You are?"

I said, "I'm going to drive out."

"W-H-O-A, man! You're going to the tribe?"

"Yes."

Stew said, "I remember me and Bracy were supposed to go to Arizona, or somewhere with you, man. One of them tribes, I don't know why we never got there, ha ha."

"I'm going out there, and I'll work and try to finish this story."

"You'll be there for a while, man?"

"I'll be there for about four months."

"Oh, that's nice."

"I hope so."

Stew said, "Yeah, that's an excellent move, you know. The best thing when you're writing your books, you have to move like that, ah, you might change it around after a while."

"O-h-h-h, I'm sure."

Stew added, "Because there's a powerful period of time in there. There's that period of time when, when this particular incident happened. There's that period of time about the history of all the people that were involved there, and, and the movement of their life happens, to happen after that, because it's almost like an impossibility for Bill at that time, to have committed the crime he did under the auspices, ah, under the method that he did, and to be alive at that time he was alive. All men that had committed that have gone to the chair."

"I know it."

"They faced, ah, ah, an un-revocable death sentence (Stew meant irrevocable)."

I said, "Absolutely."

"And Bill escaped that for some godly reason."

"Well, that was because they never found the gun."

"Yeah, yeah, I know that."

"That was the biggest---"

Stew interrupted, "That was the big thing."

"That was the big thing. They never found the gun, and they said he didn't go there to kill the cop."

"Right, he didn't."

I said, "No, but they got him for second degree."

"Second degree!"

"He was lucky."

Stew said, "Wasn't he lucky, man? That crime, at that time in this city-U-N-B-E-L-I-E-VA-B-L-E!!!"

"Yes, it was unbelievable. I told you, it was the eighteenth cop since 1912 and the seventh cop killed since 1926 by gunfire in the city, and I should mention the second police sergeant killed by gunfire."

"Unbelievable, man!"

"Like I told you, the sergeant was a hero. He saved lives during the 1938 hurricane."

"That's what I'm saying. For some reason, Bill was walking under a blessed star. He was walking under some serious blessing."

"Yeah, I guess."

Stew added, "Well, it could of gone a lot of different ways. All the elements were there, and, and, and all the real elements somehow disappeared."

"Did you know his buddy there that did the crime with him?"

"No! I, I, I might have, but I don't know."

"He didn't mess with him in prison. He didn't like---"

Stew interrupted, "No, he didn't like him. I ah, ah, I know I did know him, but he was not a part of my life."

"He finally went to the new State, but he didn't do the time that Bill did."

"But, I had to have met him. Not met him, but have had to seen him."

"Sure."

Stew said, "Bill had to have pointed him out to me. He had to, because you know how you watch those others."

"He was acne-faced, severely. He was not a very big kid."

"Yeah."

I said, "But, ah, he was a punk."

"Yeah."

"Yes, he was that. He used to come to the house."

"Really?"

"Oh yes!"

Stew asked, "This was prior?"

"Yes. When Bill started hanging around---"

"Did you meet him at that time?"

"Oh yeah! But none of us liked him."

"W-H-O-A!!"

I said, "None of us like him. Nobody in the house liked him!"

"W-O-W!"

"We'd all leave the room. Bill would take him down the corridor to his room."

Stew said, "Y-E-A-H! Y-E-A-H! You all said---and Bill didn't know?"

I said, "He knew, yeah, he knew!"

"He knew you didn't like him?"

"Oh yeah, because we said to him, 'What the hell is that guy? Fucking punk! Get him the fuck out of here!'"

Stew inserted, "O-H-H, man!"

"So, are you getting hungry?"

"Yeah, I'm ready to fix me---"

I interrupted, "No you don't. Let's go out to eat, man. I told you I'd take you out to lunch."

"You did?"

"Yes!"

Stew said, "Well, I could take you too, but we'll take each other. You want to go to the Japanese restaurant?"

"Whatever!"

"I'm a particular eater."

"Well, whatever. You show me where you want to go, Japanese, Chinese, Korean, whatever."

"Yeah, Korean and Japanese place."

"Whatever you want, remember it's on me. Okay?"

Stew said, "All right, there's both of them together. I think we'll go to a place where we can pick our own stuff, you know man."

"Let's go!"

I thanked Stew for the opportunity to have spent this time together. He is a warm person and I didn't like seeing him so ill. Bracy had said his time was coming. It was a happy and sad time for me.

Stew asked me again, during the latter part of our conversation, if I had called Bracy. I hadn't because I was visiting with my family and also preparing to spend four months in New Mexico. Stew asked because he hadn't heard from Bracy in a while, and prior to my visit, they saw or talked to each other constantly. For some reason, that stopped abruptly.

According to Stew, he thought Bracy was going through some changes for whatever reason, and Stew didn't know why. Bracy walked out of his apartment one day, left an unfinished alcoholic drink on the table, and had not called or showed up at his place, which seemed unusual. Stew didn't proceed on his own to find out why, or what was going on. The two of them have been friends too long to just separate like that. I'm sure, and I pray that they resumed their friendship, and not let it pass too long before it consumes their friendship and it becomes alien. Personally, I believe it is just a passing event. There is too much love between them for it to end.

I called Bracy on the telephone while visiting Boston ten months after this interview to say hello, and to ask if anything had changed between him and Stew. He informed me that Stew had passed away in September 2003. Bracy and I knew that Stew had stomach cancer, but I didn't know how far advanced it was, or his exact prognosis. Bracy informed me that Stew's family had taken him to Pennsylvania for internment. Stew had told me that he had children living there. I felt sad that I didn't have the opportunity to say good-bye, or to meet his family and tell them of all the help Stew gave me to complete this story. It also saddened me that Stew never had a chance to read this manuscript

# EPILOGUE

William Goudas' crime is unforgivable. In most states today, it is punishable by lethal injection, or a sentence of life in prison without parole. In the days when he committed the crime, it would have been the electric chair. Lethal injection is more passive compared to hundreds of volts passing through your body, although the end results are the same. William escaped both.

Would I say he was lucky to avoid the extreme penalty? That would be difficult to answer, and there would be many opinions on that subject. Bill spent almost half his life behind prison walls in maximum security, except for his short stay in the Colony. Of course, that was considered a piece of cake compared to old State, and it was a lot better than the new state prison he lived in until his release. That's a lot of penalty time. I'm sure some of you would say it was not enough.

When he was finally paroled, he was given his freedom, but it was a freedom he could not capitalize on. The one love of his life was his guitar and it was the one existence that became his second downfall, because he couldn't perform before the public's eye, knowing that his background would have to be divulged. It became his second killing. It was a slow death! Some would say he deserved it, but no matter where your opinion lies, I believe he paid for his crime.

The one area where Bill was lucky was the night of his capture. Having a bullet lodged in his left foot, and not getting the proper medical treatment after shooting himself, he set himself up for complications. The police, after they got a confession out of him, sent him to the hospital for treatment. The police reported that gangrene was setting in the wound and the doctor treating him was able to remove and treat the infection.

If Bill had not been captured, the gangrene would have spread and who knows what the results would have been. Possibility of amputation would not have been out of order, and if it went for a longer period, maybe death. I would comment that Bill was fortunate under those circumstances.

As for the family, we were not so fortunate. We had to carry internally the shame for his crime. We could no longer carry our proud heads as high as before. Those with the Goudas name said their name softly, hoping that it wouldn't be recognized, or that it wouldn't be attached to Bill. My sister and I were the lucky ones, we had a different last name, but we also carried the burden. After all, we were from the Goudas family, and we had the same address. Only neighbors and friends knew where we lived.

It was easier to hide that Goudas connection, especially as the years moved on. As for the Goudas name, only time, and a lot of that, removed the stigma that was attached to it. Even then, the embarrassment continued. They were afraid that Bill's history would be with them forever. Of course, after years of removal from the crime, people forget names, places, and incidents. Old crimes are forgotten, new crimes prevail. This helped the easing of personal guilt for the family, although the secret of Bill still prevails for the most part. I really don't know who has said what to whom, but I know we don't, as a family, say anything nor have discussions about Bill.

The family has had three reunions over the last twenty years, and Bill's name was never mentioned. It is like he never existed. Of course, he had no children, and the legacy he left is not one anyone wants to talk about. Now that there are grandchildren and great grandchildren, I'm not aware that anyone wants to tell them the story. Like our generation, we didn't tell our children until much later in life. I would assume the same plan of not telling until they become older would continue, if at all. Maybe this book will put to ease that burden.

A few months after Bill's arrest, a family friend informed my aunt that there was an article featured in a detective magazine about Bill. Either Christie or Madeline purchased the detective magazine to find out what they had written. The writer labeled Bill "The Whistling Bandit." As we read the story, the author claimed that when the police entered the house to arrest Bill, he was sitting at the kitchen table whistling. Of course, this was far from the truth, as Bill was terrified when the police knocked at the door. He knew who was at the door, and when the detective came briskly down the corridor, pointing a pistol directly at him, whistling was not on his agenda. In fact, his attitude that day was very solemn, definitely not jovial.

For the family, the magazine article was another blow to our integrity. It's one thing to have to endure that a family member committed a hideous crime, but to say that he was a happy killer on top of that, well, you can imagine how upset and angry we all became. Christie wanted to write the editor and ask for a retraction. After some discussion, it was decided that it wouldn't do any good. The story had already made a false impression, and who would see the retraction, even it came forth. It was too late!

Another story appeared in another detective magazine, but they related the crime and arrest more accurately. Although it produced more embarrassment for the family, there wasn't anything we could do about it. We endured it the best we could.

Family friends remained family friends, and those that felt sorry for us, knowing the ordeal that we were facing, expressed it in many ways. It was those persons who helped us to go on with our lives. Without them, we would have become isolated in a sea of neighbors.

The older women in my grandmother's apartment gave her solace. They were very understanding and comforting to her. They all realized that if it were their son, they would want the same condolences. There wasn't one that turned their nose up at my grandmother. All of this compassion was a blessing for her and the family. It was one of the big factors that got all of us through the ordeal we were facing.

The younger members of our family, mine included, all liked Bill. He was gentle with them and associated with them, and they accepted him as a lost uncle who returned home from far away. They had no reason to dislike him. Bill seemed very happy to be around the children.

When I drove to the Canadian Exposition of the late sixties, my wife and I decided to take Bill with us. We also brought our three older children; two daughters, fourteen and twelve, and a son, ten. We drove to Montreal in our new 1967 Pontiac Bonneville station wagon and found a campsite in Montreal to pitch tents. It was the first time that Bill ever went camping, and the only time he visited another country. Of course, the Exposition was a real treat for all of us, but Bill had the time of his life. With all of the pavilions and ethnic foods, who could not have a great time? The children enjoyed the Exposition, but they also loved being with their newly-found uncle. It was the happiest I ever saw Bill. I've seen him through all his moods, but never again like that. It makes me feel good, even now, that at least one time in his life he enjoyed life, and himself, immensely. He felt free as a bird!

I'm satisfied that my wife and I could contribute some happiness, for what it was worth, in Bill's adult life. Not like his trip to New Orleans, where he couldn't be totally himself. Bill did have a good time with his brother Christie and his wife, but there was a bracelet attached, like a handcuff, limiting what he really wanted to do. Of course, that was to perform and play his guitar with the best of the best. In Montreal, he could be just himself. No desires connected to his guitar.

Knowing that Bill had spent all those years in confinement, and being removed from the family in general, he didn't leave many positive remembrances. He was generally a quiet and reserved individual when in family situations, and he made no disgruntled waves in the family. If you accepted him, then he accepted you. I'm sure deep down internally, he felt the philosophical awkwardness that was prevalent in some family members, especially when he was present. Those that ignored him, ignored him, but verbal or physical occurrences never happened with him in attendance. I can't speak for what happened behind closed doors.

Bill's crime was not a crime of love, an accident or premeditated. It was an act of murder. It was an act that couldn't be reversed. It was an act that carried the most extreme penalty. Bill was spared that. The officer's family was not. They lost a devoted husband and father. Their loss was permanent. No more picnics, no more family dinners, and all the ramifications that go with the loss of a husband and parent. It is bad enough to lose a parent through an accident or sickness, but to lose one because someone killed them recklessly, that puts it into another realm.

For those families that have a relative, whether a son or daughter, cousin, uncle or aunt, whatever, that commits murder, I hold deep empathy for you. I'm aware of what you're experiencing, and I wish dearly that you overcome the guilt that you will or have acquired. The shame that is placed upon you is not your own, it is on the individual that committed the crime. Remember that! I know it will be difficult, but just remember that. I pray for you!

We know William Goudas's act of murder was not an act of premeditation or an accident. It was a state of passion of the wrong kind. It was the violent act of a desperate man. William Goudas did have alternatives. STOP! RAISE HIS HANDS! DROP HIS GUN! William put himself into a position, a position of no return.

The following pages are a biographical synopsis of Bill's immediate family, and his older sister's husband, my sister, and me, the author. Family members have passed on, leaving two of us at the time of Bill's crime–my sister and me that were living in the house with him.

We still carry his guilt, but those feelings are practically forgotten now. We're senior citizens, and far too many years have passed. As we all know, time heals all wounds, for the most part. Even though those events are far behind us now, we will never forget. How could we?

# APPENDIX

## Penelope Goudas

Penelope Goudas, my grandmother, was born in Epirus, Greece, which was under Turkish (Ottoman Empire) control. The year was 1895. Penelope got married when she was fourteen, and gave birth to my mother (Rita) when she was fifteen; it was an arranged marriage. Penelope's father came from one of the two wealthiest families in the village. The other wealthy family was Penelope's husband's family. Her family owned land and were importers. Her husband's father's family owned a hotel and a store in the nearby city. Both families had doctors, lawyers, judges, priests, etc. in their background. Penelope's father was a priest in the Greek Orthodox religion.

My grandfather, Thomas, came to America in 1910, Penelope and Rita followed in 1920, and they settled in New England. The rest of the siblings were born in this country. During and after the Depression, Thomas worked in his own barbershop on Kneeland Street in the downtown area of Boston. Money was tight, but the family was fed and clothed. Rita left the house when she married at sixteen. One more sibling, Nicholas, was born after that.

Thomas, the father, died a few years before Bill got into trouble. The two oldest boys were in the service. That left Penelope with three children at home. Bill didn't work, but Nicholas and Madeline helped out the best they could.

When Bill got into trouble, Penelope had a hard and difficult time accepting the fact that her son, the one that was supposed to be too ill to work or play, was the only one to get into trouble, serious trouble.

Penelope was a serious-minded woman. She liked to tease somewhat, but always knew the limits. She loved her religion, and prayed, went to church, and kept a lit icon in her dining room. One of my duties, while I lived with her, was to keep the flame lit in front of the icon; a wick floating on olive oil was the method used. I refilled the glass container, making sure the flame stayed lit.

Penelope wasn't a gossiper, but she had her friends. She loved to play cards for entertainment. She liked Greek music, but she also had her favorite American tunes. She learned to read and write English, but she had that typical accent that most Greek immigrants have. She loved to cook, make her own phyllo dough for spanakopita or baklava, yogurt, and homemade soap. The two virtues that she always possessed were her calmness and quietness.

When Bill got into trouble, she kept her composure and went on with life. It wasn't that she wasn't hurt; she just kept it all inside. She didn't harp on the incident or the aftermath. She went to visit Bill, but not on a regular basis. I believe that she couldn't believe that Bill could do such a thing, but coming from a country that had been war-ridden, had thieves in the countryside, and was ruled by Turks, had given her an impression of an unruly world. Men are the violent ones, and Bill was a man. She had no control over their actions.

Penelope lived to be ninety-seven. She died on the day I returned from her home village. She had never returned to her village, but she always talked about her home, and I knew she loved it very much. I put into her casket a few small stones that I brought back from her village street. It was the least I could do for my grandmother, whom I revered and loved as my mother.

I spent many times with her over the years until her death in September 1992. I never heard her make any disparaging remarks towards her son Bill. It was like she just put him aside. It wasn't that she didn't love him, but what he did was against all that she was brought up to believe. It was the only thing she could do! I must also say, that she really didn't say anything about Bill, unless someone brought it up in a conversation, and then she wouldn't say much.

Her relatives didn't help her much when Bill was in trouble, neither monetarily nor emotionally. She did have friends that comforted her.

She had grandchildren to deal with, as the years passed by. Eventually, she became the matriarch of five generations. This was a role she adored. Luckily, she had good wits about her, and her memory never lapsed. I pray for her every day.

## Rita Goudas

Rita was the oldest child of the Goudas family. She was born in Epirus, Greece, and moved to America when she was ten years old, with her mother, her mother's older sister and husband, and their three children. When she turned eleven she had a sister, Madeline. Rita was educated in American schools and managed to learn the English language without an accent, and she received her American citizenship. She went to an industrial school for girls and learned the skill of sewing. For the rest of her working years she was employed in the garment industry as a stitcher.

Rita was matched (arranged) to marry my father, and they married when she was sixteen years old (1926) and he was twenty. That arrangement was something that was still in use in that part of Greece when they arrived in America, and it was carried over here, but ended in the family with my mother. The marriage ended in divorce ten years later, although she left her children and husband after five and a half years of marriage. She moved to New York and eventually married Dominic Igneri.

Two years after Bill became a felon, Rita moved back to the New England area, after leaving and divorcing Dominic. She lived four houses from her mother.

On moving back, she immediately got a job in the garment industry, as she was a member of the International Ladies' Garment Union. Finding a job quickly was one of the advantages of belonging to that union. This also gave Rita the opportunity to be with her pregnant daughter and her future grandchildren. This closeness to Bill allowed her to visit her brother in prison. She visited Bill with Dorothea, or Christie, or Madeline, or her mother. It wasn't like she went every month, but she did visit a few times a year until Bill was finally released.

During those years, while living in New England, Rita went to the West Coast to visit her aunt and uncle and cousins. This was the same family that she had come to America with. They moved out West in the late 1940's. She came home with a man that she had met, and then got married for the third time. This marriage lasted about as long as it takes for corn to mature from seed to ear. Whatever happened is pure conjecture. I was too busy working and raising my family to know the whodunits about whomever. All I ever knew was that one day he was gone. He returned to the West Coast to never be heard from again.

After going through three marriages, Rita ended the marriage circuit. After the end of her last marriage, her career as a stitcher would last about another decade until she retired. She lived alone for a few years, until one of her grandchildren, a young lady, moved in with her to assist her in her aging years. She was active until she reached her middle seventies, when she developed asthma. She never smoked cigarettes, but all three husbands did.

From the time she got sick, she took care of herself, until the last couple of years, when she developed severe osteoporosis that disabled her physical movements, and she became almost bedridden. Her granddaughter was a great help with her medical and physical needs. Eventually, after being in and out of the hospital, Rita finally relapsed and was hospitalized for about a month before she passed away at age eighty-five.

Until her death in 1996, she was a feisty woman, but the medical team complimented her on her good disposition, even though she was in extreme pain. Rita was interred in the same cemetery as her two brothers, her mother, and strange as it may seem, with my father, her first husband, although they hadn't spoken to each other civilly in over sixty years. Not only are they buried in the same cemetery, they are only a few feet apart.

## Madeline Goudas

Bill's second oldest sister, Madeline, was always one of my favorite relatives. Even though she is my aunt, I've always related to her as my older sister. Now this is not meant to take anything away from my blood sister, but Madeline and I related more in our thinking and way of life. One other reason for our close connection is that she is only nine years older than me.

When I was six years old, Madeline took my sister and me to see the original King Kong movie. I can remember hiding behind the movie seat sobbing because I was scared. It might have been the first movie I went to, and of course radio hadn't that kind of effect. My sister was eight and Madeline was fifteen. That seems so long ago.

Madeline moved out of her mother's home a couple of years after Bill went into prison. At the time of the crime, Madeline wanted to deny his guilt, even though he had confessed, and all the evidence pointed to him. It was really hard on her. I assumed it was partly because she knew Bill was treated differently, because of his institutional early years, and she had been the one to protect him as he was growing up, especially since she was the older child in the home, seeing that my mother had married and moved out.

Madeline married and had three daughters. During Bill's confinement years, Madeline always visited and brought him things that he needed or asked for. Because she had children, she had less time to visit. Plus, she worked outside of her home. Madeline did clerical work to supplement the family's income. Her husband worked, but he never made a lot of money.

Eventually Madeline and her husband separated, and then finally divorced. It was a mutual separation, and they still saw each other over the years during holiday seasons, until his death. I guess I would state that they tolerated each other, and did it for their children, and eventually for the grandchildren.

When Madeline's oldest daughter reached her early forties, she contracted cancer and went through medical procedures, and eventually she passed away. Like my sister, years earlier, Madeline also lost her first-born. Losing your child does not seem natural while the parent is still alive, but this had been more common over the centuries, especially before the medical revolution. Generations are living longer and the young ones today get better medical treatment. This loss to Madeline took a toll on her and she has never gotten over her daughter's death, to the point that she was still depressed up to her own death.

When Bill was released, he visited Madeline and her children. Bill visited Madeline right up to the time of his own sickness, and then his death. Madeline knew that Bill wasn't getting the treatment that he needed, but Bill proceeded to see the doctor of his choice. She also believed that this was to his detriment, and lead to his death. Madeline had a hard time with Bill's death, and maybe this was the beginning of her increased depression, for it wasn't many years later after Bill's death that her daughter died.

When Bill was released, Madeline, like other members of the family, hid from her children the fact that Bill just been released from jail. The story that got around the family was that Bill lived out West and had returned to the East Coast. Of course, her children finally learned about Bill's crime, and where he had been spending his years. None of her children had any problems accepting this, but they, too, kept it a secret among their friends. I don't know when, if ever, that they finally told someone outside of the family.

Madeline had many medical problems, and considering her depression, I believe some of her medical conditions were due to her losing her daughter. In 2012, she passed away at the age of ninety.

## Gregory Goudas

Gregory, the eldest son, as far as I'm concerned, is a hero. As a young man of eighteen he enlisted in the U.S. Army before the outbreak of World War II. In January 1942, one month after the bombing of Pearl Harbor, Gregory was shipped over to the Pacific Islands to fight the Japanese. His whereabouts were never known. The only address was an APO, which told you only that he was somewhere six thousand miles away. Gregory was not one to relate war stories, but he would say that he had seen a lot of battles. Gregory returned from that distant war zone one month before the Japanese surrendered in July 1945.

Gregory had to be one of the luckiest of soldiers, for the whole time he was there he was never wounded. His only problem was he broke his nose and contracted jungle diseases, endemic to where he was stationed at the time. From what I understood, his outfit moved around the Pacific war zone, being in the Americal Division.

When Gregory was discharged, he returned to his mother's home and roamed the area, chasing ladies and trying to make up for all the time he had lost as a young man. A number of times, those war diseases caused him some problems, but through medication and time, they were released from his body.

Gregory was a good-natured man, and he was one to always joke around and makes us all laugh. He worked and earned his spending money, but he never accumulated any wealth. Gregory got married twice, and had two daughters and a son with his second wife. Neither marriage lasted very long. My personal take on it is that what Gregory endured all those years in combat had a great psychological effect on his psyche, and he was unable to shake it off. Today they call it post-traumatic stress.

As the years rolled by, Gregory would disappear for weeks or months on end. In fact he became an enigma in our family. Of course, one of the reasons he wouldn't be seen for a while was that he became a truck driver, but even with that he got lost from us. Gregory used to call or see his sister Madeline, but in the last decade or so, she lost contact with him, and she would get word about his goings-on through a mutual woman friend.

When he got older, he spent a lot of time with one of his grandnephews, and it seemed that he was returning to the depths of our family. I was happy about that, because everyone in our family loved Gregory, for he had a good sense of humor. Actually, he was the family funnyman. The children loved his antics, and I would put him in the order of a Pied Piper.

I have never heard Gregory mention anything about Bill during his confinement, when he was released, or after Bill died, but I must mention that I probably wouldn't be the one he would confide in anyhow. Years had gone by before we saw each other, but we did get to see one another, briefly. Gregory had been to my home only once in the last thirty plus years. He passed away in 2009. He was eighty-six.

## Christie Goudas

Christie was the fourth child of the Goudas family. He was one year older than Bill, and he took on the job of his brother's keeper. When Bill came home from being institutionalized for his sickness as a young boy, Christie protected him as well as Gregory and Madeline.

Christie took on that same role when Bill was released from prison. Christie took him into his home with his wife and two young children, and helped Bill adjust to the outside world.

During the Second World War, Christie joined the Marines, and after basic training, he was shipped off to the Pacific region. He was wounded in the Mariana Island of Saipan. He earned several medals for his wartime activities, including the Purple Heart. Christie returned to the United States, was treated for his wounds, and was honorably discharged in the spring of 1944. Christie returned briefly to his mother's home to find work and to recover from his battle experiences.

Christie had an even temperament and was good-natured. I always got along with him and liked him very much. He helped his mother as much as he could. Christie also got along with other members of the family, although sometimes there was tension with his youngest brother Nicholas. Nicholas teased excessively, and Christie would have nothing to do with it.

Christie eventually moved out of his mother's home, found satisfactory work, and dated pretty ladies. He purchased a convertible, and to say the least, he was very proud of it. Eventually he met his future wife a dozen years later and settled down. She was a charming and pretty lady. They had two children, a boy and a girl. They moved out of state and raised their children in a quieter atmosphere, away from big city life.

During Bill's imprisonment, Christie visited him more than anyone else in the family. He was Bill's connection to the outside world. He gave him money and whatever Bill asked for. He never gave up on his younger brother, but he didn't approve of the crime he had committed. Christie was very disappointed in him, but he knew or felt that Bill was not a hardened criminal. As you read, he went to all the trial days, helped tremendously to raise money for his defense, and cared for him until Bill moved away and finally took care of his own welfare.

Christie and Bill kept their communication in force up until Bill's death, although it became more infrequent towards the end. You might say that Christie did his very best for Bill, but Bill's bitterness and depression got the best of him. There was probably no one in the world that could have helped Bill the way he needed to be helped. Bill had to do it himself or else!

Christie's wife died of cancer. It was a terrible blow to him and the children. Both of his children are married, but only the son has children--two boys. Christie kept busy working part time, as a senior citizen, at his job of many years. Retirement was not on his agenda.

Christie finally told his children about Bill, but only after they were grown and Christie thought they could handle the fact. Of course, the children grew up with Bill around them, and they loved his company, especially when he played his guitar for them. What they saw was a loving man, and that impression has stayed with them. They have no reason to think otherwise, and if they were disappointed in the disclosure, it would be understood, but the daughter told me she liked him very much.

Christie told me that he disclosed to one of his closest friends about Bill's past, but that was when Bill was released from prison. Like the rest of the family, we kept it hidden, except for wives and husbands. I don't know what Gregory did when he married.

Christie died eight days after his eightieth birthday from complications of a blood disorder. His death occurred in the winter of 2004. Christie never got the chance to read this story, but we did discuss its progress and its contents. He ratified its contents, knowing at the time he would not live to see it published, if ever. Christie wished me the best, as I did him.

## Nicholas Goudas

Bill's younger brother Nicholas, after going away to the Merchant Marines, never spoke, wrote, or saw Bill again, except for one time before Nicholas moved to the town where Bill was in prison. How ironic is that? Their relationship ended abruptly when Bill was arrested for the killing of the police officer. Nicholas's inquiry about Bill's status in life, except for what sentence he received when Bill was found guilty, stopped in full force.

Nicholas eventually left the Merchant Marines about one and a half years after Bill's arrest and returned to his mother's apartment. Nicholas found work with a large food chain store, unloading sides of meat from freight cars and trucks. He worked the night shift. Nicholas was also the biggest and strongest member of his family.

Nicholas's act of teasing was still a discourse among family members, especially his sister and me whenever I lived there, although after Bill's confinement, my stay at my grandmother's declined. When Nicholas met his future wife, he became occupied with her, which didn't give him time to deliver his teasing. They married a few months after they met and moved into their own apartment, about two miles away from his mother.

Still working for the same company, Nicholas advanced to the ranks of authority. Nicholas's new position allowed him and his wife to purchase a new home. As the years passed, he moved up into a higher position of management, and with an increase in salary they moved again into one of those new places called condominiums.

On New Year's Eve, 1981, while getting dressed for an evening gala, Nicholas was struck with a heart attack. Nicholas never recovered from this deathly onslaught and was pronounced dead at his home. His poor wife was in a state of shock, as she was looking forward to their going out to celebrate. Nicholas was only fifty-four years old. He and his wife had three boys and one girl. They were all young adults by then.

Nicholas's family, after his church service and internment, was having a dinner and a get together at his home. I went to see Bill, to ask him if he was going to attend the gathering, knowing of the separation between him and Nicholas. Bill was very reluctant to attend, but after I spent some time trying to convince him to go, he finally acquiesced, but, as I said, with reluctance. We drove in Bill's auto and arrived after most of the family and friends had gathered at his brother's home.

Bill was very nervous when we arrived, and while he was parking he started to tell me that he really didn't want to go in. Once again, I had to persuade him that we should go in and pay our respects. I also reinforced the fact that we didn't have to stay too long. I, of course, wasn't the reason. The reason it was difficult to go inside was Bill. We finally went inside and paid our respects, but the atmosphere became heavy when people noticed Bill entering the room where everyone was assembled. One family-in-law made an openly disparaging remark. It was ignored. The family knew of Bill's and his brother's separation.

Bill did as well as could be expected, knowing that his younger brother had nothing to do with him for thirty-five years. I could see that his smile was strained and his posture somewhat stooped. I know he did his best mingling among the family, but deep down inside he wanted to be miles away.

Bill and I stayed for about forty-five minutes, telling family members that Bill had to be somewhere else, and we couldn't stay very long. There wasn't a lot of hubbub about the fact that we were leaving so soon. I'm sure whatever tension there was when we entered was alleviated when the two of us passed through the portal leading to the outside world. Bill didn't sigh visually, but I could see the electric tension emanate from his body. On the ride home, we didn't discuss where we had just been. He had done more than his brother had since their estrangement, and now it was all over.

## Dorothea Kaltsos

My sister Dorothea married when she was eighteen years old. That was a couple of years after Bill committed his crime. She was working at one of Boston's large old established banks.

My sister and her husband moved into an apartment and then started a family. Dorothea had two boys, a girl, and then another boy. When her oldest boy was sixteen, he was swimming with some friends. He and another boy got into trouble out in deep water in the pond; her son drowned. Some boaters who heard their calls for help saved the other boy. It was a tragic end to a fine young man. He was an excellent student and a promising saxophonist. It took a toll on my sister and her husband. The only thing that heals the mind is years of time, plus the fact that she had three other children to attend to.

Eventually Dorothea's husband moved into a position from menial jobs to a more lucrative situation. They purchased their own home with a rental downstairs to offset their bank payment. A couple of decades later, they sold this home and moved into a single residence in which they still live today.

Dorothea returned to work after her children were all in school. She worked in a meat refrigeration room in one of those chain food stores in the New England area. She did this for many years, and the end result was that she developed bronchitis, which has plagued her for years. She finally retired from that job, but she worked part time cleaning homes. It is not because she or her husband needed the money, she just liked to work and keep busy, plus she always kept a very neat household, so cleaning, I'm sure, is just second nature for her, and a lot of seniors prefer to work than just sit around and watch their life pass on by.

Over the years, while Bill was in prison, my sister would visit and bring Bill items he would request by mail or when you visited. Her visits to the prison diminished over the years, but they never stopped. Dorothea and Bill always had a good rapport between them.

Dorothea is a likeable person, and she has a gentle personality and always had a beautiful smile, which would melt the hearts of men. I had mentioned much earlier in this story that she was very pretty, and she still is an attractive person.

When Bill was released from prison, he visited Dorothea and her husband many times, until the last couple of years that he remained alive. I'm not aware if they communicated by telephone.

Dorothea and her husband live a quiet life and attend church regularly. She is a typical proud grandmother of nine. This gives her a lot to do, and on holidays their household is full of family and joyous affection. They love to entertain their children.

As the years have gone by, Dorothea and I don't see each other very often. The last time we saw each other was when our aunt Madeline died. There is no animosity or estrangement between us; we just live our own lives, which unfortunately don't intersect. Another factor is that we live a couple of hundred miles apart. I love my sister and I know the feeling is mutual.

## Dominic Igneri

My mother's second husband, Dominic, was raised in New York City. He was a first generation American. His parents were from Calabria, Italy, and many members of his family were associated with the so-called Mafia. When I finally realized this, it came to me as a surprise.

I met Dominic at my grandmother's, for the first time, when I was fourteen. At that time, I only knew of him as my mother's husband. He was personable and very nice to me. I had the opportunity to meet him again, when I was fifteen, in New York City when visiting my mother's home for the first time.

Dominic was working on the Brooklyn docks and Bill was working as a doorman when I visited my mother's home when I was fifteen. I had no idea what Dominic did on the docks at that time, and the subject never was brought up. I did meet some of his brothers, uncles and aunts, brother's wives, children, etc. They were all comfortable in their lifestyle, and they lived in beautiful homes throughout New York City, but mostly in the Bay area of Brooklyn. When I returned almost two years later, I found out that Dominic was a carpenter boss on the Brooklyn docks, and had connections to the Mafia (read--"*The Boy Who Was Shanghaied*"--2014) that controlled the docks.

In 1951, a senator from Tennessee led a senate probe into organized crime, and from these investigations organized crime was ousted from the New York docks. The Senator, Estes Kefauver, was credited with their ouster. Dominic lost his job and through connections he moved to Boston, the same city as my mother. He became a numbers racket bookmaker working in a bar and living across the street in a run-down hotel. It is difficult for me to say that he was Mafia connected then, but all the bits of information I could put together led me to believe that he was.

In 1955, six years after he became a bookie, Dominic was found dead one day in his hotel room. The coroner described his death as strangulation. The fact is that he was murdered. Sometimes if you don't pay off on large wagers, or you're found to have slipped some money into your own pocket, you pay the penalty. I can't say for sure this is the reason, but I can speculate. No one was ever indicted for his death. His family transported his body and had him interred in New York City somewhere.

Dominic had a wonderful demeanor and a great personality. He was generous with his pocket money, and he always made you feel at home. I give him a lot of credit for helping our family, and especially Bill, when all that trouble landed at our doorstep. There was no hesitation on his part. It was probably because many in his own family, as I found out later, had been in trouble with the law. I believe all the men in his family had been in jail at least once. It was part of their MO.

When I lived with my mother and Dominic for a short period, just before I moved back home and entered the military, I spent many a Sunday dinner with his brother, their wives, and children. All of them were Italian, except my mother and me. It was always a great time. We ate fantastic Italian dinners from soup to nuts. There was nothing but laughs and maybe some family disagreements, but it all ended in good humor.

Rita left Dominic and moved to Roxbury. My mother and Dominic had nothing to do with each other after their divorce, but I visited him near where I worked. I was going to school on the GI bill during the day, and working nights trying to support my wife and two children. I used to visit Dominic at the Silver Dollar barroom, located on Washington Street downtown Boston

(Combat Zone), where he booked numbers. He was always glad to see me, and always asked me if I needed any help. It was in reference to helping me if anyone was giving me trouble. In other words, if someone was bothering me, he would have their kneecaps broken or whatever I wanted. Luckily, I was leading a peaceful life, and had no one in my face. I never told my mother that I had been seeing Dominic, only my wife.

I felt bad the day I found out that he had been found strangled. He had his own life, strange as it may seem, but he was always good to me. I always liked his one famous line: "That dirty degenerate rat bastard!!!"

## Bonnie Goudas

One year after I started research on this project, I learned the whereabouts of Bonnie Goudas, Bill's ex-wife. I was very excited as I hadn't seen her since their divorce. I also knew that I could get some insight into their relationship beyond what I knew, and what others might tell me. I also liked her as a person. How she made her money for those years she was with Bill didn't bother me. She obviously did what she wanted. Plus, she was good to Bill while they were together. I also wanted to learn about her life after Bill.

I went to the town that Bonnie lived, and I thought I found her home. When I knocked on her door a man answered. He informed me that Bonnie had passed away during the past winter season of 2000. It was now early summer. I was told that she had become a Jehovah Witness, and her daughter and grandchildren were living in the same town. This gentleman told me where her daughter lived. I made a visit to Bonnie's daughter, but the daughter was not home. Bonnie's three grandchildren were home and I explained that I was an old friend. I didn't pursue it any further, just expressed my condolences. I left knowing that a great opportunity had been missed. I felt sad, as I really was looking forward to seeing Bonnie.

## Angelo Kaltsos

When I wrote the first edition of this story I did not include myself in the Epilogue. Readers told me that I should have included that material, so you will now read a brief history of me. My sister and I left my father when I was fourteen and my sister was sixteen, and we went to my grandmother's home at 118 Cedar Street in Roxbury, Massachusetts. I'm not going to relate reasons why we left, (read "*The Boy Who Was Shanghaied*" 2014) only to say that life with my father was not pleasant.

When William Goudas committed that crime, we were living with him at our grandmother's home as you have read in this story. That incident had a large effect on our lives.

When I turned eighteen, I joined the US Army and served a couple of months fewer than four full years. Towards the end of my enlistment I met my wife in Louisville, Kentucky, and we married five days after my discharge. We returned to Boston, and she and I found jobs. I returned to school to get a higher education under the GI Bill, and she had seven children.

I worked for Raytheon after graduation and performed top secret research on the first Doppler System for the B-1 fighter bomber that carried an A-bomb, and also supervised technicians on the system when it went into production. While at Raytheon, and during my last days there, I did environmental component research for the first flight to the moon.

Leaving Raytheon, I started teaching electronics and science at an industrial arts high school, Rindge Technical High School in Cambridge, Massachusetts. Of course, I had to take educational courses at the local colleges to acquire the state's teaching certificate. My teaching career lasted twenty years, at which time I decided to retire from that job. Attending the University of New Mexico I did independent ethnological research on an Indian reservation. While attending the university I initiated an English tutoring program on five pueblos. I taught English to teenagers on one of the pueblos. After retiring from public education I taught Southwest Indian culture in Cambridge and Boston.

After twenty-one years of marriage, my wife died from cancer. She was forty years old. My children matured and started to have children, adding sixteen more to the family. My oldest daughter died when she was forty, leaving two children. Of course, after all these years there are now seven great grandchildren.

I eventually moved to Maine from Massachusetts permanently in 1999, having rented property in Maine from 1967-78. Eventually I purchased my own cabin in western Maine in 1978. I started to write in 2000, and I have published a poetry chapbook, a cookbook, four non-fiction novels, another non-fiction short story ready for publication, and the rewrite of this novel.

My website: *www.westbranchbooks.com*

## Article tid-bits

It should be noted that one of the criminals that entered 24 Fayette Street on October 2, 1946 escaped the premises without notice by anyone. His whereabouts after his getaway were unknown to the officials. This individual, Joseph F. Moore, was never captured, even though there was a manhunt for him.

The following articles appeared in one of Boston's newspapers approximately eight years after the killing of Sergeant William F. Healey:

### Warden Kin Widowed By Convict

"One of the armed convict foursome who staged the revolt at state prison represented a personal tragedy to Warden John J. O'Brien, for prisoner Fritz Swenson caused tears in the warden's household less than eight years ago.

The warden's wife had reason for sorrow. She is the sister of Mrs. Margaret Healey of West Roxbury, whose husband, Police Sgt. William F. Healey, a police Medal of Honor winner, was shot to death by gunmen looting an apartment.

Fritz Swenson was one of the trios, although the actual shooting was done by Swenson's pal William Goudas."

### Held Fort Four Days

"After them came the four ringleaders of the revolt: Theodore Green, the bank robber who had openly wept during the conferences; Joseph A. Flaherty, once known as Boston's Public Enemy No. One; Walter A. Balben, who not only broke out of Norfolk Prison Colony but is the only man to ever break into State Prison, and Fritz Swenson who is doing life for participating in an armed robbery during which his pal, William Goudas, shot a Boston police sergeant to death."

## Swenson Pal Killed O'Brien Kin
### By JOHN HICKEY

"A drama-within-a-drama is taking place at State Prison. As Warden John J. O'Brien wrestles with the back-breaking problem posed by the four rebellious inmates, he is tackling a problem produced in art by the man who brought tragedy and suffering into the warden's own home.

Theodore Green and Walter Balben may be giving the warden his worst headaches of his 26-year penal career, but the man who has brought him the greatest heartache is Fritz Swenson.

The warden's wife is the sister of Mrs. Margaret Healey of West Roxbury, whose husband was Police Sgt. William Healey."

Printed in the United States
By Bookmasters